NEW

"A varied and interesting cast of suspects moves in and out of the action, and of action there is plenty. . . . This one maintains the high standards readers have come to expect from these novels."
The Seattle Times

"Conan Flagg's many fans will enjoy his latest involvements. As always, this series is top fare."
The Columbus Dispatch

"Ms. Wren has a real gift for getting inside her characters and making their motives and emotions seem very real and plausible. The strands of mystery are tightened into a death-grip hold."
Salem Statesman-Journal

"Another in the series of straight, ratiocinating whodunits taking place in an Oregon coastal town. The solution is sensible and yet a surprise, and M.K. Wren has all sorts of intelligent things to say."
Library Journal

D1021119

Also by M. K. Wren
Published by Ballantine Books:

CURIOSITY DIDN'T KILL THE CAT

A MULTITUDE OF SINS

OH, BURY ME NOT

NOTHING'S CERTAIN BUT DEATH

M. K. Wren

BALLANTINE BOOKS • NEW YORK

Copyright © 1978 by Martha Kay Renfroe

All rights reserved under International and Pan-American Copyright Conventions. Published in the United States of America by Ballantine Books, a division of Random House, Inc., New York, and simultaneously in Canada by Random House of Canada Limited, Toronto. Originally published by Doubleday & Company, Inc. in 1978.

All of the characters in this book are fictitious, and any resemblance to actual persons, living or dead, is purely coincidental.

Library of Congress Catalog Card Number: 77-76962

ISBN 0-345-35000-6

Manufactured in the United States of America

First Ballantine Books Edition: December 1989

Dedicated with love to Katharyn Miller Renfroe, whose birthgift to me was music, who sustained me with faith that never precluded amazement, and who transcended motherhood to become a loving friend.

CHAPTER 1

February ninth was the night of the full moon, and Max Heinz, like any experienced bartender, was well aware of that astronomical happenstance despite the fact that the moon was obliterated tonight by a pounding black storm.

Beyond the Surf House dining room's wide arc of windows, the Pacific Ocean offered ranks of thundering cataracts performing furious prodigies, but it played to shadows and empty tables; the only customers at this late hour were gathered on the upper level in the amber recesses of the Tides Room, as indifferent to the sea's glory as it was to them, drowning the sounds of rain and surf in raucous song and laughter.

Still, for all the noise, it was a small crowd. Monday. Always chancy, and so was the rain. Sometimes it brought them in droves, but not tonight.

There were only five people Max classified as real customers, and he didn't know any of them, although the couple in the corner had been in before and he could identify them as scotch on the rocks and whiskey sour. The three loners at

1

the bar were travelers, but not tourists this time of year. Salesmen, maybe.

All the noise came from the group around the baby grand, but most of them Max didn't classify as customers, even if they did pay for their drinks; they were Surf House employees. One of them, Brian Tally, was his boss.

Conny Van Roon was actually a customer, of course, but on such a regular basis that he rated a special classification. So did the young woman playing the piano but for entirely different reasons. She was in a class by herself.

And Conan Flagg.

Max had never succeeded in classifying Conan Flagg, except perhaps as one of the things that made life in Holliday Beach, a very small dot on Oregon's map, interesting.

He was standing on the far side of the piano, looking down at the keyboard, the light from the overhead spot making strong shadows under high cheekbones, negating itself on straight black hair and under the angled lids of black Indian eyes but reasserting itself in the occasional flash of a smile.

Those smiles were generally for the pianist.

Isadora Canfield, whose graceful, brutally powerful hands would two days hence be shaping the demanding complexities of the Liszt *Concerto No. 1 in E-Flat* on a concert grand in London's Albert Hall, had for the last hour served as accompanist for a loud and only rarely harmonious sing-along.

And she was loving it.

So was Conan Flagg, but then he'd be equally enthralled if she were playing "Chopsticks."

At 6 P.M., Isadora had arrived at his door—in an Alfa Romeo, this time—out of a limbo of months and miles, to inform him that she had the evening free. At 2 A.M. she must leave for Portland International Airport or her jet would turn into a pumpkin, but she was Cinderella until then if he cared to be her Prince Charming.

He cared to. For Isadora or her music—*and* her music— he cared to be almost anything.

"Suuuure, a little bit of heaven fell from out the sky one day . . ."

Brian Tally was leading the chorus in a clear Irish tenor a little muddied with whiskey, which was probably also Irish. He leaned on the piano across from Conan, turning blue eyes appropriately heavenward as he sang, the spotlight firing his red hair, putting into high relief his flushed, blunt-featured face; the kind of face women called ruggedly handsome and men were simply comfortable with. Isadora looked up at him, laughing, and exchanged a telling glance with Conan while her fingers danced through flamboyant arpeggios and maudlin tremolos.

"And nestled in the ocean in a spot so far away . . ."

Brian pulled a solemn face, lost the melody, and broke into laughter, swaying as he draped an arm around Tilda Capek's shoulder. At first it seemed she might fall under his faltering weight, but she managed to get him in balance and on the melody, leading him in a soft, husky alto.

"And when the angels found it, sure it looked so bright and fair . . ."

Tilda was smiling, but it didn't reach her eyes, which were fixed on Brian's face with a troubled concern that was revealing. But Conan wasn't surprised at that revelation any more than he was at the affectionate presumption of Brian's embrace. This had been a long time coming.

Tilda Capek had been hostess and dining room manager at the Surf House Restaurant for three years, and for many of its male customers, she was its main attraction. No doubt she was aware of that, but she never seemed to be, always warmly gracious, yet as unapproachable as a Meissen porcelain and as artfully beautiful: champagne-pale hair and fair skin; large, changeable gray eyes framed by dark lashes. She spoke with a hint of an accent and seemed as unaware of its beguiling charm as she was of her beauty.

But at the moment Tilda was aware of only one thing: Brian Tally.

He was drunk.

"They said suppose we leave it, for it looks so peaceful there . . ."

With extravagant gestures, Brian played conductor to the ebullient chorus, and even if he was unsteady on his feet, his phenomenal memory for lyrics didn't fail him.

But he was drunk, and Conan did find that surprising.

As owner and host of the Surf House, Brian had long ago learned the art of pacing and subterfuge as well as developing an impressive tolerance for alcohol. Conan had never seen him actually drunk, but tonight he seemed to be deliberately working at it.

Tilda wasn't alone in her concern. The matronly soprano issuing from the woman next to her tended to wander from the melody whenever the sharp eyes behind the jewel-rimmed glasses wandered toward Brian.

Beryl Randall, Brian's bookkeeper. "Born with an adding machine for a brain," Brian always said, and Beryl always laughed. At least when *he* said it.

"So they sprinkled it with stardust just to make the shamrocks grow . . ."

Beryl lifted her chin fastidiously as Howie Bliss, who was living up to his surname, staggered against her. The sentiment of the song was overwhelming him; tears flooded his puffy cheeks, and his face was neon pink to the balding dome of his head.

If Brian wasn't so near oblivion himself, Conan knew he'd be watching Howie closely; his history as a cook at the Surf House was checkered with alcoholic disaster.

But if Brian was indifferent to Bliss's alcohol content, Claude Jastrow wasn't. Jastrow, still in his chef's white, contributed to the musicale with a resonant baritone while casting looks of withering scorn on his subordinate.

" 'Tis the only place you'll find them no matter where you go . . ."

Jastrow also bestowed occasional withering glances—equally unavailing—on the man standing next to him at the end of the piano, a meager, middle-aged man who seemed to have outfitted himself for a vacation in Palm Springs ten years ago and never made it.

Conny Van Roon. Everyone called him Conny, but the sign outside his real estate office read, "F. Conrad Van Roon," and Conan had it on good authority that the F. stood for Frederick. He had other things about Van Roon on good authority, too, but tonight Conan could only regard him with warm tolerance as Conny la-da-da'ed along, off-key, off-beat, grinning his vacant contentment.

"Then they dotted it with silver to make its lakes so grand . . ."

Isadora ran a flashing arpeggio while the choraliers took a concerted breath in anticipation of the finale.

"And when they had it finished, suuuure, they called it IIIIIII-er-land!"

The music dissolved in hectic laughter, and Brian shouted, "Erin go brath!" or a close approximation, kissed Tilda resoundingly, then treated Isadora to the same accolade.

"Oh, Dore! You've gotta have some Irish in you somewhere. Isadora, Dore, our own adorable Dore!" He started to make a song of it, then turned, arms raised, and sighted Max Heinz at the bar. "Pour another round for ever'body, Max—on the house!" He surveyed the room and laughed. "Safe enough, the size of *this* house."

Isadora rose but didn't join the general movement toward the bar; she turned to Conan, her hand finding his.

"Five minutes till midnight. Let's go home."

He drew her under the arc of his arm. "Home? You sound like an old trouper. Where's home for you? Any place you hang your Steinway?"

There—that shadow smile again; Conan sighed.

"Home is where the heart is," she said.

"Mm. Then what are we doing here?"

"Hey, Dore!" Brian shouted. "Conan—come on, you two. Berry up to the—" He doubled in a spasm of laughter. "B-barry up to the bell! Oh, damn. What'll you have? Hey, Max, fix the little lady a drink."

Isadora gave Max a brief shake of her head, then smiled for Brian.

"Thanks, but save your booze. It's nearly midnight."

He produced a despondent sigh. "Pumpkin time, right? And that's when your glass slippers crack up."

Conan and Isadora found that amusing for reasons of their own and, if this Cinderella still had two hours grace, neither of them felt it necessary to reveal the fact.

Isadora gave Brian a sisterly hug.

"It's been a marvelous ball. Thanks so . . . much . . . ."

She had lost his attention.

His gaze was turned on the entrance of the bar with a fixity that created a chill vortex; it moved out from him, silencing voices, paralyzing motion. The terrain of his face was suddenly uncharted territory.

And into this silence, someone said in elegantly ironic tones, *"By the pricking of my thumbs . . . Something wicked this way comes . . ."*

Conan glanced behind him, seeking the source of that astounding pronouncement. Claude Jastrow's mouth was tight with a smile, but there was no humor in it, and no one was laughing. They were all, like Brian, staring transfixed at the entrance where the catalyst of this incomprehensible chemistry paused, perhaps intimidated by the many eyes so abruptly focused on him.

A spare, slightly stooped man who could be no more than thirty-five, yet at first glance seemed elderly. He wore a tan raincoat, the shoulders soaked with rain. His pale hands moved nervously to unbutton it, revealing a dark suit, pristine white shirt, and a narrow, unpatterned tie. The shirt collar was unfastened and the tie knot a little loose, but the vest was neatly buttoned, and Conan almost expected to see a gold watch chain looped across it.

Black tie and tails would be no less inappropriate here, and that made the hat crowning the ensemble all the more curious. A Homburg wouldn't have surprised Conan, but the man wore an odd, soft-crowned hat of rough brown tweed, its floppy brim pulled down over his forehead to protect his glasses from the rain. But to no avail in this storm. The lenses were so spattered with light-catching droplets, he seemed blind, which only added to the impression of vulnerability.

Yet Brian's words to him were spoken in a seething, guttural tone that made Conan's pulse accelerate.

"Goddamn you, Nye!"

The man stiffened, eyelids moving rapidly behind the glittering lenses.

"Mr. Tally, that's hardly—"

"What the hell do you want? Can't you leave me alone?"

Conan was watching Brian and the man he called Nye, but he was aware of shifting movements: Beryl Randall taking up a position near Brian on his right; Tilda Capek standing close enough to reach out for his left hand. But he waved her back, as if to keep her out of the way of potential danger. Max was coming warily out from behind the bar, and even Jastrow and Bliss were on their feet, watching, ready.

Nothing about this encounter made sense, and apparently it didn't seem odd to anyone here that Brian Tally, over six feet tall, weighing no less than a hundred and eighty, and none of it superfluous, might need their support, moral or actual, against this antagonist—an owlish man with thin, white hands, looking up at Brian in rain-dazzled myopia.

And Nye, his brow furrowed earnestly, proved willing to brave the united front to approach Brian.

"Mr. Tally, I *must* speak to you. It's very important."

Brian exploded, "Five days, Nye! Then your goons can come in with their damn orders in triplicate and board the place up! You can *have* it—right down to the last cocktail fork! But I've still got five days, so why in hell can't you leave me *alone*?"

Beryl was making clucking remonstrances, while Nye shook his head and moved even closer, which to Conan's mind showed remarkable courage. Or perhaps it was only literal and figurative short-sightedness.

"No, you don't *understand*," he insisted, evidently obliv-

ious to Brian's clenched fists and certainly to his state of
inebriation; he seemed cold sober. "Mr. Tally, I've come
across something that—well, it changes the picture drasti-
cally. Please, it's imperative that I discuss—"

"Damn it, haven't you done enough? What do you *want*?
My blood along with everything else?"

Nye drew himself up. "Mr. Tally, that's entirely uncalled
for. After all, I have a job to do."

"You've done it! You've done *me*!"

Brian closed the remaining distance between them, shaking off the anxious protests and restraining hands, while Nye
persisted in explaining himself.

"Believe me, I'm very sorry about what's happened, but
I'm trying to tell you that I've found something—"

"Sorry!"

That was a poor choice of words.

Beryl screeched, "Brian!" as his sledge-hammer fist
cocked back, level with his shoulder.

Conan moved in, impelled more by instinct than conscious
intention, and discovered that Nye's reflexes were faster than
he anticipated.

Nye dropped.

For Conan, he simply vanished. But the flesh-and-bone
hammer of Brian's fist was launched on its trajectory, and
now Conan was in its path.

In the last millisecond, he saw the raw chagrin on Brian's
face, but he could no more stop that hurtling missile than
Conan could evade it.

It was an earthquake, a tidal wave, and a bolt of lightning
all in one.

A phenomenon, but for Conan one of brief duration.

He didn't even know when he hit the floor.

CHAPTER 2

Conan drove to the bookshop the next morning. Usually he walked the two and a half blocks, but he wanted to find out if he could manage the XK-E's manual shift with his left hand in a cast.

He admitted, grudgingly, that it wasn't as bad as he expected; his thumb, index, and middle fingers were free, which gave him enough grip to control the wheel while he shifted gears.

A fracture in the fifth metacarpal. That was Dr. Nichole Heideger's diagnosis after she studied the X-rays at the hospital last night. The break was accompanied by a gash that took ten stitches to close. Nicky X-rayed his aching and swollen jaw, too, and pronounced it intact, although she advised him it would produce a colorful bruise.

She also advised him, with some relish, to stay out of barroom brawls.

He told her it was an accident, which was as true as it was incredible; the broken bone was a result of hitting his left hand on the edge of a table when he went down after inadvertently putting his face in the path of Brian Tally's fist.

Brian was at the hospital, too, repetitiously and blearily apologetic, looking more in need of medical attention than Conan. Tilda and Max took him away finally after Conan mouthed the words of understanding and forgiveness Brian seemed to need so desperately.

But a true spirit of forgiveness came hard, especially when he had to say good-by to Isadora in the sterile glare of the emergency room with a curious orderly, a nurse, and Nicky as witnesses, and his left hand immobilized in wet plaster.

It was asking a great deal of a man to forgive that.

Two blocks east of his beachfront home, Conan turned left into a parking lane paralleling Highway 101, drove a half block, and stopped directly in front of the bookshop door. That was sheer perversity. Miss Dobie considered it a stone-etched tenet of good business that the best parking places must be left for customers, and she always parked a considerate distance from the shop, even if it meant trudging through a drenching typhoon to reach the door.

And Conan didn't even have the excuse of rain.

Last night's storm was well gone, sweeping east to the Cascades; the air was crystalline, the west wind salt-scented and bracing; the sun poured out a beatitude of warmth upon the row of ramshackle old shops facing the highway, of which the Holliday Beach Bookshop was the largest as well as the oldest and most ramshackle.

This was his most prized possession, yet today he surveyed it with an atypically jaundiced eye, noting that three shingles were missing on one of the upstairs gables, and the trim needed painting.

When he got out of the car, he slammed the door, which was also atypical; the Jaguar was another prized possession, and although its inner workings were to him analogous to the Delphic mysteries, he always treated it with awed respect.

But it had been a long night. A long *solitary* night.

The bells on the door jangled, and Beatrice Dobie, at the counter across from the entrance, offered a sunny smile.

"Good morning, Mr. Flagg. Isn't it a lovely day?"

Conan muttered, "Good morning, Miss Dobie," and went to the door behind and to one side of the counter. It was equipped with one-way glass and a sign reading "Private," but he left it open. That was simply habit.

This room, which he insisted on calling his office, was also a prized possession—rather, a small space serving to house some of his prizes: the Kirman on the floor; the Hepplewhite desk; a cast-iron half ton of an antique safe; the drawings, prints, and paintings—which included a Ben Shahn—crowding the paneled walls.

In the exact center of the desk reposed another of his prizes, although he never made the error of thinking of Meg as a possession. He suspected she considered *him* a possession, however.

He sat down in the big leather chair behind the desk, bringing his head nearly on a level with Meg's.

"Good morning, Duchess."

Siamese cats, Miss Dobie maintained, were descendants of royal houses, to which he always retorted that they had been ratcatchers in the temples. But Miss Dobie adhered to the royal house lineage, adding, irrelevantly, that Meg was a *blue*-point Siamese, as if that made her blood even bluer.

At that moment, the Lady was occupied with her postprandial ablutions, making a pretzel of herself, one hind foot pointed as gracefully as a ballerina's so that she might wash each dainty, daggered toe.

Conan didn't disturb her, knowing that cleanliness is next to repletion in the feline lexicon, nor did he start checking the morning mail, which was generally his first order of business; Meg was sitting on it.

He only slumped deeper in his chair, remembering, when Meg spared him a curious glance, that Isadora Canfield's eyes were exactly the same shade of sapphire blue.

And Isadora was in London.

He was still glumly nursing that thought when Miss Dobie came in carrying a ten-pound tome bound in brown leather, her square face inflated with a beaming smile that made her look incongruously cherubic. She admitted to fifty-five years, but Conan always accepted such feminine admissions with private skepticism.

"Look what came in the mail, Mr. Flagg." She put the book down on his desk with a triumphant thump and paused meaningfully.

But Conan didn't comment, nor even move, and Meg, startled by the seismic impact of the book, unwound herself and departed, muttering inscrutable comments all the way to the door.

Miss Dobie watched her go with an absent frown, then turned to her employer and offered enlightenment.

"It's the Gaston *Portland: Its History and Builders*. The third volume. Remember, that collector in Kansas City—oh, what *is* his name? Chalmers. That's it. F. T. Chalmers. Well, he offered fifty dollars for volume three to complete his set, and I found this at that estate sale in Amity last week and made a bid for ten. Of course, the asking price was forty, but I told Mrs. Jenks I can't pay that kind of money and make anything on my time, and it wasn't very likely she'd find anybody else who'd even offer ten for a single volume out of a set, and what did you do to your face, Mr. Flagg? And—oh, dear—did you break your wrist?"

Conan regarded her with frank amazement, then waved toward the safe where the coffee pot wheezed.

"Will you pour us some coffee, Miss Dobie? No, I didn't break my wrist. It was a metacarpal bone."

She filled two mugs, placed one in front of him, and sat down in the chair across from him with the other.

"Well," she said to his metacarpal, then her gaze shifted to his empurpled jaw. "What happened to your face?"

Conan grimaced as he seared his tongue on the coffee.

"I was in a barroom brawl."

"Oh?"

He lit a cigarette, ignoring her lifted brow and the pendant question in that syllable. When it became apparent that he didn't intend to elaborate, she leaned back and crossed her legs with an air of studied indifference.

"By the way, there was a call for you this morning."

Obviously, she was feeling as perverse as he.

"When? Who was it from?" His first thought was Isadora, which was nonsense; when she was on tour her communications were limited to an occasional post card.

"Oh . . . it was a little after ten; about half an hour ago. Earl Kleber."

He flicked his cigarette irritably against the rim of the ashtray.

"What did he want?"

"Well, I don't know, but he said it was important. He wanted you to call him as soon as possible."

"He's probably selling shares in the police pension fund." Conan eyed the telephone as if it might explain the vagaries of Holliday Beach's chief of police, but he didn't make a move toward it.

"I wondered," Miss Dobie drawled, "if it might not have something to do with the terrible thing that happened at the Surf House Restaurant last night."

Miss Dobie's mind worked in mysterious ways, and he read that as a probe; he had refused to elucidate on the barroom brawl. Still, he didn't understand why she characterized that abortive scuffle as "terrible," or how she happened to know about it.

Of course, the Holliday Beach grapevine was extraordinarily efficient, and the bookshop was one of its main exchange centers, second only to the post office. Conan couldn't guess why Chief Kleber would be interested in last night's comedy of errors, but it was possible.

He shrugged. "Well, I can't think of anything else Earl would want to talk to me about."

Her eyes went round. "You *know* about it, then?"

"Know about it?" That knowledge was not only painfully, but visually evident. "How could I *not* know about it?"

She frowned in obvious confusion, which made it mutual.

"You mean, you were *there*?" she asked.

Conan was considering going home and starting the day fresh; it might make more sense the second time around. The ring of the phone came as a welcome diversion, and he answered crisply, "Holliday Beach Bookshop, may I help you?"

"Conan? Oh God, I hope so."

He stared across the desk at Miss Dobie but only because she happened to be in front of him; he wasn't seeing her. The voice was Brian Tally's, and the husky tension in it sounded an immediate alarm.

"Brian, what's wrong?"

"It's about what happened last night. Conan, I've got to talk to you."

"Last night?" He laughed uncertainly. "Look, I'm not going to sue you, so will you just forget about it?"

"*Forget* about—" A spluttering pause, then, "Oh. I see what you . . . no, I didn't mean—I guess you haven't . . . heard about it, then."

Conan brought his eyes into focus on Beatrice Dobie, who seemed to be concentrating her every faculty on the task of lighting a cigarette.

"No, Brian, apparently I *haven't* heard about it."

"Well, it's that . . . oh, damn"—he stopped for a long breath—"that IRS auditor."

"What IRS auditor?"

"Nye. His name was Eliot Nye. He was the guy who came into the bar last night. The one I . . . I tried to . . ."

Conan closed his eyes wearily. Leave it to Brian Tally to take a swing at an Internal Revenue Service agent.

"Is *he* suing?"

"Suing? Oh, Lord, I wish he was." His next words came out with wondering hesitancy, as if he doubted their veracity himself. "Conan, he's *dead*."

Finally, it was all beginning to make sense.

That was the "terrible thing" that happened last night at the Surf House. Miss Dobie was still pointedly not listening, but under her auburned curls her ears were pink.

Conan said into the phone, "I assume he didn't die of natural causes."

"No. He was . . . murdered."

"How did—" He stopped, hearing Brian in a curt exchange with someone else; a man's voice.

Brian concluded that conversation with an impatient, "All right, I said I'd tell him. Conan, Earl Kleber's here. He wants to talk to you. You're a witness."

"A witness?" The only thing he could testify to was Brian's unsuccessful attempt to treat Nye to a mouthful of fist. But perhaps that was a large "only."

That bungled assault was meaningful in relation to Nye's death only if Brian was a suspect. A murder suspect.

"Brian, where are you?"

"The restaurant. Howie found him here. Nye, I mean."

Brian was mumbling unintelligibly. Conan asked, "Did you say Howie Bliss found him?"

"Yes. He was . . . the body was in the walk-in."

"The what?"

"The freezer. Damn, what a hell of a way—somebody shut him in there; hit him on the head and left him there to . . . to freeze to death."

Conan felt the muscles around his mouth tighten; he crushed out his cigarette with hard jabs.

"You can tell Kleber I'm on my way."

CHAPTER 3

The morning was a gift of spring all the more generous because it was premature. Conan drove south on Highway 101 with the windows down, the heady wind tingling against his face, but the glory of the day stung in some obscure sense, as if it were a personal affront, a gaucherie comparable to laughter at a funeral.

Being a rational and educated man, he recognized the magnificent indifference of natural forces to the triumphs and tragedies of humankind. Still, at times the veneer of rationality cracked, and as he sped to the site of death, he could only regard the shining day with irrational resentment. The occasion demanded gray rain.

But he came by such unreasonable lapses reasonably enough. He was born on a cattle ranch in Eastern Oregon, a semidesert land in which survival was literally dependent on the whims of nature. A drought could sear the pastures into blowing dust flats devoid of sustenance. A badger hole could cripple a horse and leave a man stranded miles from help or water. A lightning-ignited range fire could raze crops, herds, homes, and hopes in a matter of minutes. And in a high desert blizzard, the temperature could drop to forty below and cattle could freeze on their feet.

One of Conan's clearest childhood memories was of a winter night when he was thirteen. He stood at the open door of the old house at the Ten-Mile Ranch, shivering in the agonizing blast of blizzard wind, and stared out at his father on the porch only a few feet away but nearly invisible in flailing curtains of snow.

Henry Flagg faced that keening white oblivion with both hands raised, convulsed into fists, and howled curses into the storm.

He would not curse his God, but he cursed the icy wind that had torn down the power lines; he cursed the cold that even the sturdy walls of this stone-cased house couldn't rebuff; he cursed the mountainous drifts that lay siege to his keep, that no vehicle, no horse, no man, could break through; he cursed his human impotence against that vast omnipotence while his wife and younger son lay dying of pneumonia, and the nearest doctor was thirty miles away in infinity.

Henry Flagg dealt with the forces of nature on a highly personal basis, and now, when the skies laughed in the face of a human tragedy, Conan discovered that he hadn't, after all, interred that with his father's bones.

He roused himself in time to turn right at a junction where a billboard urged him to. The Surf House Resort, a hundred motel units, two swimming pools, sauna, tennis courts, beauty salon, gift boutique, and easy beach access. Plus Tally's Surf House Restaurant and Tides Room Lounge.

Within a distance of two blocks, he went from one axis of Holliday Beach's existence, the Coast Highway, to the other, the beachfront. When he reached Front Street, he crossed onto a field of asphalt around which the resort complex clustered, forever celebrating and waiting for summer.

The restaurant was west of the parking area and beyond

the outdoor pool. The sun made glowing jewels of the lights atop the three police cars, two marked with the insignia of the Holliday Beach police, the other with the star of the county sheriff. The crowd of resort employees and townspeople was small, which meant the cars had been here for some time; curiosity had given way to boredom.

Conan roused a stir of interest as he passed between the cars, exchanging greetings with the onlookers he knew. He felt their stares at his back as he traversed the covered walk beside the swimming pool to the glass doors bearing the legend, "Welcome to Tally's Surf House Restaurant."

It was a little difficult to read at the moment. Standing in front of it was a young man of formidable height and breadth, wearing a blue uniform with a .38 holstered in black leather at his side.

Conan nodded, returning his smile.

"Hello, Billy."

Sergeant William Todd opened the door for him, taking no offense at that familiar greeting; he had been a Holliday Beach Bookshop habitué since he was old enough to read.

"Chief Kleber's waiting for you, Mr. Flagg."

"Yes, I'm afraid so."

Sergeant Todd restrained a smile. "Good luck."

Another policeman was posted ten feet down the hall where a narrow passage opened to the left. Along that passage were the restrooms, a phone booth, and at the end of it, a door opening into the kitchen. That explained the guard; the freezer was beyond that door.

Another ten feet down the entry hall, the opaque glass screen on the right angled out, making the entrance to the bar, and a few feet farther, the hall ended in five slate steps descending into the dining room, a spacious room with a warm, lush atmosphere enhanced by banks and hanging pots of Boston fern. The west wall was a curving panorama, its windows framing an unspoiled span of beach, surf, and sky.

Conan looked to his left where there was another opening into the kitchen. A second police guard was posted there. The other occupants of the room were seated by the windows in a numb tableau presided over by Chief Earl Kleber in his blue uniform and Sheriff Gifford Wills in brown.

Brian was slumped at a table across from Tilda Capek, his head cradled in his hands, while Tilda watched him silently, one hand resting on the table near him. Beryl Randall sat at the next table to the left, and the sunlight wasn't kind to her, betraying the artificial consistency of hue in her reddish hair, the lined irregularity of her scarlet mouth, the harsh curves of overdrawn brows behind the rhinestoned glasses. It also betrayed, when she looked at Brian, the anxious bewilderment in her eyes.

Claude Jastrow sat across the table from her, his attention fixed on the contemporary chandelier in the center of the ceiling. There was something oddly self-conscious in his posture and the studied cant of his head; something also evident in the perfectly matched pants and sweater combination, both designed to play up a slender, but well-proportioned body, and stylishly accented with jewelry at the neck. He wore his brown hair long, brushed straight back, calling attention to a high forehead that was the best feature of a face otherwise notable only for exceptionally fluent eyebrows, which he used to maximum dramatic advantage.

Conan wondered if Jastrow chose to sit so near Howie Bliss with that same self-awareness. They had in common their profession, but it was obvious, even without tasting their respective wares, that Claude Jastrow was a *chef*, while Howie Bliss would never be more than a cook.

At the moment, it seemed unlikely that Bliss could manage a hard-boiled egg. He looked as if he'd been deposited in the chair like a sack of potatoes, the front of his white jacket gapping in zigzags, his round face gray, mouth slack, bloodshot eyes shifting from Kleber to Sheriff Wills in resentful alarm, although their attention was turned elsewhere.

Part of Bliss's problem was undoubtedly shock—he had found the body—but it could also be attributed simply to hangover, and in that he wasn't alone. Across the table from him was another hard-hit victim.

Conny Van Roon's costume hadn't changed since last night except that it was rumpled as if he'd slept in it, and the plaid jacket seemed to have stretched, or he had shrunk within it. Perhaps he had combed his thin, dark hair, but he hadn't shaved. Obviously, he needed the coffee beside him on the table, but he only slumped bonelessly, staring down at his limp hands as if he was wondering how they worked.

Van Roon was oblivious even to Kleber, who was standing near him but occupied at the moment with Max Heinz. Kleber, notebook in hand, had Max thoroughly intimidated, which Conan found both unexpected and surprising. Life behind a bar had inured Max to human folly, and he usually dealt with it with capable tolerance, but he seemed out of his depth now and looked as sick as Van Roon or Bliss, although the only physical reason could be lack of sleep; Max never drank.

Now he threw up both hands helplessly.

"Chief, I told you, I didn't know those five. They paid cash; no credit cards or room charges and none of them was anywhere near eighteen, so I didn't see any IDs."

"All right, so what about this"—Kleber checked his notebook—"this Canfield woman?"

Conan descended the steps and started across the empty expanse of the room, and Brian surged out of his chair.

But Kleber spoke first.

" 'Bout time you showed up, Flagg."

Giff Wills, bluff and bland and blond, was more polite; his job was, after all, elective. He offered a smile.

"Morning, Mr. Flagg."

"Good morning, Sheriff." He glanced at Brian, who had come up beside him, but again Kleber intervened.

"We're getting everybody together who was here last night when Nye came in. I understand you're friendly with this piano player."

"Pianist," Conan said.

Kleber raised a heavy black brow. He was well into middle age but retained a thick crop of dark hair. His eyes were equally dark, but his complexion was fair so that his jaws were always shadowed with incipient beard.

"You know where I can find her?"

"Isadora?" Conan shrugged. "She's out of the country."

"Out of the *country*?"

"On a concert tour."

While Kleber pondered that, Wills nodded sagely.

"Sure, I remember her now. She's Senator Canfield's daughter, Earl. Remember a few years back when the senator got murdered? You was in on that, right, Mr. Flagg?"

"Yes."

Kleber remained unimpressed. "Still ought to get a statement from her. Maybe by phone."

Conan asked sharply, "You're taking statements now?"

"No. Just asking a few questions. And we don't need any advice from amateur lawyers."

Wills oiled the waters adroitly. "Right now, we're waiting for the county DA and the state medical investigator, Mr. Flagg. I asked for a state crime scene team, too."

Conan's eyes narrowed at that. Calling in the state police was certainly an available option for the sheriff, but Wills wasn't famous for his grace in surrendering any part of his authority.

On the other hand, Wills wasn't famous for burning his hands on hot potatoes. Wills seemed to sense Conan's unasked question and cast an anxious glance toward the kitchen.

"When Earl told me who that guy was—I mean, him being

with the IRS—well, I figured this thing might get a little complicated. 'Specially this kind of homicide.''

"What kind is that?''

"Well, the kind where it ain't just a matter of robbery or a couple of drunks having at each other. The kind where you can't say right off the bat who did it.''

Earl Kleber was looking past Conan straight at Brian, and if a confrontation was to be avoided, some distance would have to be put between them.

Conan said to Wills, "I'd like to talk to Brian for a few minutes. We'll be up in the bar.''

Wills, being a peaceable as well as politic man, nodded amiably, but Kleber sputtered, "Now, just a damn minute! I've got some questions to ask you, Flagg, and anyway, you've got no right to leave here, either one of you.''

Brian retorted, "We're not *leaving*, and you've got no right to hold me—unless you want to arrest me here and now.''

Kleber's face went red, but that silenced him. Conan took Brian's arm and aimed him for the steps.

"We'll be within calling range, Chief.''

Kleber turned away with a snort of disgust, while Wills smiled benignly, and Jastrow laughed and murmured, *"Virtue itself of vice must pardon beg. . . .''*

Brian muttered, "Shut up, Claude,'' and marched off, pausing only long enough to send Tilda an uncertain smile.

In the wan solitude of the Tides Room, Brian went behind the bar and stood looking blankly around him.

Finally, he asked, "Can I get you something?''

Conan saw a glass coffee server steaming on a hot plate.

"Coffee, Brian. Straight.''

He fumbled about filling a cup, which clattered in the saucer when he put it on the bar for Conan. Then he opened the refrigerator under the back counter, took out a quart bottle of tomato juice, and when he came around the bar and sagged into the chair next to Conan's, gulped down a third of it, then sat with his eyes closed as if he were waiting to see how his stomach would respond.

No doubt that was questionable. He had repaired his appearance with a shave and change of clothes, and as befitted the host of the Surf House, he always dressed well, but his physical state seemed past remedy and aroused Conan's sympathy. No one should have to contend with Earl Kleber, much less a murder, when he was so pitifully hung over.

"Last night was the full moon," he said at length, apparently getting a reasonably favorable verdict from his stomach. "I should've known."

Conan lit a cigarette and offered him one.

"What's this about the full moon?"

"Don't laugh," he said sharply, although Conan hadn't. "Call it superstition, but it never fails. The night of the full moon, you can always count on trouble in a bar."

Conan took a long drag on his cigarette while Brian got his ignited, a feat of coordination that demanded his full attention.

Then he said grimly, "Conan, I called you because I can read the writing on Kleber's face and I know I'm in trouble. I also know you're a card-carrying private detective, even if you don't seem to like admitting it."

He shrugged. "I just don't like to jeopardize my amateur standing."

"Okay, but I was around when you pulled Dore Canfield out of that hole when her father got . . . murdered." He seemed to have trouble with that word. "Anyway, she was happy with your work, and—damn it, Conan, I need *help*."

The desperate plea in that made both of them uncomfortable. Conan nodded through a veil of smoke.

"I'll do what I can, but I never make any promises."

"I'm not asking for any." Then he began tugging at one finger, finally freeing a ring. "This was my granddad's. A gen-u-ine antique." His mouth shaped a twisted grin. "Sounds like Bea with her damn *heirlooms*. Anyway, that's a three-carat diamond. So, take it. Call it a retainer."

Conan only frowned at it uneasily.

"Why don't you wait until—"

"Take it now, or you'll end up with nothing. When the IRS finishes with me, there won't be anything left but flesh and bone, and I have a feeling Kleber intends to take care of that."

Conan took the ring. It was quite ordinary; a heavy gold mounting for a stone impressive for its size, but he recognized it as something precious to Brian Tally; something surrendered in desperate reluctance.

"All right, Brian. You're my client. First, you'd better tell me about you and the IRS."

He called up a laugh. "I thought you were supposed to ask first if I . . . if I'm guilty."

"Of murder? You said Nye was shut in the freezer. If he died of a blunt instrument the shape of your fist, I might wonder. Even then, I'd call it accidental."

Brian turned away and again seemed to be consulting his stomach.

"He's still in there. Did you know that? He's still in that damned . . . It doesn't seem right."

"Wills called in the state lab people; the body can't be moved until they have a look at it."

"I know." He eyed the tomato juice, then took a puff on his cigarette instead. "As for me and the IRS, that's a long story. It started six months ago. August thirteenth, *Friday* the thirteenth. I got a letter from the IRS, then they sent a field auditor from Portland a few days later."

"That was Nye?"

"That was Nye. He walked in with his briefcase and adding machine, and they might as well have sent a bomb to blow the place up. When he finished his audit—it took a week—he told me I owed the IRS fifty-three thousand two hundred seventy-three dollars."

"Good God!" Conan nearly spilled his coffee at that.

"Sure," Brian said dully. "Good God."

"On this, I *will* ask first if you're guilty."

"Of tax evasion? *No.* Nor tax fraud, civil or criminal. They've been trying to put the screws on me with that."

"Fifty thousand in tax represents a lot of income."

"Oh, that's for three years and includes penalties and interest," he replied airily. "Adds up fast, you know."

"But Nye didn't pull a tax deficiency like that out of his hat."

"Why not? He had to come up with something to fill his quota, didn't he? He talked a lot about averages. They've got it all down. Exactly how much it's supposed to cost to put a steak in front of a customer and how much to put a martini in his hand. Nye didn't like our averages."

"Do you?"

He gave that some consideration, then shrugged.

"I've had this place for fifteen years, and it was six before I began to break even. After that it got better every year, and the last five years—well, I wasn't complaining. I don't know how our averages compare to McDonald's, but anything in the black looks good to me."

"How closely do you check your books?"

Brian responded defensively, "You mean how close do I check my bookkeeper, don't you?"

"If she's solely responsible for your accounting."

"Beryl Randall's been with me since I opened up here, and after the first year I turned all the bookkeeping over to her. Oh, I can run a profit-and-loss sheet, but I know damn well I'm better on the grill, or behind the bar, or just working my jaw with customers than I am with figures, so I leave that to Bea." He paused, smiling to himself. "She's one of the fixtures here, you know, and I love this place. Don't ask me why when it's meant working my butt off twelve to sixteen hours a day all these years."

Conan laughed. "They tell me it gets in the blood. Like show biz."

"Maybe. Anyway, about Bea—she may be a little dotty in some ways, but there's one thing I'll stake my life on: she's a hell of a good bookkeeper, and she's honest."

Conan didn't point out how much he *had* staked on that.

"Then you're convinced the IRS doesn't have a case?"

"I *know* they don't, but that doesn't seem to bother them. What it comes down to is I can't *prove* myself innocent, so that automatically makes me guilty."

"Did you try to get outside help?"

"Sure. I went to a big tax lawyer in Portland and paid him two thousand bucks to tell me to take my licks and pay up. I don't know where he thought I'd get the fifty thousand to pay up *with*. Business has been good the last few years, but not good enough to put back that kind of reserve."

"I suppose you considered making a settlement with the IRS?"

His mouth made a thin, hard line.

"Oh, they talked about that when the Collection Division moved in. They also tried to slip a Form 870 waiver past me. Just a formality, Mr. Tally. But I'm damned if I'll settle for anything more than *zero*. That's what I owe!"

Conan turned his attention to his coffee.

"Brian, how much is this place worth?"

"I had an offer not long ago for five hundred thousand." Then his narrowed eyes, glacial blue, fixed on Conan. "You're about to give me some good advice, right? If I don't come up with the fifty thousand—and I can't, even if I was willing to—they'll slap a seizure order on me and put everything up for sale to the highest bidder, and market value doesn't mean a damn thing. If they get ten cents on the dollar, they'll be happy; they'll get *their* money. So, you're going to tell me to settle while I still have something to settle with. Isn't that how that tune goes?"

Conan shrugged a silent admission, and Brian hesitated, a little embarrassed at his own vehemence.

"Well, it's probably good advice, Conan, and I've come close to taking it. They wear you down, you know. They keep making deadlines and shoving forms at you and shunting you back and forth from one office to another. And all the while you're waiting for the guys in the suits and ties to walk in with the papers and padlock, to take away everything you ever . . ." He stared blindly at his own image in the mirrors behind the bar. "I haven't got any family. I mean, like a wife and kids. It's just me. At least . . ."

He seemed to lose track of what he was saying, and Conan had to prod him with a question.

"So, you're going down with your ship?"

He managed a transient smile.

"Well, why not? What's left after it sinks?"

"What about selling? You said you had an offer for five hundred thousand."

"Sure, that sounds good, doesn't it? After taxes—what the IRS *says* I owe, plus the taxes on the sale—I might have enough left to get a fresh start somewhere else, right? Trouble is, I don't like where the offer came from. It's dirty money, Conan, and I guess I'm still a country boy and probably not too smart, but I wouldn't touch it with a ten-foot pole." He took a slow drag on his cigarette, exhaling with a sigh that seemed to come from his soul. "Besides, I don't think I have what it takes to make a fresh start. I mean, why should I? Why should I fight it? There's no way you can win anymore."

Conan might have asked more about the source of that tainted money but deferred his questions, silenced by the depth of hopeless bitterness he read in Brian's eyes.

"What I don't understand," he went on huskily, "is how they get away with it. The FBI or CIA steps out of line, and they get the press, the ACLU, and Congress on their necks. But nobody even squeaks at the IRS. They take your money *before* you owe it—and that's just out-and-out confiscation—and never pay a damn cent of interest, and if a taxpayer happens to get a refund at the end of the year because the IRS made him pay more than he owed, damn, he acts like it's a gift from heaven. And maybe it is. When you think what they can do to you, I guess you're lucky if they let you have some of your own money back." He took a last puff on his cigarette and crushed it viciously in the ashtray.

"They can't lose. They've got the deck stacked so they just can't lose. Like, once Bea and I were trying to figure out some damn rule on capital improvements, so we called that toll-free number they advertise like it was another gift from heaven. Before it was over, we called three times, got three different people, and three different *answers*. So, what do you do? Flip a coin? The hell of it is, if you get called down for doing the wrong thing, you can't say, well, your agent, Joe Blow, *told* me this was what I was supposed to do. They just say, sorry, Joe didn't know what he was talking about, so pay up. With penalties. And interest. They don't pay any interest on *your* money, but they damn sure collect it when they think it's *their* money. And they can break you—all legal and neat—they can take everything you own, and what can you do? Sue them?" His laugh was an acid parody of amusement. "Sure, you can go to court, all the way to the Supreme Court—*if* you're a millionaire. A good tax lawyer gets seventy-five bucks an *hour*. And even if you win—hell, the IRS can be dead wrong and they don't even have to pay court costs. Oh, Conan . . ."

He closed his eyes, then after a long silence brought his hands up to rub them, finally propping his elbows on the table to support his head.

"You know, I think I *could've* killed Nye. It was his audit that started this whole thing. And last night wasn't the first time I wanted to ram my fist down his throat; it was just the first time I was ever drunk enough to try it. Damn, he was so *smug*. 'Mr. Tally, the figures speak for themselves.' The *figures*! What about me? Why was it when I tried to speak for myself, it just didn't count?"

Conan said with the bitterness of similar experience, "Maybe you didn't speak his language."

"What language is that?"

"Accountese. A language with no adjectives or adverbs, no qualifiers."

"Well, I never was very good at languages. I nearly flunked Latin in high school. Conan, maybe I could've killed

Nye; I had plenty of motive, and I guess that's why Kleber's looking at me so hard, but I *didn't* kill him.''

Conan nodded unconcernedly. ''I'm working on that assumption, Brian. Last night you said something about having five days left. What did you mean by that?''

''Did I . . . well, I've had my *final* final notice. In five—no, four days, they'll be here with the seizure orders and padlocks. That'll be another Friday the thirteenth.''

''But Nye was an auditor. He wasn't with the Collection Division. What was he doing here last night?''

Brian frowned, patted his shirt pocket for cigarettes, and when he came up empty, accepted one from Conan.

''Thanks. I don't know about last night, but he showed up last Thursday and said he wanted to see my books again.''

''Why?''

''I don't know. I didn't talk to him; I passed the buck to Bea. Damn, it's a wonder she hasn't had a *real* heart attack over this. Anyway, I said I didn't care if he went over the stuff with a microscope, I just wanted him out of my hair, so he put everything in a box and carted it off to his motel.''

''All your records?''

''Everything for the three years in question, anyway.''

''Did you see him again? I mean, before last night.''

''Not to talk to him. He was in and out, but I made a point of being out every time he was in.''

''Did he talk to Beryl?''

''Well, not much, I guess. He was checking procedures, inventories, that sort of thing. And getting in everybody's way. Claude threw a bowl of chowder at him one night.'' He smiled tightly. ''Missed, though.''

''What was Nye talking about last night? He said he'd found something that 'changed the picture.' ''

''I don't know. I didn't even hear . . . well, the whole thing's a little fuzzy.''

''That happens to the best of memories. I had the feeling he thought he was bringing you good news.''

''Nye never brought me anything but disaster.'' But after

a frowning pause, he added, "That's what Tilda told me, though. I mean, about it maybe being good news. Max, too. That was when we were driving back from the hospital. Maybe it *was* at least better than the kind of news he'd *been* bringing me. But I guess I'll never know."

Conan checked his watch, taking two runs at it when he automatically looked for it first on his left wrist.

"Brian, you'd better give me a fast rundown on what happened here last night."

Either the question or Conan's search for his watch on the wrong wrist jarred Brian with remembrance of at least one occurrence of the night before, and his face reddened.

"Damn, I didn't even think to—how . . . how's the hand?"

"Well, fortunately, I'm right-handed."

"I guess you'll be eating on the right side of your mouth, too. Oh, Conan, that was so . . . I'm sorry."

"Yes, I know. You made that clear last night." He laughed with that, but Brian couldn't manage it. "Look, the state troops will be arriving soon; we haven't much time. So, start with what happened *after* you laid me out."

He took a puff on his cigarette, frowning sourly at it.

"Well, it was a little confused, and like I said, everything's sort of fuzzy. I was too busy trying to bring you around and stop you from bleeding all over the new carpet to notice what happened to Nye, but I guess Bea got an arm lock on him and took him out of the bar. I think he left then."

"Left the restaurant? Did anyone see him leave?"

"I don't know. I haven't really talked to anybody about it except Tilda, but she was with me the whole time."

"Okay, I remember vaguely being walked out to a car. You and Tilda and Max were with me, and Dore."

He nodded. "We took you to the hospital in my car. Dore followed in yours."

"Did you close the restaurant before you left?"

"No. Bea came out of the ladies' room just as we got out into the hall, and I told her to tend bar till Max or I got back, or just to close up if she wanted to."

into the hall, and I told her to tend bar till Max or I got back, or just to close up if she wanted to.''

"What did you do after you left the hospital?"

"Well, Max was driving. Let's see, first we dropped Tilda off at her apartment, then when we got back here, I told Max to go on home."

"Did he?"

"Yes. I saw him drive off, anyway. You can ask his wife when he got home."

"I'll leave that to Kleber. It'll be something to keep him busy—along with tracking Dore down."

Brian laughed curtly, then asked, "How come he bristles up so much when you come around?"

"I don't know." He paused to light a fresh cigarette, smiling obliquely. "As a matter of fact, Earl should feel rather kindly toward me. I helped make him chief."

"*You* did?" His brows nearly met his red hair at that.

"I sent his predecessor to prison, and that opened up the job for Earl. I'll tell you that story sometime over a few drinks, but right now let's get back to last night."

He sighed. "Where was I? Oh—after I sent Max home, I came in here to the bar and told everybody else to go home."

"What time was it then?"

He had to think about that. "Maybe one-thirty."

"Who was 'everybody'?"

"Bea, of course, and Howie and Claude. They were still here, but Bea had closed up and locked the front door."

"Who has keys to that door?"

"I do, and Bea and Claude. And Howie. He usually opens up in the morning."

"Anyone else?"

"No. Why?"

"Well, it might be useful to know who could've gotten in here last night—assuming none of the doors or windows were jimmied."

Brian hesitated, eyes averted in an oddly sheepish manner. "Nobody would've had to jimmy any doors or windows.

You see, I . . . didn't get around to locking the front door again. Howie said it was open when he came in this morning.''

Conan's black eyes turned opaque; he was afraid he knew what was coming, but he had to ask.

"When did you go home, Brian?"

He shrugged and muttered, "Well, I didn't. After everybody left, I decided to have another drink, and I guess it got to be quite a few. Finally, I just . . . stretched out on the bar and went to sleep. When Howie came in at seven, he found me. *Heard* me, I guess. He said I was snoring to raise the—'' He swallowed hard at that. "Anyway, Howie woke me up, and I went home to try to pull myself together.''

"That was at seven? When did Howie find the body?"

"Nearly eight. That's when he phoned me.''

"That's almost an hour.''

"He had to set up for breakfast first. It wasn't till he started pulling stuff for lunch that he had any reason to open the freezer. When he called me, I thought he'd just been hitting the booze too hard, but . . .'' He stared into nothingness, but what he was seeing in memory was undoubtedly something that would haunt him forever. "I told him to wait for me, then I came down and . . . and looked in the freezer.''

Conan didn't ask what he saw; it was highly unlikely he'd observed any meaningful details.

"You called the police then?"

"Yes. I gave Howie a shot of whiskey—and he needed it—then I phoned Kleber. And don't worry, I didn't touch anything. I didn't even go back in the kitchen.''

"Did you go into the kitchen for any reason last night?"

"I didn't set foot in the kitchen after the dining room closed. That was at ten.''

"After Nye left the restaurant last night—did you see him at all?"

Brian frowned quizzically. "See him? How could I? I was at the hospital until nearly one-thirty, and then—well, I told you the rest.''

Conan turned, distracted by a noise in the entry hall. The angled opening precluded visual access, but he could hear footsteps and voices passing, one raised in surly complaint. He recognized Kleber's voice effectively squelching the surly one.

Brian said, "They must've found Johnny."

"Who?"

"Johnny Hancock." He pulled a wry grin. "*John* Hancock, yet, but ask him who the father of our country is, and he thinks it's the first line of a dirty joke. I tried kidding him once—told him to put his John Hancock on his time card, and he just looked at me and said he always signs his name Johnny."

"Mm. So, *Johnny* works for you?"

"Yes, he's our night man."

"Your what?"

"Janitor, really. All the cleaning has to be done at night after the dining room closes. I guess that's why they call them night men."

"Was he here *last* night?"

"Sure. He goes on at ten . . ." He stopped short, then, "Oh, damn, I forgot about him. He came into the bar to clean up about an hour after I sent everybody else home. I think it was an hour. Anyway, I told him to leave, too."

Conan sighed. "You didn't just happen to see anyone *else* here in the course of the night?"

"No, but that doesn't mean nobody was here. I think it was right after Johnny left that I decided to take a little nap on the bar. Conan, I haven't slept at all for three nights and—well, I was bombed out of my mind."

Conan puffed at his cigarette, refraining from comment on the advisability of getting bombed and catching up on lost sleep on the bar the night his freezer acquired a body.

"Brian, do you have a lawyer?"

He stared at the cigarette in his hand, apparently unaware that it had burned itself down to the filter.

"Well, Herb Latimer takes care of all our legal business here at the restaurant."

"Herb isn't exactly a qualified criminal lawyer. I know a good one, though, and he owes me a favor."

Brian finally dropped the cigarette butt in the ashtray.

"You know, yesterday I thought things couldn't get any worse. Not unless I found out I had a terminal disease. And now . . ." He gave a bitter laugh because he was on the verge of something else. "How in the hell did I ever get *into* this? How does something like this—"

He choked off the words and turned away, and Conan tried to think of something meaningful to say, but with no success. Then he frowned, again distracted by sounds from the hall.

The front door had opened; a shuffle of footsteps tangled in a murmur of voices moved past and into the dining room where Kleber's and Wills's respectful greetings were audible.

"The state has arrived," Conan said. "We'll have some action now, one way or another."

Brian roused himself for a flippant, "Well, with my luck, it won't go my way. I guess I'm one generation too far removed. The Irish luck ran out." He finished off the tomato juice with a sick grimace. "Whoever decided this stuff is good for hangovers?"

Conan put out his cigarette as he rose.

"Some tomato-juice canner, probably. Come on, we might as well—"

"I'll be damned. You just never know who you're going to run into."

Conan turned, startled both by the unexpectedness and the familiarity of that dry, drawling voice.

The man slouching against the screen at the entrance was tall and rangy, with dust-colored hair that always looked windblown and sage-gray eyes set in a habitual long-distance squint. He wore a dark suit replete with tie, but even after twenty years he never seemed comfortable in city clothes. Levi's, boots, and a Stetson would suit him better.

Conan gave him a slow smile.

"No, Steve, you just never know." Then to Brian, "Your Irish luck hasn't run out yet. Brian Tally—Steve Travers. We used to ride fence together when we were kids." He paused, then added, "Steve is Chief of Detectives for the Salem division of the state police."

CHAPTER 4

In the dining room the suits and ties of the newcomers gave
the gathering a straitly formal aspect. Besides Steve Travers,
there were three members of the crime scene team carrying
odd-shaped cases, tools of their trade, and a thin, sardoni-
cally handsome man with a trim mustache and beard: Dr.
Daniel Reuben, state medical examiner. He sent Conan a
brief smile; they had met before in similar circumstances.
Also present was Owen Culpepper, Taft County district at-
torney, looking paler and more dyspeptic than usual, one
hand moving repeatedly to his face to push his glasses up on
his nose.

There was one newcomer whose attire was anything but
formal. While the official contingent deliberated, Conan
turned to Brian and asked, "Is that Johnny Hancock?"

Brian nodded, eyes narrowing as he looked over at the
man standing near Tilda's chair being thoroughly ignored.

At first glance, he seemed an unkempt and rebellious eighteen, clothed in artfully ragged Levi's and sweatshirt, long,
lank hair constrained by a beaded band, the lower part of his

face obscured in an attempted beard, the upper part by dark glasses. On second glance, however, Conan decided he was closer to thirty than eighteen.

"Right, Mr. Travers. You just holler if my office can help out in any way."

Sheriff Wills was making his exit, trying not to let his relief at surrendering this particular case to the state seem too obvious. He was in such a hurry, he didn't notice that the relief at his departure was mutual.

With Wills out of the way, Kleber turned to Steve.

"I guess you'll want to look at the body first, Mr. Travers."

"Yes. Who are those people?"

Kleber glanced toward the windows. "That's everybody who was here last night when Nye came into the bar. At least, everybody we had a name for and could round up. I figured you'd want statements from all the witnesses."

"Witnesses? You mean you have witnesses to the murder?"

"Well, not exactly to the murder, but there was a scrap between Nye and Brian Tally, and Tally tried to—"

Brian said hotly, "I didn't even touch him!"

"Well, it damn sure wasn't because you didn't try!"

Owen Culpepper turned even paler and put in, "Uh, Earl, maybe you'd better hold off on any, uh, official comments?"

Steve frowned impatiently and headed for the kitchen, waving to the crime scene men and Dr. Reuben to follow.

"Come on, let's see what we've got. Conan, you might as well come, too."

That last was put so casually, it was only when Conan started after Steve that Kleber came to with a startled, "Now, wait just a damn minute!"

When Steve turned on him questioningly, he assumed a more conciliatory tone.

"Mr. Travers, he's only here as one of the witnesses. He's got no business in official police business."

Steve said in a velvet-gloved drawl, "Chief, I've known

Conan for a long time, and this won't be the first time he's been involved in police business—sometimes on request.''

With the state firmly established in command, Steve led the way into the kitchen, Conan only a pace behind, Kleber hard on his heels, Dr. Reuben and the crime scene team trailing after them.

The entourage marched through an anteroom of sorts, which Brian always referred to as the pantry, an area devoted to preparation of the accessories of a meal. On the left-hand wall was an ice well, coffee brewers, water, soft drink, and milk dispensers, and under the counter, racks of glasses and cups.

On the right-hand wall in the corner was a cash register, and Conan wondered about that; there was another in the dining room where customers paid their dues. Above this one was a blackboard with the remains of hasty messages incompletely erased. One was still there. ''86 prime.'' In the code of the kitchen, that meant prime rib had been deleted from the menu due to temporary shortage.

Centered in this wall was a pass-through from the cooking area, and below it a wide counter cluttered with condiment racks, bread baskets, and butter warmers. Beneath it were stainless-steel drawers, miniature ovens for warming bread and rolls.

The far wall was divided, the left half given over to a salad counter, the right a doorless opening into the kitchen proper. To the left of the opening, behind the wall, was a narrow tier of five steps and a door.

Behind that door, Conan knew, was the corridor giving access to the restrooms and connecting with the entry hall.

Beyond the pantry, the kitchen loomed large in every dimension. It was shaped roughly like a reversed L, and they were entering at the toe of it. The initial impression was a maze partitioned with worktables and carts. Folding itself around the corner of the L were ten stainless-steel yards of dishwashing apparatus, looking like an aborted assembly line; enigmatic machines squatted here and there like cast-

iron trolls, and esoteric tools and instruments hung over
shelves bearing in gargantuan containers the ingredients of
gastronomic delight.

Past the side entrance, a short wall extended back to make
a corner with a transverse wall. Against the short wall was a
table surfaced in laminated wood two inches thick, and on
the transverse wall, a wooden door mounted with a heavy
metal latch.

The door was at least eight inches thick. Conan could see
that because it was ajar, but it didn't open into the freezer as
he expected when he saw the kind of door it was.

A cooler. He waited while Steve and Kleber conferred,
aware for the first time of the level of noise here; a constant
roaring rush. He looked back into the cooking area where a
huge metal hood revealed the source. Exhaust fans. The
sound seemed to emphasize the ghostly inactivity of this place
designed for work.

Steve turned to enter the cooler, and Conan was ready at
his side.

"Am I still welcome in this part of the business?" He had
to lean close to make himself heard.

Steve laughed and nodded. "Just watch your hands and
don't give Kleber a chance to say I told you so." Then over
his shoulder to Dan Reuben, "Close quarters. Let me take a
look, then I'll get out of your way."

Inside the cooler the mechanical roar was augmented by
refrigeration equipment pouring cold air out of a duct above
the door. The cooler was about twelve by six feet, its shelves
inundated with crates of fruits and vegetables, giant steel
stockpots of soups and gravies, gallons of dressings and
sauces, butter in sixty-pound blocks, bacon in twenty-pound
cartons, eggs in boxes of thirty dozen, hotel pans filled with
whole prime ribs, steaks, preformed hamburgers, boned
chicken breasts, crab, oysters, cocktail shrimp, breaded
prawns and razor clams, scampi, sole, and whole salmon
staring glassily.

It was stultifying, the realization of the quantitative mass of food processed in this kitchen each day, skillfully prepared for the delectation of demanding diners, a large portion of it inevitably returning as garbage.

A waste, but a great deal in life could be called a waste. And some lives.

On the wall to the right of the cooler door was another identical to it. The latch wasn't closed. Steve pushed the door open with the back of his hand.

The freezer was a third the size of the cooler, three of its walls lined with shelves, the food on them nearly all contained in white boxes or wrapped in frost-filmed plastic. Another duct poured out a glacial wind, misting the air with cold steam, and for the second time in a single day, Conan was reminded of his thirteenth winter.

The open space in the center of this boreal pocket was small; the body filled it. Even then, it was cramped into a fetal position.

Many cultures in human history considered that position appropriate for the dead.

And what culture advanced enough to find it necessary to collect taxes didn't despise its tax collectors? Conan thought, Poor little tax collector, curled in a frozen womb, who despised you this much?

Eliot Nye lay on his left side, right hand near his face, his head toward the door. It had been pressed against it, in fact; his hair retained the flattened impression. At the back of his head the hair was matted with brownish frost; the blood had frozen. It was impossible to assess the wound, but it had bled freely. The floor was thick with the same grim frost.

Steve went down on one knee.

"He wasn't dead when he was put in here."

"No. And he didn't stay unconscious."

The spilled boxes on the floor, the bloody imprints of desperation on the lower shelves were silent evidence of that and of unthinkable terror. There was blood on the shoulders of the raincoat; Nye had been partially upright for a short time. Conan touched the coat. It was stiff with frost.

"His coat was still wet."

Steve frowned. "Did it rain here last night?"

"Torrents. I know it didn't stop before 3 A.M. when I finally got to bed."

The glasses were askew, the lenses frosted. Conan remembered the raindrops sparkling on them last night and tried not to think about the fact that there had been no light in this frigid tomb. He stared at the right hand, at the purplish cast of it; blued flesh under a mottled casing of frozen blood. The blood must have come from the head wound; the hand itself didn't seem to be injured.

"Oh, damn." Steve breathed the words in a near whisper as he turned to look at the inside of the door.

There was blood on the push knob and in smears around it, but opening the outer latch with that knob took both strength and the leverage of a standing position. Nye's strength had been drained with the blood that rimed the floor, and he'd been incapable of standing; none of the rust-brown blotches left by the beating of his fists were more than three feet above the floor.

And no one heard his desperate poundings. This chill cell was insulated to preserve its deathly cold; it might as well have been soundproofed, and outside in the kitchen there was the noise of the exhaust fans.

Were they on last night? Brian would know.

Then, as his eyes followed the ghastly smears down toward the bottom of the door, Conan felt the outer chill closing around his heart.

There was a shape and purpose to some of those smears.

Letters. Two letters, canted to the left, drawn crudely like a child's first efforts; drawn in darkness; drawn in his own blood by a man in the black shadow of death.

The first was relatively clear, although the horizontal lines lapped too far over the vertical. Still, it was readable as a B. The second looked like a grim, asymmetric crucifix with the horizontal crossbar overbalanced to the right and at that end sagging down, then failing with the failing strength of the hand that shaped it.

But it was legible. The letter T.

From the cooler door, Earl Kleber said, ''Thought you might be interested in that, Mr. Travers. Sort of a dying testament, you might say.''

Steve rose and faced him.

''You have somebody around here with the initials B.T.?''

Kleber smiled grimly. ''Matter of fact, we do. You met him. Name is Brian Tally.''

CHAPTER 5

Conan stayed out of the way while the criminologists and Dr. Reuben went about their business. He wandered the sterile reaches of the kitchen, feeling as empty and useless as the silent machines, the suspended pots and tools, the dead ovens.

He explored the upper part of the L, passing the pastry table and baking ovens, pausing to look into two storage rooms. There was a door at the end of the L. He tried it, using a handkerchief, although he was sure too many people had access to everything in this kitchen for fingerprints to mean anything. It was unlocked. Beyond it was a long passage lined with plastic garbage cans.

When he realized that he'd been staring at the ranked cans for a full minute without moving, and certainly without seeing them, he turned away, closing the door behind him.

What he had in fact been seeing was those two bloody letters.

B T

B T: Brian Tally.

With those letters Nye had pointed an incarnadined finger of accusation.

Yet it didn't make sense. Conan could no more accept the possibility that Brian had murdered Eliot Nye—at least not in this particular fashion—than he could accept an assertion that the sun rose in the west.

But neither could he deny the reality of those letters.

He returned to the front of the kitchen where an occasional strobe flash indicated that the crime scene crew was still at work in the cooler and freezer. Dr. Reuben was supervising the removal of the body; it was on a stretcher and decently covered, but there was something grotesque about the hunched shape of it under the sheet. It wouldn't give up its fetal position. Conan watched two policemen maneuver the stretcher out, faces reflecting more than physical strain.

Dan Reuben was shaking his head. "Steve, I can't do anything until it thaws out, and I hope you don't expect me to give you an estimated time of death."

"Well, we know it had to be sometime between midnight and eight o'clock this morning."

"Based on rigor?" Reuben asked ironically.

"No. Oral flux."

"Well, I can tell you this much: it was closer to midnight than eight. That's based on the state of freezing. Look, I've got an autopsy to do in Medford this afternoon. I'll have to take care of this one tomorrow morning."

Conan had come up to eavesdrop. He asked, "What about the head wound? Any idea what hit him?"

Reuben shrugged. "Probably the usual blunt instrument. That's all I can tell you now."

Conan nodded and offered nothing more to detain him, thinking that there were undoubtedly more lethally sharp instruments than blunt in this kitchen. He roused himself when Steve went to the cutting table near the side door.

"Personal effects, Conan. You want to look them over?

Chief?'' This to Kleber, who was hovering nearby. ''I'd like to talk to that janitor. What's his name?''

''Hancock. You want me to bring him back here?''

''Yes, thanks.''

Conan studied the meager pile on the table. A ring of keys, some change in which a paperclip had gotten mixed, a ball-point pen, a notebook without a remaining note, a pickup slip from a local drive-in restaurant. A billfold. Its contents had been removed: two twenties and a ten, four credit cards, a photograph of a pretty, dark-haired girl; it looked like a graduation portrait. There was also a driver's license and a plastic card inscribed with the Lord's prayer.

Conan turned the license to read it. Eliot Ussher Nye. Thirty-four years old. Restriction for corrective lenses.

Steve said, ''Ussher. As in House of, maybe?''

''It's spelled with a double S. As in Archbishop.''

''Okay, I'll bite. Who's Archbishop Ussher?''

''He was an accountant, too, in his way. Seventeenth century. He went through all the begats in the Bible and calculated that the world was created in 4004 B.C. I think it was October twenty-sixth at something like nine in the morning.'' Then he frowned. ''Chief?'' But Kleber was gone.

''I don't think Earl can tell you whether that was standard or daylight-saving.''

''What?''

''The creation of the world.''

''I was hoping he could tell me where Nye was staying. What motel, I mean. He's been in town since Thursday.''

''Has he, now? Well, I can save you making yourself be-holden to Earl. Nye was staying at the Seafarer Motel a cou-ple of blocks south of here. In fact, the chief has already put a guard on his room and car.''

''Well, you have to give him credit. But what I want to know is where is Nye's motel key? I can't believe he'd walk out at midnight and leave his room unlocked.''

Steve studied the scant assortment on the table, the long-distance squint reaching out a few more miles.

"Good question. And he *did* lock the door. At least it was locked when Earl's sergeant arrived for guard duty. We checked all of Nye's pockets, which wasn't easy. It must've been raining buckets here last night; his coat was soaked through. And frozen through."

Conan started as if he'd been physically prodded.

"Damn. His hat, Steve. Where's his *hat*?"

"Oh, Conan, for God's sake, how would I know—"

"Never mind. Here's our night man."

"Our what? Oh. Hancock."

Kleber led Hancock into the kitchen, curtly cautioned him not to touch anything, then presented him to Steve.

Hancock still wore his dark glasses, which was as revealing as dilated pupils. His mouth slackened as his head turned toward the cooler where the lab men crowded the confined space, but when he faced Steve, his arrogant slouch served notice that he didn't intend to volunteer anything.

Steve asked pleasantly, "What time do you usually get to work, Mr. Hancock?"

He hesitated, but perhaps it was only because he wasn't accustomed to being addressed as "mister."

"Ten o'clock," he admitted.

"And how long a shift do you put in?"

"Oh . . . usually till four. Depends."

"When did you leave last night?"

"Early. About two, maybe."

"Why did you leave early?"

"Brian told me to."

"That's Brian Tally? Okay. Then you were here at midnight?"

"I told you, I come on at ten."

Steve smiled. "I mean, were you here in the kitchen?"

"Sure. I don't usually finish up in here till about one."

"You start your cleaning in here?"

"Yeah."

"So, you were here in the kitchen from ten until one. Did you leave at any time?"

One shoulder twitched in a shrug. "No."

"All right, now this is important. Did you see anybody here in the kitchen during that three-hour period?"

He paused, only briefly, but Conan found himself resenting the dark glasses. He had the feeling something vital was going on behind them; something lost to him.

Finally, Hancock's mouth stretched in a malicious grin.

"Yeah, I seen somebody. It was Claude. Must've been about midnight."

"Claude?"

Kleber explained, "Claude Jastrow. He's head cook here."

Hancock snickered at Jastrow's unintentional demotion, but the hard look he got from Kleber sobered him.

Steve said, "Chief, I'd like to talk to . . ."

But Kleber was already on his way. "I'll bring him."

"Thanks. Okay, Mr. Hancock, tell me about Jastrow."

"You mean when he come in here? Well, I just got back from taking out the last load of garbage, and here he was, standing about where you are now."

"You didn't see him come into the kitchen?"

"Well, no. Like I said, I was taking the—"

"Yes, I got that." There was a hint of chill in his tone. "How long does it take to get the garbage out?"

"Oh, hell, I don't know. Some days they collect a ton of garbage here."

"And you take it outside the building?"

"Yeah. The dumpster is . . . out at this end of the parking lot." He was beginning to realize his error.

"Give me a rough estimate. How long were you *out* of the kitchen while you were hauling off a ton of garbage?"

His hands opened and closed nervously.

"I . . . well, it takes maybe an hour altogether. But I was, you know, sort of in and out the whole time."

Steve didn't seem impressed with that qualification.

"Did you see anybody else here in the kitchen at any time after midnight?"

Another pendant hesitation, then, "No. I didn't see nobody."

He was spared further questions for the moment. Kleber returned with Jastrow, who gave Hancock a heavy-lidded look of transparent contempt and said in honeyed tones tending to Old Vic English, "What a relief it must be, Johnny, to answer police questions about something other than your own transgressions. Ah—is it *Chief* Travers? Your title precedes you, sir, if not your fame, which I'm sure only reflects the benightedness of this backward corner of the world."

Steve needed a moment to digest that speech, which would have been sickly obsequious except for the drawling irony in it.

"I never use the 'chief,' " he said, "but you'll have to fill me in on the etiquette for 'chef.' "

Jastrow threw back his head to laugh at that.

"Ah, very good. And I never use the 'chef.' You have some questions for me?"

"Yes. Were you here in the kitchen about midnight last night?"

"Of course I was." This with a wry smile for Hancock. "My purpose, Mr. Travers, was to look in on Johnny, who has an unfortunate tendency to knit up his 'ravel'd sleave' at every opportunity, *or* to avail himself of the cooking wine, which reduces his usual low efficiency rate to zero."

Hancock's whiskered chin jutted out belligerently.

"Damn it, you got no right putting me down like—"

"Oh, no doubt, Johnny. *Treat every man after his desert, and who should 'scape whipping?* Certainly not you."

"Never mind," Steve put in before Hancock could retort to that. Then to Jastrow, "Can you pin down the time a little closer? I mean, when you came into the kitchen?"

"It was twelve-fifteen," he replied flatly. "I remember looking at my watch when I left the bar."

"Okay, could you tie it in with what was going on in the bar then? Was Nye still there?"

"Ah, the little Sadducee. No. Actually, the alarums and excursions were over by then, and Mr. Flagg had been assisted from the field on his shield." He spared Conan a sympathetic smile.

Steve only glanced obliquely at Conan, then asked Jastrow, "Did you see anybody else in or near the kitchen?"

"Other than Johnny? No."

"How long were you in here?"

"Oh, perhaps five minutes. Long enough to see that Johnny had neglected to empty the grease traps on the grills. I also noted and informed him that he'd done his usual slipshod job mopping the floor."

Hancock snarled, "A couple of scuff marks! You could *eat* off that floor!"

"Perhaps *you* could; I assume your digestive system is inured to coexisting with filth, but mine isn't, and I—"

"You know what you can do with your digestive system!"

Steve noted testily, "Look, I'm not from the Health Department. That'll be all for now, unless . . . Conan?"

Conan had glanced up from his frowning survey of the floor to catch Steve's attention with a raised eyebrow.

"Claude, where were those scuff marks?"

"Here." He took a step backward to the corner of the cutting table. "Johnny apparently managed to eradicate them the second time around, but there were two of them, approximately parallel, about—oh, two or three feet long and angling off toward . . ." His eyes completed an arc ending at the freezer, but if he drew any conclusions, Hancock gave him no opportunity to voice them.

"So *what*? A couple of sh—of measly scuff marks! And, damn it, they wasn't even there when I mopped the floor!"

Conan demanded, "They weren't there? Are you sure?"

Jastrow laughed mockingly. "Mr. Flagg, Johnny's perceptions aren't always exactly clear, shall we say."

"Those marks wasn't there when I mopped!" Hancock

insisted. "Hell, you probably made 'em yourself just so you'd have something to bitch about!"

"I hardly need to go to that much—"

Conan interrupted impatiently, "Johnny, when did you mop the floor?"

"Well, I mopped this end before I started on the garbage. The floor was still wet when Claude come in and tracked it up while he was looking for something to bitch about."

"You weren't finished with the mopping? Where was the mop then—and I suppose you use a bucket of some kind?"

"Sure. It's a regular mop bucket with a wringer on it. I left it right over there by the dishwasher."

Conan might have pursued the subject, but Kleber's patience was obviously wearing thin, and he decided not to try it further. He nodded his satisfaction to Steve, who thanked Jastrow and Hancock and sent them back to the dining room.

When they were out of earshot, Kleber asked, "Mr. Travers, what about getting those statements from the witnesses?"

Steve studied the work in progress around the freezer.

"You have a stenographer available?"

"Amy Marstand's waiting at the police station."

"Okay, have somebody take the, uh, witnesses to the station, but before we get started on that, I want to see Nye's motel room. Jeff?"

One of the men from the crime scene team turned. Lieutenant Jefferson Kaw, whose Indian blood was as obvious as Conan's and not as diluted.

"Yes, Steve?"

"When you get through here, the next stop is Nye's motel room. I'm going to take a look at it now."

Kaw nodded. "Just keep your hands to yourself, okay?"

"Don't I always?" He frowned as a Holliday Beach policeman came into the pantry and beckoned to Kleber.

"Phone call for you, Chief."

Conan followed Steve and Kleber back into the dining room, noting that the tableau by the windows hadn't changed appreciably. Brian looked at him as if awaiting a divine sign, but got only a vague shrug. While Kleber took the call on the phone by the cash register, Steve was buttonholed by the D.A. Conan caught part of that conversation.

"Luther Dix," Culpepper said, wringing his hands. "Assistant district director. That's in the Portland IRS office. I, uh, told him you're in charge of the case?"

Steve grimaced. "I'm afraid so. What did he want?"

"Well, uh, I think he just wanted to find out, well, what progress you're making. Oh—he seemed, uh, quite concerned about any IRS papers Nye had in his possession?"

Steve said curtly, "I'll call him as soon as I can."

Kleber hung up the phone with a satisfied grunt.

"Mrs. Randall?"

Beryl Randall looked up with a startled, "Yes?"

"That was the state patrol. They found your car."

She sighed gustily, "Oh, thank goodness!"

"Your car?" Brian asked with a perplexed frown. "What's this about your car?"

"Well, it was stolen. When I woke up at seven, it was gone. That's why I was late this morning, then when I got here and found out what . . ." Brian had paled, and she bit her lip, then turned to Kleber. "Where was it?"

"Down at the Shag Point state wayside just south of Holliday Bay. Somebody had a short ride."

She blinked in bewilderment. "Why, that's only a mile from my house. How strange."

"Maybe not. It won't start. It's being towed up to the police station. We'll have to go over it, you know."

"Oh. Yes, of course." She added absently, "I've been having trouble with the starter. I suppose . . ."

"I guess that's why it was such a short ride. The car seems to be all right otherwise, though."

"Well, that *is* a relief. I'd certainly hate to have it stripped up, or whatever they call it."

"Yes, ma'am. Mr. Travers? You ready?" He carefully

ignored Conan, even when he fell into step with Steve as he
headed for the entry hall.

Conan heard Brian saying to Beryl, "You should've told
me about your car, Bea. Damn, that's a hell of a note."

And her long sigh. "It just seemed . . . such a trivial
thing. I mean . . ."

She didn't finish. Everyone knew what she meant.

CHAPTER 6

"**N**ye must've been trying to save the taxpayers some money when he picked this one," Steve commented dourly.

Conan nodded, surveying the arc of small, aging cottages. Still, they were freshly painted, the peaked roofs newly shingled, the crescent of lawn as trim as a putting green.

"Noah and Wilma'll be here in the office, Mr. Travers," Kleber said as they approached the cottage at the hub of the arc. "Nice folks, the Appletons. Been in Holliday Beach for thirty years. That's where Nye was staying: number ten." He pointed to the third cottage from the north end of the semicircle. A Ford sedan was parked in front of it, and a policeman guarded the door.

Inside the office, Noah Appleton was snoring softly in an armchair facing a dark television screen, but his wife was on duty at the counter.

She said in a stage whisper, "Noah! Wake up, for heaven's sake." Then with an apple-dumpling smile for Kleber and entourage, "Good morning. Noah runs the night shift here, y'know. Thinks he's still home in bed."

But Noah was on his feet now, producing a smile even before his eyes were fully focused.

"Morning, Earl." Then when Kleber introduced Steve, "Well, now, it's a real pleasure, Mr. Travers. Anything Wilma and me can do to help out, we'd be proud. Morning, Mr. Flagg. Bet you had to get out your detective badge again." His knowing laugh garnered a black look from Kleber.

Conan shrugged. "Just tagging along, Mr. Appleton."

"Sure, sure. Well, Mr. Travers, I guess you'd like to see the cottage where Mr. Nye was staying."

"Yes, but I'd like to ask you a few questions first. When did Nye check in?"

Appleton had the registration card handy on the counter.

"Let's see, that was February fifth; last Thursday."

"Is there a phone in his room?"

"Yep. We've got phones in every unit, but they're extensions; all the calls go through our switchboard here. You'll want a list of his calls, I expect. Wilma?"

"Here you are." She produced a file card with a small flourish. "These are just the long-distance calls. We don't charge for local calls, but any long distance we put through the operator ourselves and get time and charges. Otherwise, we'd be mortgaged to the phone company."

Steve obligingly laughed, letting Conan study the card over his shoulder before he passed it on to Kleber. The only calls were dated February ninth; yesterday. Three between two and five o'clock all to the same number, then three more between five-thirty and eight to a second number.

"I remember those calls," Mrs. Appleton declared. "Person-to-person, but Mr. Nye couldn't seem to get hold of the *right* person. That first number, now that was the *In*-ternal Revenue Service in Portland."

Steve raised his eyebrows, properly impressed.

"Do you remember the name of the person he was calling?"

"Oh, dear, let's see now. The first name was Luther. Don't hear that much these days. But the last name . . ."

"Dix?" Steve asked tightly.

"Why, sure, that was it. And the other number was for him, too. His home phone, I guess. Must've been out to dinner or something. Mr. Nye didn't get hold of him till—well, there it is. The last call. Eight o'clock."

"But he *did* get hold of him? Okay, can you think of anything unusual that happened while Nye was here? Did he have any visitors you noticed, for instance?"

She puffed herself upright. "Sure did. Just last night, in fact. Noah, you better tell him about it."

Noah seemed to be looking forward to it.

"Well, it was twelve-twenty—I noticed the time because it was late for customers—and this fancy foreign car drives up, rumbling like it had two motors under the hood."

"A foreign car? Did you notice what make?"

"I wouldn't know one from another. It was real low; one of them racing types, just room enough for two people, and you wonder how. And it was red. Fire-engine red. Anyhow, the car stops outside here and a woman gets out."

"Was she driving?"

"No, there was a man driving. Young, dark hair and a mustache; sort of a sporty-looking feller. He got out and opened the car door for her."

"A gentleman. All right, tell me about the lady."

"It was the lady who came into the office." Then with a sly laugh, "I figured that was a real switch, but it turns out she didn't want a room. Told me her name was Lorna Moody Nye—used three names just like that—and she wanted to know what unit her husband was in. Eliot Nye."

Appleton paused to relish the surprised stares that engendered, then admitted, "Well, now, that sort of took *me* back, too. She said she come to see Mr. Nye, that it was real important, and she knew he was staying here but didn't know which unit.''

Steve had recovered himself. "Did you tell her?"

"Well, sure. Didn't seem any reason not to." He frowned and asked anxiously, "You don't suppose them two had anything to do with what happened to Mr. Nye?"

Kleber laughed that off. "Not considering the circumstances, Noah."

Conan sent him an oblique glance. They didn't yet know *all* the circumstances.

"What happened then?" Steve prompted.

"Well, she went back to the car, and they drove off around the circle here to number ten."

"Did you see them go in?"

"No. I didn't figure it was any business of mine. Anyhow, I was in the middle of the late movie."

"Do you know what time it was when they left?"

" 'Fraid not. You'd think I would've heard that car, but it was raining like heck last night, and what with the TV, well, I never heard when they left. About one, when I was walking over to the house"—he cocked a thumb southward—"I didn't see the car, so they was gone by then."

"What about Nye's car?"

"It was there, right where it's sitting now."

"Any lights in his cottage?"

"No, not a one."

Conan put in casually, "By the way, did Mr. Nye leave his room key with you when he went out last night?"

Appleton seemed a little surprised at the question.

"No, but he never left his key with us, Mr. Flagg. Matter of fact, he hardly ever went out the whole time he was here."

"What about yesterday? Was he in his room all day?"

Appleton surrendered the floor and the question to his wife, who explained, "I was around cleaning the units or here in the office all day yesterday. I don't think he went out but once, and that was about suppertime. Maybe six. He didn't stay long, and when he came back, he was carrying a couple of white sacks, like he'd brought his supper in.''

Steve squinted thoughtfully over that, then asked, ''Do you have an extra key for number ten we could use?''

Appleton nodded and rummaged under the counter until he produced a key on a plastic oval.

''Here it is. This is the spare.''

''The only spare?''

''Yes, but we've got a master key, so you can keep this one till you're finished up there.''

''Thanks. We'll look at the room now, then a lab crew will be over later.''

Kleber took the lead as they crunched across the gravel drive to number ten. He introduced Steve to the sergeant guarding the door; Conan he was still trying to ignore. Steve examined the door and lock carefully before opening it; there was no evidence of forced entry. Once inside, he flicked on the wall switch, using the key as a lever.

Conan followed him in and surveyed the room, bleak in the light of the single ceiling fixture, holding on to the night with the shades drawn. There was a peculiarly sterile tidiness about it and few indications of occupancy; the bed hadn't been touched since it was last made.

He opened the closet where a suit, two fresh shirts, a bathrobe, and pajamas were neatly hung.

''His hat isn't here.''

Kleber, standing at the door, elbows angling out so he could hook his thumbs in his gun belt, snapped, ''You making an inventory of his clothes already?''

Conan responded coolly, ''I just want to know what happened to the hat he was wearing last night. It was an oddlooking thing, sort of a tweedy brown cloth; looked like it was handmade.''

When Kleber snorted contemptuously at that, Steve sent him an impatient frown but offered no comment. He was bending over the dresser, which Nye had turned into a desk. Conan went over to look at it. There was a typewriter at one end, an old-fashioned electric adding machine at the other. The space between was uncluttered, only a stapler, a few paperclips, a pencil sharpener, five pencils of various lengths, and a yellow legal pad without a mark on it, or even the ghost of an indentation, although half its pages had been torn out.

Conan knelt with Steve when he opened the attaché case on the floor by the dresser. Inside they found blank IRS forms and bulletins in stultifying variety, a fresh legal pad, and one file folder. Steve opened it, handling it by the edges, and disclosed a sheaf of tax forms and schedules.

He read, "F. Conrad Van Roon, 429 Coast Highway, Holliday Beach. You know him, Conan?"

"Yes. He's one of the . . . witnesses. I wonder if this means *he's* being audited, too."

"Could be. Luther Dix ought to know."

"But will he tell?"

Conan rose and stepped aside for Kleber and, as he surveyed the room once more, felt a warning chill at the back of his neck. He turned the survey into an outright search, looking in the closet again, opening every drawer, even checking under the bed.

Steve was busy with his own search, but Kleber seemed to find Conan's activities fascinating, finally demanding, "Flagg, just what do you think you're doing?"

At that point he was back at the dresser-desk, scowling down into the wastebasket.

"Looking for something else that's missing. Steve, look at this wastebasket. Empty."

Kleber said curtly, "They empty the damn things every day. Maybe Nye just didn't have anything to throw in it yesterday. Doesn't look like he was doing any work here with everything laid out so neat."

"No," Conan agreed, "it doesn't *look* like it, but we know he was here most of the day yesterday, so what was he doing? Chewing up and swallowing the Surf House Restaurant accounts for three years?"

"The *what*?" That startled inquiry came from Steve.

"Nye took all the records from the restaurant last Thursday and, according to Brian, put them in a box and carted them off to his motel. But they're not here, nor are the contents of this wastebasket, nor any of the sheets torn off that legal pad; there's not a note or memo or even a piece of scratch paper with some stray numbers on it in this room. So, what happened? Where are the Surf House records?"

Steve pronounced that another good question, but after a moment, Kleber had an answer for it.

"Somebody walked off with them. The *same* somebody who killed Nye. That's why we didn't find his motel key on the body. Whoever killed him used that key to get in here and grab those records and all that other stuff so there wouldn't be anything left of them."

Steve's response to that was to ask Conan, "Do you know anything about Tally's problems with the IRS?"

"A little, yes."

"Everybody in town knows he was having trouble with the IRS," Kleber put in hotly. "So, maybe he figured he could get himself *out* of trouble if all his records disappeared *while* they were in the hands of an IRS agent. I mean, they might have a hard time proving anything against him without the records, and he could say it was *their* fault they got lost."

Conan restrained the tendency of his right hand to make a fist.

"You're saying that Brian methodically removed the records and any evidence of them from this room, then left Nye's *body* in his freezer while he slept peacefully on the bar, giving himself no alibi at all?"

Kleber only shrugged. "Well, I don't figure he *meant* to leave the body in his freezer, but he'd hoisted a few—he said so himself—so maybe by the time he got around to deciding what to do about the body, he just plain passed out."

"Oh, for God's sake, you can't—"

"He was alone in that restaurant from two o'clock on. Now, Mrs. Randall said that after Tally belted you when he was trying to lay Nye out, Tally told him he'd talk to him later. So, maybe that later was after two o'clock.''

"You don't *know* that."

"Not for a fact, but I'll tell you one thing I *do* know, Flagg, and you can't talk your way around it. Nye left a message in his own blood, and the initials were *B.T.* .''

Conan felt an aching in his left hand; he was trying to make a fist of it, too. He had no answer for those initials. But there was one. In the name of all that was reasonable, there *had* to be an answer.

"Now, here's something interesting."

Conan turned abruptly toward Steve, who was delving into the suitcase on the rack at the end of the bed.

It was a business-size envelope. Steve extricated its contents carefully and spread them on the bed. Kleber studied them from over Steve's right shoulder, while Conan took a vantage point on his left, his bruised jaw still painfully tense.

The return address was the Multnomah County Sheriff's office, and the two documents were weighted with fustian authority. The first was a summons, the second a complaint in dissolution of marriage filed by Lorna Moody Nye.

Conan said softly, "Well, it seems even tax collectors have private lives. And private problems."

Steve sighed. "Almost makes them human. This is dated February third. I wonder if he filed a response—'' The door opened, and he frowned, ready to give a curt order, but never got around to it. "What is it, Jeff?"

Lieutenant Kaw pulled a plastic evidence bag out of his coat pocket as he approached.

"Thought you'd want to see these, Steve. We just found them in the cooler at the restaurant."

The brown-wrapped marijuana joints were easily identified; so were the orange Dexedrine tablets in one bottle and the red Seconal capsules in the second.

Steve said, "I'll be damned. Well, those bottles should give us some nice prints."

Kleber's narrowed eyes moved from the drugs in Kaw's

hand to the documents on the bed, and Conan wondered if it was coming through to him that there might be unexpected complications in his open-and-shut case.

But he only shrugged indifferently as he turned away.

"Mr. Travers, maybe we should get down to the station and talk to those witnesses."

CHAPTER 7

Conan went to the police station and offered his duly sworn statement but didn't ask to sit in on the questioning of the other witnesses. He had Steve Travers' promise—made discreetly out of Kleber's hearing—that he would let Conan see copies of the statements, and since he wouldn't be free to ask his own questions, attending the inquiries didn't seem worth a confrontation with Kleber.

He waited outside the station, propped against Brian's blue Buick convertible. The weather was still a premature miracle as the day turned to afternoon, but he didn't find his surroundings inspiring. The Holliday Beach police station, a cement-block building with the architectural austerity of a WPA project, and not as much flair, was on a side street two blocks east of the highway where the snarl of passing log trucks was still audible.

When Brian emerged from the station, Tilda Capek was at his side, looking as fresh as a Tyrolean peasant girl with her pale hair in a single braid at the nape of her neck. Brian looked far from fresh, but he produced a smile for Conan.

"Well, they let me out *this* time."

"And told you not to leave town, I suppose. Hello, Tilda. I hope the grilling wasn't too grueling."

"Not really. Your friend Mr. Travers is a gentleman."

"So he is, and if Brian believes in prayer, he better say a few in gratitude that Steve was assigned to this case."

"Oh, I have," Brian sighed. "I've said a lot of prayers lately. So, uh, you come up with anything yet?"

"Questions, that's all. And I have a few for you. Like, were the exhaust fans on in the kitchen last night?"

"I hope so. We never turn them off. All the grills and ovens run on gas. If any of the pilot lights go off, the place is less likely to blow up with the fans to pull the fumes out."

Conan nodded. "Okay, here's another. One of Steve's men found some drugs in the cooler—not the over-the-counter variety. You have any ideas about that?"

Tilda gave Brian a rueful, I-told-you-so look, while he screwed up his face in annoyance.

"Damn. They probably belong to Johnny Hancock. And I thought—I hoped he'd seen the light."

"You knew he was on drugs, then?"

"Half the kids I hire are on drugs. That's just a fact of life. Trouble with Johnny is he decided to use the restaurant for a retail outlet, and I won't stand still for that."

Tilda said gently, "But you did, Brian. You can't reform one like that, not even with a threat."

He put his arm around her, nodding down at the ground.

"I guess not, but I thought he'd be better off here than in prison. I mean, he was working at something constructive and pulling a good wage."

Conan said, "Concentrate on the kids; it's too late for Hancock. What kind of threat were you using to reform him?"

"Well, about six months ago, I caught him selling joints to one of the busboys, and I read him the riot act; told him to get out and not to bother to come back."

Tilda put in, "Then Johnny told him his life story and said he had never even known his father's name."

Brian retorted weakly, "*That* much is probably true. The threat was a signed confession, Conan, that he'd been using and selling drugs. The idea was I'd give him another chance, but if he didn't keep his nose clean, I'd hand that confession to Kleber. I thought . . . well . . ."

Conan sighed. "I know. Where's that confession now?"

"Oh, hell, I threw it away."

"But did Johnny know that?"

"No, he didn't, but what does this have to do with Nye?"

"Probably nothing." He shifted his weight against the car, frowning toward the highway. "Brian, did Kleber—or anyone—tell you about the initials?"

Brian only blinked in mild perplexity. He didn't know about them. Conan was sure he hadn't seen them in his brief, shocked glance at the body—he wouldn't have held that back—and apparently they hadn't been mentioned when he was questioned. Kleber would want to save that until Brian was arrested; it might shock him into a confession. Steve would simply want to wait until all the facts were in. And Owen Culpepper—well, the prosecution on principle reserves its big guns for the trial.

Brian asked, "Conan, what do you mean? What initials?"

Conan told him, and Tilda went pale, her breath catching, but Brian only stared at him and at first tried to laugh it off as if it were a joke in questionable taste.

"*My* initials? Come *on*, now. How could . . . why would Nye . . ." The last vestiges of his smile faded, leaving his features strained in unnatural lines. "Oh, no . . . oh, God, no. Why? Conan, it just doesn't make *sense*!"

"Not yet, anyway. That doesn't mean it won't eventually. So, go on home and get some rest. You look like you need it. Tilda, you'd better see to it."

She slipped her arm through Brian's. "That's exactly what I intend to do."

Then she frowned, her head turning as she watched a tow

truck emerging from the alley behind the station. "Isn't that Beryl's car?"

A maroon Mercedes-Benz 450SE was being dragged ignominiously behind the truck, which bore the identifying legend, "Driskoll Garage—24 Hour Tow." The driver waved as he passed, while Brian swore irritably, but not at Rafe Driskoll.

"I forgot. Beryl told me she had to send her car to Rafe's after they were through with it here. Something about the starter. She'll need a ride home."

Tilda only smiled forbearingly, but her relief was obvious when Conan offered, "I'll take her home. I want to talk to her anyway."

"This is really awfully nice of you, Mr. Flagg," Beryl said as he turned the Jaguar onto the highway. "What a terrible time to have my car stolen. Nothing like this has *ever* happened to me."

"Well, if it had to happen, you're lucky the car wasn't stripped or wrecked."

"I suppose so. Oh, I *do* hope Brian will go home and get some sleep. He's just exhausted. All these months of . . . and now *this*."

Conan glanced at her; she was very near tears.

"Did he tell you he hired me as an investigator?"

"Yes, and I'm so relieved. He can be *so* stubborn, as if it were unmanly to have to ask for help. Anyway, I hope you know that I'll do anything I can to help *you* help *him*."

"I was counting on that, and I'd like to ask you some questions." They were passing the bookshop, and he gave it a proprietary survey. Judging by the few cars in the parking lane, Miss Dobie wasn't being overwhelmed with business.

"If you'll turn right on Laurel Road," Beryl directed, "that's the easiest way to get to my house. Oh, dear, there it is, poor thing."

That stopped him until he saw that she was looking toward

the other side of the highway and Driskoll's Garage where
her Mercedes was being disengaged from the tow truck.

"It's a beautiful car," he offered conversationally.

"Yes. I suppose some people would call it extravagant. I
mean, Mercedes-Benz really doesn't make a cheap car. But
they *do* make a *good* car, and actually it's an excellent investment. This is the first trouble I've had with it in five
years. The starter, you know. Here's Laurel Road. Actually,
the least expensive car you can buy is a Rolls-Royce. My
mother always used to tell me that."

"The *least* expensive?"

"Well, a Rolls will last a lifetime, so if you average the
cost per year, you come out way ahead of American cars
when you have to replace them every few years."

Conan smiled at that as he turned onto Laurel Road.
"Road" was an optimistic designation for a rutted dirt lane
that wound its way over the shoulder of Jefferson Heights
through the oldest residential district in Holliday Beach.

Beryl apparently noticed that he was having difficulty with
the necessary shifts of gear.

"Oh, Mr. Flagg, I meant to ask you about your hand."
But she didn't give him a chance to tell her about it. "Brian's
been under such a *terrible* strain these last few months. I've
known him for fifteen years and never once—well, *only* once
before have I seen him really . . . inebriated. I suppose he
told you about his experience with the IRS?"

"Yes, and it doesn't seem to be much of a secret around
town."

Her mouth puckered, deepening the radiating creases
around it, and he found himself wondering exactly how old
she was. He'd have guessed late forties, but he'd never actually taken a long or close look at her before.

"Brian is *so* trusting," she complained. "I mean, there
are some things a person in business just doesn't tell *any*one.
Of course, keeping a secret in a small town is always difficult, but he actually told some of the employees."

"Which employees?"

"Well, Max Heinz, but then Max is thoroughly trustworthy. And Claude Jastrow. It was probably he who told Howie Bliss, and I'm sure Brian told Miss Capek."

Conan made a note of that cool *Miss* Capek.

"Did Johnny Hancock know about it?"

"Oh, I'm sure he did. Once Howie found out, there was no stopping it. Howie has something of a drinking problem." She sighed copiously. "Oh, it's so *unfair!*"

Conan frowned as he maneuvered through a tight curve.

"Howie's drinking problem?"

"Oh, no. You'll have to forgive me if I seem a little . . . well, I'm just beside myself, really." One hand fluttered to her bosom. "And I *must* be careful about getting too wrought up. I was thinking of poor Brian. It makes you wonder what kind of world it is when a man like Brian is so burdened with disasters. There's Front Street up ahead. Turn right, then it's about two blocks to my house."

"How did Brian get so burdened with the IRS?"

"I don't really know. I've been right in the thick of it with him, but I *still* don't understand it. My books balance perfectly; they always have."

She paused while he made the turn onto Front Street as if to make sure he did it correctly, then went on, "The IRS insists we aren't showing enough profit in ratio to our costs. Well, what can you do? You can prove what you *spent* with invoices and receipts, but you can't really prove what you did or *didn't* make. And, of course, the IRS doesn't have to prove anything. They say we *must* have made so much, and it's up to us to prove we didn't. Oh, it's just been awful, and you know what I think? It's the third house on the left—the one with the carport in front."

Conan looked ahead to a small house flanked by vacant lots gone to salal and beach grass. It had probably been built twenty or thirty years ago as a weekender, a tidy little bungalow with silver-shingled walls and roof, the space in front given over to gravel and driftwood rather than lawn or garden.

"No, what do you think, Mrs. Randall?"

"*I* think the IRS audited Brian on an informer's tip. After all, they still pay an informer's fee, and 10 per cent of fifty-thousand dollars is a lot of money."

Conan considered that as he came to a stop in front of the house.

"What makes you think there was an informer?"

"Well, of course, they're very careful to protect their Judases, but when Mr. Nye first came—that was in August—he said they *had reason* to believe Brian hadn't reported all his profits. But later when I asked him point-blank about that reason, he backed off and said it was only a random audit; Brian's number was pulled out of the computer's hat."

"Who would turn informer against Brian?"

One painted brow came up cynically.

"You don't think he has enemies? Not that he ever hurt anyone; in fact, he bends over backwards to help, but some people will always bite the hand that feeds *or* helps them, and some people will always envy success, and Brian's a very successful man. Would you . . . care to come in, Mr. Flagg?"

"Yes, if you don't mind. I have more questions I'd like to ask." One was why she seemed so hesitant with that invitation, but that one he wouldn't ask.

Beryl waited for him to come around and open the door for her, then accepted his helping hand in getting out.

"A car like this keeps you limber, doesn't it?" She smiled as she straightened her skirt, ran a hand along the XK-E's shining black fender as if she were checking for dust. "What a lovely car. You must enjoy it very much."

"I do. I consider it an art object, but *this* car can't be regarded as a practical investment."

She laughed and began foraging in her purse for her keys as she walked toward the house.

"Well, it wouldn't be an art object if it were practical, would it?"

"Art doesn't *preclude* practicality, I suppose. Mrs. Randall, have you any idea who would be enough of an enemy to Brian to call down the IRS on him?''

''Not really.'' She unlocked the front door, which took some time; there were two locks. ''But I still think *someone* informed on him. My, it's almost too warm in here. Solar heating, you know. When the sun shines, I get a double dose: from the sun and from the reflection on the ocean.''

She led him down a short hallway ending in a filigreed metal screen on the right, while the left-hand wall continued to form the south wall of the living room. The west wall was solid glass and ocean view.

''Would you like some coffee, Mr. Flagg? It'll only take a minute. Just make yourself comfortable . . .'' Her voice trailed away around a corner into the kitchen, but he was hardly aware of her absence.

He had walked into a modest little cottage and found himself in a miniature mansion. The floor was parquetry oak graced with a beautiful Aubusson carpet, and in the center of the coffered ceiling a crystal chandelier spun rainbows out of the sunlight. The drapes were silk brocade in shades of rose to compliment the rug, and the same cloth covered the north wall. The other walls were paneled in dark wood to set off paintings in massive gilt frames, idyllic landscapes sleek with heavy varnish.

On the south wall was a fireplace decorated with Belgian tiles and flanked by bookshelves, but there were only a few books on them, old leather-bound volumes which after a closer look he decided were chosen for decorative purposes rather than content or rarity. Otherwise, the shelves served to display an astonishing array of vases, pitchers, bowls, plates, cups, stemware, and figurines. And the display wasn't limited to the bookshelves; the entire room was a showcase. Porcelain, hand-painted china, cut glass, blown glass, art glass, ivory, exotic woods, ormulu, bronze, silver, even gold. And if the objects showed too strong a tendency to sentimental ornateness for his taste, they were still unquestionably genuine and all fine examples of their genre and period, which was almost exclusively nineteenth century, although a few pieces were late eighteenth. The furniture was of the same ilk, tending to plush, fat Victorian, and in keeping with the decorative philosophy of the period, not one flat surface in the room was free of bric-a-brac lovingly placed on embroidered runners and polished so that not a single mote of dust would have the temerity to settle on them.

He accepted the truism that a person's home is a mirror of character, but he was too overwhelmed to fathom exactly what this lavish private museum revealed about Beryl Randall.

The mistress of the house emerged from the kitchen carrying a tray laden with a silver coffee pot, crystal sugar and creamer, and two dainty cups, and Conan wondered where she intended to put it down. But she managed nicely, balancing the tray on one arm while she cleared a space on a table between two chairs.

"Why don't you take this chair, Mr. Flagg? It's very comfortable."

He went to the upholstered wing chair indicated, thinking that Chippendale had designed for a shorter generation if comfort had in fact been his aim.

Beryl filled the cups with a silver flourish, then with a sugar cube poised in silver tongs, asked, "Sugar or cream?" When he declined, she presented his cup to him. "How do you like my little home?"

He would have preferred to offer comment without prompting, but managed it with a smile.

"It's lovely. I'm sure I could spend hours in this room alone and not see everything; at least, not appreciate it as it deserves."

She beamed over the gilt rim of her cup.

"How nicely put. Thank you." Then, holding on to her smile through a long sigh, "It's my only heritage from a more gracious time. The house belonged to my late husband, but the furnishings are from my family home; all that could be saved after . . ." She paused, then renewed her smile for him. "But you aren't here to listen to tales of old tragedies and fortunes lost."

"No." Then he added, "I mean, I'm afraid I can't take the time when I have a fresh tragedy to deal with." He put down his cup with a cigarette in mind, but in all this clutter he could see nothing resembling an ashtray, so he took the hint.

"Yes, of course," she agreed to his priorities, then went on as if nothing had intervened, "Actually, I *do* have in mind—well, a *suspect* for the informer."

That came as no surprise. "Who is it?"

"Well, I hesitate to say anything because I really have nothing to support my suspicions, but I was thinking about who stood to gain if Brian were backed into a financial hole, and although spite or jealousy might be motives, I think financial gain is generally a stronger motive."

Conan smiled and tried his coffee.

"In some crimes, at least."

She shrugged. "Yes, well, at any rate, if you consider financial gain in this case, then I know of only one person who would benefit from Brian's ruin." She paused to give him an opportunity to ask the question, and when he only waited attentively, she answered it anyway.

"Conny Van Roon."

He obliged her this time. "How does Conny stand to gain from Brian's ruin?"

"Well, eight months ago, he approached Brian about selling the restaurant. He wanted to act as agent, of course, and his commission on a sale that large would be impressive. And he was so—well, *rudely* insistent. At first hardly a day went by when he didn't try to corner Brian and talk sale. Mr. Flagg, he was *desperate*."

Conan nodded. "If you believe the local grapevine, there isn't much left of his business; he drank it away."

"I can vouch for the fact that he drank a great deal of it away in the Tides Room, and liquor isn't his *only* vice, you know. He's a regular at the Elks Club's backroom casino *and* the casinos in Las Vegas and Reno." Then as if Conan were doubting that, she added, "That's not gossip; that's from Conny himself. He talks a great deal when he's had too much to drink, and he's so *proud* of his big trips to Vegas and Reno. He even claims to have a foolproof system, like any inveterate gambler. If you ask me, *he's* the fool, and the proof is on his whiskey bottles."

Conan laughed at that, wondering if it was original.

"So, you think his desperation for the commission on the sale of the restaurant is sharpened by his expensive vices?"

"Well, that's obvious, and I think it's very interesting that when Brian asked him if he had a commitment from a buyer, he said he had 'moneyed backers' ready and willing to pay up to five hundred thousand dollars. He *also* described these backers as *Nevada* interests."

"Apparently he made some friends on his trips south." And that explained the dirty money Brian wouldn't touch with a ten-foot pole.

"If that's what you call them. As far as Brian was concerned that killed any possibility of a sale." She put her cup down and leaned forward to make her point. "He told Conny absolutely no; never. And within *two* weeks, Brian got that first letter from the IRS. Now, is *that* coincidence?"

"On the surface, no."

She sniffed. "Of course not. Conny was counting on the IRS to put Brian in a position where he'd be *forced* to sell, and even if he still refused—and he has—then Conny expected to buy the restaurant for a pittance at a tax sale."

Conan's eyes were narrowed to black ellipses.

"Did you ever discuss this with Brian?"

"No." She toyed with the lace doily on the arm of her chair, the sea-cast sunlight flashing on an antique diamond solitaire. "I saw no reason to discuss it when he was so distraught. He . . . well, sometimes his temper *does* get out of hand." Her eyes chanced on Conan's bruised jaw, dropped to the cast, then to the floor, but a moment later she offered brightly, "Would you care for more coffee?"

"No, thank you, but I hope you'll bear with me a little longer. I need some general background information on some of the employees, and I doubt anyone else is in a better position to give it to me."

"Well, I've certainly seen enough of them come and go."

"At the moment I'm only interested in the ones who were in the bar last night. Let's start with Howie Bliss. He's been with the restaurant a long time, hasn't he?"

Her mouth pursed unflatteringly. "Off and on, one might say. He's living proof of the old saying that all cooks are drunks, and proof that with *some* people kindness just doesn't pay."

"Whose kindness? Brian's?"

"Of course. Howie used to be head chef, and he was rather good at it in spite of his drinking. When he drinks he's all sentiment, you know, until he reaches a certain point, and then—well, you just never know *what* he'll do. One night about five years ago, he hit that critical point and went out to the parking lot with a dough hook and smashed the windshields on every car there, and if you think *that* didn't cost both Brian and the resort a young fortune. And when Brian tried to stop him, Howie turned on him and sent him to the hospital with a concussion."

Bliss in the role of berserker was a little difficult to imagine, but Conan didn't doubt Beryl's account.

"What happened to Howie?"

"He spent a year in the state prison, and then . . ." She blinked behind her jeweled glasses as if confronted with solid evidence that water flows uphill. "When he got out he had the *gall* to come crawling back to Brian asking for a job. And Brian *gave* him one. Of course, in the meantime he'd hired Claude as head chef, so he put Howie on as morning cook. I'll admit he's done rather well, although he hasn't stopped drinking, but the thing that really disgusts me is the way he feels about Brian."

"What do you mean?"

"Well, wouldn't you think he'd be grateful? No one else

would even hire him as a dishwasher, but Brian gave him the best job he could. Of course, with Brian he's all sugar, but *I* hear things around the restaurant that don't get to Brian, and I can assure you, Howie Bliss *hates* him. And do you know why? His reason, if you could call it that? Because Brian didn't give him back his job as *head chef*."

"Does Brian know how he feels?"

"Oh, I've tried to tell him, but he just shrugs it off. Howie's really harmless, he says, and what would he ever do without his job?" She concluded with a martyred sigh.

"How does Howie feel about Jastrow?"

"Strangely enough, they get along quite well. Claude is a bit overbearing for a person of his station, but that doesn't seem to bother Howie. I think he really likes being bullied, and sometimes I wonder if he doesn't know, deep down, that he can't hold a candle to Claude as a chef. We're very lucky to have him, you know. He trained at the Four Seasons in New York and worked at the Royal Garden Hotel in London, the Nine Muses in Hollywood, and Tarantino's in San Francisco. Not as head chef, of course."

"How long was he in England?"

"Long enough to acquire that pseudo-English accent, it seems," she replied with a smug smile.

Conan laughed at being found out. "And a fondness for Shakespeare?"

"Oh, dear—*that*. Perhaps, although he'd really like to be an actor. I think that's why he went to Hollywood, but as far as I know, his career has been limited to amateur groups or summer stock. He and Miss Capek were . . . friends long before they came here, you know."

Of course she knew he didn't know that. He offered nothing in response but a raised eyebrow, and she added, "I understand she was working as a waitress at Tarantino's when Claude was there."

"Did they come up here together?"

"No, Claude was hired first, then about a year later we lost our regular hostess and dining room manager, and Claude

sang Miss Capek's praises so convincingly, Brian offered her
the job.''

"Did she and Claude continue their . . . *friendship* here
in Holliday Beach?''

Her shoulders lifted in a nervous shrug, and the red of her
rouged cheeks deepened.

"Apparently the, uh, situation has changed. At least, as
far as Miss Capek is concerned.''

Conan couldn't quite resist putting in casually, "Yes, she
and Brian seem to have something going for them. It looks
serious.''

The flush expanded to include the whole of her face.

"Well. Yes, I suppose . . . well, I hope for Brian's sake it
isn't serious. Miss Capek is a lovely young woman, of course,
but I doubt she's inclined to lasting relationships.''

"Is Brian?'' He turned that with a laugh. "I never thought
him capable of loving anything but the Surf House. What do
you know about Tilda's history? Is she an immigrant?''

"Yes, I believe so, from Czechoslovakia; she immigrated
with her family as a child. They settled in Chicago and apparently didn't do too well; the father was an unskilled worker
with seven or eight children to feed. Miss Capek married
quite young, rather an unfortunate affair, rife with domestic
assault and battery. They had a little girl, but I understand
Miss Capek left the child with her parents when she divorced
and moved to California—like so many of the unfortunates
of the world—in search of a new life.'' She patted her hair
as if to assure herself it was in order. "Of course, I really
don't know Miss Capek too well.''

No, Conan thought, but you know a lot *about* her.

He shifted to another position in the chair, in search of
comfort, and to another subject.

"You heard what Nye said when he came into the bar last
night. Did it make any sense to you?''

She frowned thoughtfully. "Well, he wasn't really very
clear, of course, but you know, I . . . I had the feeling he
thought he could *help* Brian in some way.'' She sighed. "I

wonder if we'll ever know. And I wonder what will happen to the IRS's case against Brian now.''

"Should an auditor's demise affect it?''

"But you'd think—'' Her red lips twitched into a bitter smile. "No, I don't suppose that would make any difference to them.''

"You probably had more personal contact with Nye than anyone else at the restaurant. What was your impression of him?''

The cold tension around her eyes and mouth was eloquent, but after a moment that gave way to another sigh.

"It's difficult to separate the man from his job. He was very . . . conscientious, which should be a virtue, but he was so *coldly* conscientious. I mean, I don't think it ever occurred to him that there were real *people* behind all those numbers. Oh, I don't know. I'm afraid I'm not the person to ask if you want to know what he was really like.''

"I can understand your prejudice. I asked because I was wondering if he was the kind of man to hold a grudge; enough of a grudge to accuse, as his last living act, an innocent man of his murder.''

Her mouth sagged open. "What*ever* do you mean?''

"He left a dying testament in the freezer: two letters written in his own blood; the letters B T.''

She went white, her face masklike with the heavily drawn brows and lips stark against the pallor of her skin.

"B T . . . but that's . . .''

"Brian's initials.''

"But I thought Nye was *dead* when he . . . I mean, someone—Howie, wasn't it?—said Nye had been struck on the head.''

"Yes, but the blow didn't kill him. I *must* find an explanation for those initials because they're damning. Absolutely so in Kleber's eyes.''

She stared at him as if he'd lapsed into Swahili.

"What do you mean, damning? No one thinks—Kleber

isn't saying—not *Brian*! Oh, Mr. Flagg, that's nonsense. Surely, even Earl Kleber wouldn't accuse Brian of—of . . .''

''Unless someone can explain away those initials, it's difficult *not* to accuse Brian when you consider how he felt about Nye—feelings he made publicly clear only hours before his death—and when you consider that the body was found in the same building where Brian spent the night. Alone.''

''*Mister* Flagg! If you don't know Brian Tally better than to accuse him of this—this cold-blooded murder—''

''But I do know him, and that's why *I'm* not accusing him; because the murder *was* so cold-blooded. A bad choice of words in this case, incidentally.''

She missed any humor in that, but seemed mollified by his declaration of faith. She stared down at the floor for a moment, then asked peevishly, ''Oh, *why* didn't he go *home* last night?''

Conan carefully put his cup on the tray as he rose.

''I'm sure Brian has been asking himself the same question all day.''

CHAPTER 8

Steve Travers had exchanged his shirt and tie for an old cable-knit sweater and was whistling along to the strains of the *Minute Waltz*—no mean feat—when he left the guest room. He crossed the balcony to the stairway, then paused to look down into the living room at his host.

Conan was using the top of the Bösendorfer concert grand for a desk and had covered half of it with typewritten sheets while he hunched over a note pad, pen in hand and totally absorbed. The fingers of his left hand, emerging from the cast, moved in rhythm to the music pouring from speakers quartering the room.

A very exclusive recording, he had informed Steve, made in this room and on the magnificent piano he adapted for a desk now. The pianist was Isadora Canfield. Steve's mouth pulled up on one side in an indulgent smile as he descended the spiral staircase.

Conan hadn't closed the drapes on the west windows, he noted, although it was already dark outside and the panoramic view of beach and surf was lost. Steve sometimes wondered why he had installed drapes on those windows, and considering the size of them, it had been an expensive undertaking.

But Conan liked wide open spaces and tolerated walls only for the sake of privacy. Maybe that was the Nez Percé. Conan Joseph Flagg's middle name honored a chief.

He didn't look up nor did the scratching of his pen stop when Steve reached the bottom of the stairs; he only asked vaguely, "Find everything you need, Steve?"

"Sure. The Flagg Hilton's the best in town." The pen still didn't stop. "And having Raquel Welch up there's really a nice touch. Damn nice."

"Well, let me know if there's anything else."

Steve sighed and went to the bar on the south wall.

"What are you doing, Conan?"

Eventually, he muttered, "A schedule."

A few minutes later, after Steve had mixed two drinks, Forester on the rocks, and took them over to the piano, Conan offered, "Can I fix you a drink, Steve?"

"I'll have a double zombie. But why don't you try this first?"

Conan looked around at him and the offered glass.

"Oh—thanks. I'll be finished here in a couple of minutes. Just make yourself comfortable."

Steve recognized the sheets spread on the piano: copies of the statements made by Kleber's witnesses. He took both glasses and crossed to the Barcelona chairs facing the window wall, put the glasses on the table between them, and settled down to enjoy a view of early blackness. Still, the sky was clear and faint whispers of light hinted that there *were* breakers out there.

"By the way, Conan, I ran the names of all those people through the NCIC computers."

From behind him came a mumbled, "Mm?"

"Two of them have records. Hancock for one. Started out as a runaway and worked up through vagrancy, D and D, drug possession, to petty theft. He's done a total of three years in assorted prisons.''

Silence. Steve turned to look over his shoulder.

''Don't let me distract you, but when are we going to eat? I missed lunch today.''

''Right. Let's see, where's Jastrow—oh, here. The drugs your boys found in the cooler belong to Hancock.''

''Thanks. Is that ESP or divine inspiration?''

''Probably.'' Then after more shuffling of papers, ''What else does Howie Bliss have on his record?''

''What *else*? I guess you heard about Howie and the windshields. Well, that's about it. Was Mrs. Early here today?''

''Mm?''

''Your housekeeper. Remember her? I thought maybe she left one of her Care packages in your refrigerator.''

''Uh-huh.''

Steve sighed, then rose and stalked out to search for sustenance in the kitchen.

The Saint-Saéns *Allegro Appassionato* was pounding to its climax when Conan finally tossed down the pen, surveyed two pages of notes critically, then stacked the statements.

''Steve?'' He frowned at the vacant chair, then when Steve came around the corner from the kitchen with a fistful of cookies, his jaw working, ''Oh—are you hungry?''

He didn't answer until he returned to his chair and swallowed the mouthful.

''Whatever gave you that idea? I guess this wasn't Mrs. Early's cleaning day.''

''No. We'll go down to the Shanaway Inn in a little while. It's only second best, but the best is closed today.''

''Right now I'm truly sorry about that, but I'll settle for the Dairy Queen.''

Conan took the vacant chair and the waiting glass.

''Thanks for the drink.''

"It's on the house. Okay, what's this schedule you were working on?"

Conan crossed his legs and propped the notes on his knee while he lit a cigarette.

"I was trying to put together a chronological sequence based on those statements—and hoping to come across a glaring discrepancy in someone's testimony."

"Did you?"

"No. Of course, things get a little vague in spots."

"Yes, I noticed that."

"Well, the entire cast was bombed to varying degrees. Except Max."

"What about you? Cold sober?"

"No, only unconscious."

Steve laughed more heartily than Conan thought that deserved.

"Oh, Conan—damn, I wish I'd been there."

"Sure, it was the best floor show the Tides Room ever had. Are you interested in what I've sieved out here?"

He managed to rein his amusement. "Yes. I haven't had time to cross-check the things myself."

"Okay, we begin immediately following the floor show, which was at midnight, give or take a minute. In the ensuing confusion, Beryl Randall said Nye was still trying to get Brian's attention while he was busy determining how much damage he'd done to me, and Brian said he'd talk to Nye 'later.' Max remembers that, too, but Brian doesn't. Then Beryl took Nye out to the hall to keep the peace, and that's when Conny Van Roon stuck his nose in."

Steve frowned while he masticated the last cookie.

"What do you know about Van Roon?"

"Not much, but I learned more about him this afternoon." He started on his drink while he recounted that part of his conversation with Beryl, concluding with a question: "If Brian *was* audited on the basis of an informer's tip, will the IRS admit it? And will they name the informer?"

Steve seemed to find his whiskey excessively sour.

"I don't know if they'll admit it, but I do know that not even the Chief Justice of the Supreme Court can squeeze an informer's identity out of an IRS agent. Not unless the agent gets permission to let it out from the commissioner. That's the big man in Washington. By the way, I talked to Luther Dix on the phone this afternoon."

"What did he say?"

"Well, he's grief-stricken. Nye was the best auditor he ever had. Also, he wants the records and files Nye was working on returned to the Portland office. Now."

"Did you tell him the Surf House records are missing?"

"Sure, and he nearly had a seizure. He nearly had another one when I told him I couldn't release anything from Nye's motel room until the investigation is finished." He smiled complacently at the memory.

"What about the phone call Nye made to him last night?"

"IRS business, and in so many words, none of mine, even if I *am* an officer of the law."

Conan put his glass down harder than he intended, flinching at the clink of crystal against marble.

"I suppose if that IRS business concerned Brian, Dix considered *that* none of your business, too."

"Right. Same for the file on Van Roon. But he wants me to keep *him* informed about the investigation. I have a feeling my information is going to be inconclusive for a long time to come. So, what happened next?"

Conan consulted his notes. "Where were we? Oh—Van Roon followed Nye and Beryl out into the hall and asked Nye why he was so anxious to talk to Brian. Van Roon said he was only interested because Brian's such a good friend; Beryl said he was impertinent. And drunk."

"Well, if he *did* inform on Tally, maybe he had good reason to be interested. Conan, what did Nye actually say to Tally? Nobody seemed very sure about that."

"I'm not sure, either, except that he said he'd found something that 'changed the picture.' "

"Not a lot of help, is it?"

"No, and Van Roon didn't get any more out of him. Nye told him it was none of his business—in so many words—and he told Beryl he wouldn't discuss anything with her until he talked to Brian. Still zero. Anyway, Van Roon went back to the bar, probably looking for something to soothe his hurt feelings. Beryl said Nye told her he was sorry about all the trouble and headed for the front door, while she headed for the ladies' room. The time was approximately five minutes after twelve."

"And the rest of the cast was still in the bar?"

"Except for Johnny Hancock, who was in the kitchen, or outside at the dumpster, or at some point in between. By twelve-fifteen I was on my feet and on my way to the hospital with Brian, Tilda, Max and Dore offering support."

"What about Van Roon? Didn't he leave before that?"

"Oh, yes. I think—here it is." He turned the paper to read a cramped marginal insert. "Right. He gave up on getting any service at the bar and left the party. That was only a couple of minutes after Nye snubbed him, but he said he didn't see anyone in the hall or the parking lot."

"Nye must've been a fast walker or Van Roon would've seen him."

"Conny's vision was limited. Besides, there's a pathway through the resort that skirts the parking lot. Nye probably walked to his motel that way."

"Why would he walk in the middle of a storm? That's what I don't understand."

Conan shrugged. "It's only two blocks. It would take about as long to drive and park a car as to walk. But I'm sure he walked *to* the Surf House. When he came into the bar, he was soaked."

"Okay, so Nye left about five after twelve, Van Roon—what? Maybe two minutes later? And Beryl was in the ladies' room."

"Yes. She came out when Brian et al. got out into the hall

with me at twelve-fifteen. He told her to tend bar or close up, whichever came first. There were still those five customers in the bar, but otherwise only Bliss and Jastrow were left. Jastrow says he went to the kitchen to check on Johnny at that point, but neither Howie nor Beryl could back him up. She pleads general emotional upheaval with a hint at heart trouble, or maybe it was vapors. Howie doesn't plead; he just didn't keep track.''

Steve purloined a cigarette from the package Conan had left on the table, squinting into the smoke as he lit it.

''So, nobody is really sure when Jastrow left the bar.''

''Except Jastrow. He says he was in the kitchen about five minutes, then he returned to the bar where Beryl was encouraging the last customers to leave. Meanwhile, back at the Seafarer . . .'' He turned to the second page. ''At twelve-twenty Lorna *Moody* Nye and friend arrived.''

''Oh—I forgot to tell you. I sent Frank Carp up to Portland to notify the widow and look over Nye's house.''

''Any interesting results?''

''From Lorna, no; Frank was just notifying. But he talked to her lawyer, and he said Lorna moved out of Nye's house and life a year ago, and she filed twice for a divorce. The first time she backed off when Nye offered to contest it. The second time—well, you saw the summons. Nye hadn't responded to that complaint yet. And that's all the lawyer had to say. But it's interesting that he's on retainer for Kautsky Freight Lines, and by some odd coincidence, that's where Lorna's been working for the last year as private secretary to Luke Kautsky. He's the owner's son and a vice president. And by another coincidence, Luke drives a *red* Ferrari.''

Conan took a meditative puff on his cigarette.

''No wonder she backed off on the first complaint. Did Frank find anything in Nye's house?''

''Some insurance policies.''

''Naming his faithful wife as beneficiary?''

''To the tune of a hundred thousand bucks.''

''Well. That might do for a motive.''

Steve gave a curt laugh. "You've got a few details to work out if you expect to make a case for murder one against Lorna Nye. Or her friend."

"Maybe." He frowned at his notes. "The next entry is twelve-thirty. Beryl got rid of the customers and locked the front door, then cleared the cash register, and told Howie and Jastrow she was going down to her office."

"By the way, what did she mean by 'down'?"

"There's another story under the dining room; the banquet and conference rooms are *down* there and so is the office. And, yes, there's an outside entrance on that level."

Steve lifted his glass in a salute. "Just wondering. Jastrow and Bliss stayed in the bar, didn't they?"

"Yes, although Jastrow was out in the front hall in time to see Beryl return from the parking lot at one. She said she went out to see if her car would start, since she'd been having trouble with it. It did then and again when she drove home a short while later."

"I guess she knew how to talk to it, and whoever stole it didn't." He paused, squinting toward some inner horizon. "You know, that's kind of funny about her car."

Conan sent him a slanted glance. "Raises the old hackles, doesn't it? It *feels* like it should be connected with the murder, but I'm damned if I can see how."

"Mm. Well, on with your schedule."

"Next entry, one-thirty. After leaving Tilda at her apartment, Brian returned to the Surf House and parted company with Max in the parking lot. He went into the bar in a 'foul humor,' according to Jastrow, and told him, Howie, and Beryl to leave. They did, and all of them swore they went directly to their respective homes. Alone of course. At about two, Hancock came into the bar to clean and was also told to leave and also went home, also alone. Hancock said the front door was unlocked when he left, and Brian admits he never got around to locking it. When Howie arrived at seven in the morning, it was *still* unlocked."

Steve said with some asperity, "I *get* the point. The door

was unlocked from about one-thirty till seven, so anybody could've walked in. Right?''

"Right, and with Brian in a virtual coma, I doubt anything less than a brass band would have disturbed him. At least nothing did, unfortunately. So. End of sequence.'' He folded the sheets into an airplane and launched it, frowning acerbically when it crashed into the window. "So, what do *you* have to offer?''

"You just disposed of most of it. Kleber would have me court-martialed if he knew I let you see those statements.''

"Oh, yes. Thanks. Does he know you're staying here? Looks like consorting with the enemy to me.''

"Yes, he knows. I told him this would be a good way to keep an eye on you. Anyway, I don't have much else to offer yet. Too early for most of the lab reports, and Dan couldn't do the autopsy today. About all I have now is that those initials *were* made in Nye's blood.''

"But did Nye make them?''

He shrugged. "Fingerprints may tell us that, but not much else. Jeff said every likely surface in that kitchen was solid smudge. Nye's room didn't give us anything, either; no blood, nothing damaged to suggest a struggle. His car was locked, no sign of jimmying, and it hadn't been moved since the rain started, which the Coast Guard says was about 8 P.M. There was dry gravel under it.''

Conan stabbed at the ashtray with his cigarette.

"Did your boys pull any prints off the mop handle or bucket?''

"I'll have to check. Why?''

"That head wound bled a lot. If it was administered in the kitchen, the mop was very conveniently at hand for cleaning up the blood.''

"*If* the blow was administered in the kitchen, and *if*— never mind. I'll check it.'' He paused, swirling the ice in his glass, then asked hesitantly, "Conan, how well do you know Brian Tally? I mean . . .''

"I know what you mean: Did he kill Eliot Nye?''

"Yes, I guess that's what I mean."

Conan considered his answer through the poignant first phrases of *Für Elise*.

"We're not close friends, Steve; not what I call close, but I've known him long enough to be absolutely sure he didn't kill Nye. I'm not saying he isn't capable of it, but the MO is wrong, particularly that business about the missing records. If Brian killed him, it would be an act of passion, of rage, and entirely unpremeditated. This thing is too convoluted; Brian thinks in straight lines."

Steve mumbled into his glass, "Thank you, Dr. Flagg."

"You asked for an opinion."

"I know, and I'm not putting yours down. I just wish I had something a little more solid to work with."

"Why? You couldn't ask for a more beautifully packaged suspect." He emptied his glass, then seeing that Steve's was equally dry, rose and took both glasses to the bar.

"He's *too* beautifully packaged," Steve grumbled. "Like leaving the body in his own freezer while he went to sleep in the same building. Would a jury believe anybody could be that stupid? No, except he was also known—by a lot of people—to be drunk to the gills."

Conan put more ice in the glasses, brows drawn in an irritable frown.

"So his drunkenness explains his stupidity?"

"That's how Kleber sees it. According to his theory, Nye came back to the restaurant after everybody else left—that's the 'later' Tally says he doesn't remember—they got to arguing, and that time you weren't in the way, so he connected with Nye's cranium—"

"But the wound was at the *back* of the cranium."

"Just because he got *you* in the face doesn't mean—"

"All right, objection overruled." He brought the freshened drinks and handed one to Steve but didn't return to his chair; he stood at the window searching for the phantoms of breakers.

"Anyway," Steve went on, "Kleber figures Tally put Nye

in the freezer for safekeeping—thinking he was dead—took
his motel key and made a beeline for those records, figuring
that if they disappeared while they were in the possession of
an IRS agent, it would put a hole in their claim. Of course,
the agent was supposed to disappear, too, with no clues that
Tally had anything to do with it, but after he disposed of the
records and went back to dispose of Nye, he decided he
needed another drink to brace him up first and—''

''—and braced himself into unconsciousness. Yes, I heard
the birthing of that theory this morning.''

''Well, for Earl it's come of age by now. He's already
talked to the D.A., and Culpepper likes it, too. And I can
see why. It fits the known facts, and it has two real clinchers.
The first is motive. Who else had a better motive to kill Nye?
The IRS has a seizure order scheduled to be served next
Friday, and it was Nye who made the original audit and came
up with the tax deficiency.''

Conan nodded impatiently. ''But if Nye's picture-changing
discovery was something that would negate the threat of an
IRS seizure, then Brian *didn't* have a motive.''

Steve lifted a skeptical eyebrow.

''Conan, we don't know what Nye meant by that picture-
changing business. Maybe it was something that put Tally
even further up the creek, and if Nye did come back to talk
to him about it after two—well, unless we find out what Nye
actually had on his mind, it doesn't change the picture for
Tally as far as motive is concerned.''

''What about opportunity, then? Brian did *not* see Nye
again after midnight. He was at the hospital until one-thirty
and in the bar from then on. If Nye was in the restaurant
after two, Brian wasn't aware of it.''

''I know, Conan. That's what he *said* in his statement.''

''But he can't *prove* it.''

''Well, can he?''

Conan stared out into the blackness, feeling the ache of
protracted tension in his swollen jaw.

''All right, but someone else *does* have a motive against

Nye: Lorna Moody Nye. And/or friend. A divorce denied and a hundred thousand dollars in insurance.''

''Sure, they've got motive, but if they did it, how come Nye's body ended up in the freezer at the Surf House?''

Conan shrugged. ''The facts can also be explained if you assume Lorna and friend are guilty. I don't think they came to Holliday Beach with malice aforethought or Lorna wouldn't have announced herself at the motel office, but it's not unreasonable to assume there were harsh words exchanged when she appeared at Nye's door with this 'sporty-looking feller' in the red Ferrari—''

''We don't *know* it was Luke Kautsky's Ferrari yet.''

''But we know Lorna had an escort, so maybe the scenario went something like this: Husband, wife, and unidentified sport argue, and in the heat of the moment Nye is hit and knocked unconscious.''

Steve began to protest while he was taking a swallow of his drink; it was a moment before he got his throat clear.

''One thing we *do* know, there was no sign of a struggle and no blood in Nye's room, and as you already pointed out, that head wound bled a lot.''

Conan took that objection in stride.

''So the argument took place *outside* the room in a driving rain. Maybe Nye didn't feel hospitable enough to invite his reluctant wife and her lover in. Anyway, the blow was struck and they thought he was dead. Then if either of the lovers went into his room—which isn't unlikely—they'd see the Surf House records. Now, Brian and the resort do a lot of advertising; the name would undoubtedly be familiar to them, and the Surf House is only two blocks from the Seafarer. They probably passed it coming in.''

Steve was frowning critically, eyes down to slits.

''So they decided Tally might make a handy scapegoat?''

''Yes. Lorna would certainly know enough about her husband's work to realize that anyone he was auditing would probably have a motive against him, so to point the finger at Brian, they took all the Surf House records, then transported the body—or what they thought was a body—to the restaurant. They had to wait until the coast was clear there, but that could be scouted through the windows, and the chances of observation at that hour and in that storm were nil. Finally, after Hancock left, one of them tried the doors and, by an incredible stroke of luck, found the front door unlocked, and what better place to dispose of a body than a walk-in freezer? They could be sure it wouldn't be found until the next day, and freezing would confuse the time of death so it wouldn't be so easily connected with Lorna's appearance at the Seafarer.''

Steve gave that hypothesis due consideration while he lowered the liquid level in his glass a quarter inch.

''You're reaching, Conan.''

''Maybe I am, but nothing we know now precludes that scenario. My point is, someone other than Brian *did* have a motive against Nye, and at least you can't say it was impossible for them to kill him. And I have more to say on the subject of motive.'' He settled himself in his chair to say it, while Steve sighed and took his drink down half an inch.

''Okay, who *else* has a motive against Nye?''

''Against Nye? No one that I know of.'' He reached for his cigarettes, offering Steve one before he lit his own. ''Have you considered this possibility, Steve: maybe we're looking at the motive from the wrong angle; maybe the motive wasn't against Nye, but against *Brian*. He's the one who's so beautifully packaged as a result of Nye's death.''

''Yes, well, that would open things up a little.'' He shook his match out furiously; it had burned down to his fingers. ''Okay, elucidate.''

''As if you could stop me short of walking out. Well, I was thinking along this line: assume that someone had some compelling reason to put Brian in jeopardy and accomplished it by the simple expedient of betraying him to the IRS. But if whatever Nye discovered *was* good news for Brian—and I wasn't the only one who got that impression, by the way; Tilda, Max, and Beryl had the same feeling about it—then look at that piece of good news from the point of view of the person who wanted Brian in trouble in the first place. That person would be just as anxious to *keep* him there, and right now he's in about as much trouble as a man can get. If things looked bad for him yesterday with the IRS ready to close him up, how do they look now with a murder charge hanging over his head?''

Steve mulled that through a long drag on his cigarette.

''Then the person you're looking for is the informer?''

''Possibly. Maybe even probably. But it could also be someone else who simply took advantage of Brian's motive against Nye to frame him for his murder. Obviously, that person would also have a compelling reason to want Brian in jeopardy, but it isn't necessarily the informer.''

''Just somebody who didn't shed any tears when Tally ended up in that IRS box canyon, right? Okay, I suppose you have some candidates in mind.''

''Yes. It was Nye's announcement of his discovery, whatever it was, that changed the picture for the killer; that was the catalyst. So, the killer had to be one of the people in the bar last night. I'm not eliminating Hancock; he says he was carting garbage out, but the path—the one Nye could have taken through the resort to his motel—goes past the back door of the kitchen.''

Steve nodded absently. ''Hancock might've seen Nye on his way to the bar, then gone inside and eavesdropped from the entry hall. But what's *his* reason for keeping Tally in trouble?''

Conan related Brian's ill-fated attempt at criminal rehabilitation, smiling faintly when Steve first stared incredulously, then, his head falling back against his chair, sighed his world-weary resignation.

''Oh, my God. Did Tally—I mean, I can't believe he really thought—''

''He did, Steve. I'm afraid Brian is an unreformed reformer. He disposed of the confession, incidentally, but

Johnny doesn't know that, and the penalty for *selling* drugs
is a little stringent.''

"That all depends. Of course, Hancock isn't a juvenile,
and he's a long way from a first offense, so it probably would
be stringent for him. So, who else do you have tabbed as a
suspect? Everybody in the bar?''

Conan stretched his legs and savored a swallow of bourbon
before he answered.

"The five unidentified customers I've eliminated because
they *were* unidentified. This is a personal affair; something
between friends—or enemies. But not strangers. I don't think
you can argue if I also eliminate Dore and me.''

"Oh, I probably could, just for the hell of it.''

"But you're hungry, so you won't. That leaves Max, Tilda,
Beryl, Howie, Claude, and Conny Van Roon. I've already
told you about Van Roon's Nevada connections and his heavy
selling campaign—all according to Beryl.''

"Who also thinks he's the informer.''

"And he may be, so he's on my list. Beryl also told me
Howie Bliss has taken a very recalcitrant attitude toward
Brian; nothing arouses resentment so much as kindness. And
Howie's an alcoholic, which doesn't automatically make him
a killer, but a permanently pickled brain doesn't function
logically or reasonably, so his resentment can't be treated
lightly.''

Steve laughed. "Not when he entertains himself knocking
out windshields.''

"He also sent Brian to the hospital when he tried to save
any remaining windshields.''

"Damn, I never knew the restaurant business was so violent. Okay, who else is on your list?''

"Possibly Claude. The motive would be jealousy. Beryl
hinted that Claude and Tilda were having an affair, or whatever it's called these days, before they came to Holliday
Beach, but it's off now. Tilda's on with Brian, and the feelings
are so mutual, they eliminate her from my list. I eliminate
Max and Beryl offhand because they're both so unquestion-

ingly loyal to Brian. So, at the moment my list includes Johnny, Howie, Van Roon, and possibly Claude, and not one of them has an alibi for his time after he left the restaurant except Van Roon. He says his wife gave him hell when he came home at twelve-thirty, but I don't have much faith in spousely alibis. The scenario for any of them would be essentially what I outlined for Lorna and friend, but you wouldn't have to reach so far to cast Brian as the scapegoat."

Steve leaned forward to rest his elbows on his knees, his cigarette held in the curl of his palm as if he were shielding it from a desert wind. The Debussy *La Cathédrale engloutie*, and the tape, came to an end, leaving a silence paced by the soft rush of surf.

"You know, Conan, I could go along with you on just about everything you've laid out if it weren't for one thing, and it's the real clincher in Kleber's case."

Conan closed his eyes, listening to the endless, ageless murmur of the sea in the darkness beyond the windows, and he felt something akin to fear—fear of the unknown. He was met with an enigma that resisted rational processes.

"The initials," he said flatly. "Eliot Nye's dying testimony. *The moving finger writes; and having writ . . .*"

Steve asked almost regretfully, "What else could those letters mean?"

"Except Brian Tally? I don't know." Then his eyes assumed an obsidian glint. "But there *is* another explanation; there must be. For one, it's possible that the killer made them for the express purpose of clinching the case against Brian."

"In his victim's blood?" Then he shrugged and answered his own question. "Well, that's possible, I'll give you that. Maybe the fingerprint experts can tell us whether it was Nye's finger that made the letters."

"What would preclude the killer's using Nye's finger as a writing instrument?"

Steve winced at that. "Nothing, I suppose."

"Besides, there's another alternative. We don't know much about Nye, about the way he thought or felt about anything, and in particular the way he felt about Brian. For all we know, Nye hated Brian passionately, and we don't know how far he was capable of carrying a grudge. Maybe Nye didn't actually see who hit him—the blow was to the back of his head—and once hit, he certainly wouldn't know who put him in the freezer to die. Maybe he hated Brian enough to assume arbitrarily that he was his killer."

Steve said patiently, "Nye was dying and he must've known it. It'd take a hell of a grudge to make a man accuse somebody of his murder if he wasn't really sure he was guilty."

Conan laughed bitterly and came to his feet.

"I know. But if a question is irrational, maybe the answer has to be irrational, too." He stood silent a moment, then, "When will Kleber arrest Brian?"

Steve's downcast eyes fixed uncomfortably on his glass.

"Kleber won't arrest him, Conan. *I* will. This case belongs to the state, and I guess I'm the state here."

And he wasn't enjoying the role. Conan studied him, wondering how Steve Travers had managed over the years to stay both sane and uncalloused in his chosen profession.

"The case is yours, Steve, but you can't ignore Kleber."

"Earl is *un*ignorable. And I can't ignore the evidence. Motive and opportunity and, on top of that, a dying testament from the victim. Unless something unexpected turns up in the lab reports or autopsy, Kleber plans to take an affidavit to Culpepper in the morning, and Culpepper's primed and ready to hand it to the grand jury."

"And he'll probably have an indictment and a warrant by tomorrow afternoon."

"Probably, and I'll have to sign the affidavit and serve the arrest warrant."

"Are you apologizing for that?"

Steve didn't respond to Conan's ironic tone; he replied soberly, "No. I just don't like the feel of this thing any more than you do, but I don't have any good reason to set my heels. Not the way things stand now."

Conan turned to pick up his crashed paper airplane, frowned sourly at it, then tossed it on his chair.

"Well, an arrest isn't a conviction. Come on, Steve, let's go find something to eat."

CHAPTER 9

Conan was not and never had been a willing early riser, and since he had spent a good part of the night on his feet making repeated trips downstairs to the library, to the bar, to the kitchen, and another part of it chain-smoking at his bedroom window while he watched the moon descend to a golden rendezvous with its reflection, he didn't welcome the telephone call that routed him from hard-won sleep.

He swore and groped and fumbled for the phone on the bedside table. The illuminated numbers on the clock informed him that it was exactly 8 A.M.

"Oh, my God . . . *hello?*"

After a momentary hesitation, a masculine voice asked, "Is this Mr. Conan Flagg?"

"I think so. Yes." Then abruptly he pulled himself up into a sitting position. "How did you get this number?"

Another hesitation, then, "Oh—I see. The number *is* unlisted, isn't it? Well, the local police—"

"All right, who are you?"

"My name is Luther Dix. I'm assistant district director in the Portland office of the IRS."

Conan wondered if he expected a round of applause.

"Yes, Mr. Dix."

"I'm in Holliday Beach, and it's imperative that I speak to you, Mr. Flagg. I'll be there in ten minutes. That is, if you can spare me a little of your time."

Conan was at a loss for words, which was probably fortunate. It was clear from his tone that Luther Dix didn't consider it remotely possible that he *wouldn't* spare his time, but what galled Conan was the blithe assumption that all the world punched in at eight o'clock.

"I don't conduct business in my home," he said in as businesslike a tone as he could manage. "My office is at the Holliday Beach Bookshop. It opens at ten. I'll be happy to arrange my schedule so I can see you then."

"But, Mr. Flagg, I really must—"

"Oh, it's quite all right, Mr. Dix. No trouble at all." He smiled through that and immediately hung up, restraining the impulse to slam the receiver down.

Then he rose and stalked out of the room, neglecting to put on a robe, but oblivious to the morning chill despite his stark state. He padded along the balcony over the living room to the guest room and found the door open, the room empty, and the bed made after Steve's fashion.

Dix wasn't the only one who punched in at eight o'clock.

Half an hour later, showered, shaved, dressed, and sitting at the kitchen window with a cup of coffee and a telephone, Conan looked out at the crystal day and conceded that the early light on the breakers did perhaps have something to recommend it.

He found Steve Travers at the first number he called: the Holliday Beach police station.

"Good morning, Steve."

"Conan? Is that you? Holy mud, it's only—"

"I know what time it is. I have an appointment at ten with assistant et cetera et cetera Luther Dix. I thought I'd better check with you and find out if there's anything I should know before I come to grips with him."

"Well, I'd recommend a couple of cups of coffee first."

"I'm tending to that. At this point I'm fully awake."

"I'll be damned. Okay, well, I guess you should know that Dix arrived in your fair whistle-stop yesterday evening and went straight to the top: Chief Earl Kleber. You can figure Dix knows everything about the case Earl does."

"And what does Earl know from Dix?"

"I only saw him for a few minutes, but it didn't sound like he'd gotten any revelations from on high. Dix's main concern is those missing Surf House records, although he's a little irate about somebody killing an IRS agent."

"Of course. Sets a bad precedent. Do you have any of the lab reports yet?"

"Conan, it's early—remember? I haven't had a chance to call Salem yet. But Dan Reuben arrived about ten minutes ago. He should have a prelim on the autopsy before noon."

"He must be the fastest scalpel in the West."

"The fastest in Oregon, anyway. He's got another autopsy in The Dalles this afternoon. Call me after your date with Dix. I'll have the lab reports by then." He added wryly, "Besides, I want to hear what you find out from him."

"I'll call you anyway."

Again Conan missed his morning walk to the bookshop. He always kept the car handy when he was on a case, and with the immortal motto "Be Prepared" in mind, he made a detour to Driskoll's Garage, which was also, almost incidentally, a filling station.

Rafe Driskoll already had a customer, so Conan stopped at the Super pump and got out to wait. Beryl Randall's Mercedes was parked outside the gaping maw of the garage.

"What happened to you, Mr. Flagg? Run into a door?"

The previous customer was departing, and Driskoll turned his square, stubbly face, clefted with a grin, on Conan. He seemed tanned by exposure to grease and oil rather than sun, and his coveralls and billed cap had assumed the same yellow-brown patina as the sturdy hands he wiped with a rag the same color.

Conan laughed and touched his jaw.

"*Must've* been a door, Rafe; it sure swung hard. Just gas. Everything else should be all right."

He nodded and leaned down to remove the gas cap and insert the nozzle, holding it in place while the pump ticked.

"Oughta be all right. I went over her stem to stern last week. Any more trouble with the clutch?"

"No; smooth as silk. Say, is that Beryl Randall's Mercedes over there?"

"Yep. Now, that's one gorgeous hunk of machine. Really get a kick outa workin' on it. Only trouble is, it don't ever need much workin' on."

"What's wrong with it now?"

"*Now* not a damn thing. She's fixed. It was the cable on the starter. People shouldn't keep cars when they live right on the beach. Damn salt. Eats up the wirin' and paint." He frowned at the XK-E's rear bumper. "Like yours. Damn thing's startin' to rust again."

"That's the price we pay for the view, along with exorbitant property taxes."

"Uh-huh. Don't see you puttin' your house up for sale, though. You hear about Mrs. Randall's car gettin' stolen?"

"Well, yes, I did hear something about that. It was found down at the Shag Point wayside, wasn't it?"

"Yep, I guess it was."

"The thief didn't get very far. He should've picked a car with an intact starter."

Driskoll eyed him from under the browned bill of his red cap.

"No. He just shoulda kept *goin'*, that's all. She run like a top once she got started." The nozzle clicked off, and he pulled it out and shoved it back into its niche on the pump. "Clean your windshield?"

Only the innocent or forgetful let Rafe loose on a wind-

shield with his idea of a clean cloth, but Conan was so absorbed in his own thoughts he was almost too late with his
hasty, "Uh, no, thanks, Rafe. Just put the gas on my tab."

"Okay." He began thumb-smearing the pages of a receipt
book in search of a fresh one. "By the way, Mr. Flagg, good
luck on that Surf House murder."

The grapevine, Conan thought darkly. It was incredible.

At nine-fifty-five when Conan arrived at the bookshop, Beatrice Dobie was unlocking the front door. She seemed to be
having a hard time of it, which could be explained by the
stack of books she was balancing with one hand while man-
aging the key and the knapsack she called a purse with the
other.

Or it could be the presence of the two soberly suited men
hovering behind her.

Conan startled her when he came up beside her.

"Good morning, Miss Dobie. Here—let me help you."

"Oh! Why, Mr. Flagg, you gave me a turn. If you'll just
take the books. These . . . gentlemen are here to see you."
She didn't quite make that a question.

"Yes, I know."

He turned to the elder of the pair, who was examining him
through the magnifying lenses of his glasses.

"Good morning, Mr. Dix."

"Mr. Flagg," he acknowledged with a nod. "This is Russell Griswold, my assistant."

Since Conan had one hand full of books and the other in
a cast, handshakes were precluded, and Griswold seemed a
little relieved. He wore glasses, too, but with the youthfully
impetuous touch of lenses with a light tint.

"Mr. Flagg."

"Mr. Griswold."

The door surrendered to Miss Dobie's efforts and she bus-
tled in, beginning a conversation with Meg. At Conan's nod,
Dix preceded him into the shop, saying, "I hope you understand, Mr. Flagg, that only the most urgent—*damn!*"

This came as he tripped over Meg, staying upright by a miracle of fast footwork, while Meg made a voluble and probably unprintable, if it were translatable, comment.

Miss Dobie deposited her purse on the counter and came back to relieve Conan of the books.

"Now, Meg, you *must* learn to watch where people are going. I, uh, assume you'll be incommunicado for a while, Mr. Flagg?" This with a searching look at Dix and Griswold.

"Yes." He went to his office door, opened it, then stood aside. "This way, Mr. Dix. Mr. Griswold. Meg."

Meg, as befits a lady, entered first; Dix was careful to stay out of her way. Conan closed the door, and the three of them—four with Meg—made a crowd in the small room. When Dix and Griswold had accepted his invitation to the two chairs in front of the desk and settled themselves with their hats in their laps, Conan went to a cabinet under the west window and took out a Spode bowl, a spoon, a can opener, and a can of cat food. Meg lavished loving words on him while she made figure-eights around his legs.

"What was it you wanted to see me about, Mr. Dix?"

"Well, Mr. Flagg, we've been informed that you're more than proprietor of this . . . interesting bookshop. You're also a private investigator."

"On occasion. Damn—would you mind opening this? I can't get a proper grip with this cast."

Dix stared at the can and the opener as if they had arrived via flying saucer, but after a moment, his assistant lived up to his title.

"I'll take care of it, Mr. Flagg."

"Thanks." Meg complained bitterly at the delay.

"As I was saying," Dix went on doggedly, "it has come to our attention that you're investigating Eliot Nye's death in the interests of the Surf House Restaurant."

"No. In the interests of Brian Tally. Thank you, Mr. Griswold. All *right*, Meg, it's *coming*."

"In Mr. Tally's interests, then. Now, I'm sure you'll understand that Eliot's death is not only a personal blow to me, but a blow to all of us in the Portland office, to the IRS itself, in fact.''

Conan tapped the spoon against the bowl to loosen a scoop of boiled-liver scented hash.

"Why such a blow, Mr. Dix?"

"Why? Well, after all, I worked with Eliot for—"

"No, I wasn't questioning the personal blow. I meant the blow to the IRS. Here you are, Duchess." He knelt to present the bowl to Meg.

"Eliot Nye was a full CPA, Mr. Flagg, and one of the best auditors it has ever been my privilege to work with. He was both tenacious and conscientious, and he had a sixth sense for fraud. It was quite extraordinary, actually.''

Conan sat on his heels, watching Meg's shining canines tear into her unresisting repast.

"A full CPA? He might have made a great deal of money for himself in private practice.''

"Of course, but he believed, as I do, that, in the words of Oliver Wendell Holmes, 'Taxes are what we pay for civilized society.' Eliot considered it his obligation to see that no one shirks his fair share of the cost.''

No doubt Dix meant that to his soul, but at the moment Conan found it hard to stomach.

"And in the words of Plato,'' he replied, " 'Where there is an income tax, the just man will pay more and the unjust less on the same amount of income.' Or in the words of Justice John Marshall, 'The power to tax involves the power to destroy.' '' Then he rose and went to his chair behind the desk, adding with a smile, "And in the words of Ben Franklin, 'In this world nothing is certain but death and taxes.' Why did you send Nye to audit the Surf House books a second time?''

That succeeded in catching him off balance.

"I *didn't* send him.''

"The order came from higher up?"

Dix opened his mouth, hesitated, then said cautiously,

"Eliot asked to make another audit. As I said, he was a very tenacious and conscientious man."

"Did he have doubts about his first audit?"

Dix was solidly *on* balance now. "I can't discuss that."

"Mm. Well, I suppose he deserved a little break."

"What are you suggesting, Mr. Flagg?"

He shrugged. "Well, it made a good excuse to spend a few days at the beach at the taxpayers' expense."

Dix's face glowed pink against his white hair.

"That is a scurrilous insult to a man beyond defending himself! I can assure you, Eliot Nye came here for a good reason, and he came here to *work*, not to vacation at the taxpayers' expense."

"What was his good reason?"

"I can't discuss that."

Conan glanced at Griswold and found his features set as firmly as his boss's; no weak links here.

"Mr. Dix, did Nye often work on informers' tips?"

He frowned irritably. "No. Contrary to popular opinion, the IRS does not depend on information from informers in carrying out its investigative functions."

"But you can't ignore that kind of information."

"Of course not. Every law enforcement agency depends on information of that kind on some occasions."

"Granted. Even private investigators do, and believe me, I understand why you're reluctant to divulge the name of the person who informed on Brian Tally."

That didn't work; Dix only smiled glacially.

"I'm glad you understand, but I hope you'll note that I said nothing to suggest that the Surf House Restaurant audit was prompted by an informer's tip."

"Will you say it was prompted by anything else?"

"I won't say at all."

Well, that was something, perhaps; at least it wasn't an outright denial.

"Mr. Dix, will you say that Nye's phone call to you Monday evening *didn't* concern Brian Tally?"

"What we discussed in that call is IRS business."

"Will you say that Nye *didn't* admit he'd made an error or overlooked something in his first audit?"

"Mr. Flagg, I repeat: what we discussed in that call is IRS business."

"With Nye dead—murdered—you still consider it exclusively IRS business?" Then he brought himself up short; his temper was slipping out of control. "Well, I suppose it would be under normal circumstances, but I'm sure you're aware that Chief Kleber assumes Brian had a motive to kill Nye. Because of Nye, Brian stood to lose a business in which he had invested fifteen hard years and which was valued at half a million. But I was in the bar Monday night and heard what Nye said to Brian. It was inconclusive in itself, but three other witnesses were given the same impression: whatever Nye found that changed the picture changed it in Brian's favor. If that's true, Brian was no longer faced with ruin and no longer had a motive. That's why Nye's reason for the second audit and what he told you on the phone are so vital. Without that information, an innocent man may be condemned to life imprisonment."

There wasn't a crack in Dix's adamantine facade.

"If that information," he pronounced, "proves necessary to the prosecution of the case, it will be made available through proper legal channels."

Conan was silenced; he recognized a stone wall when he met it. He took time to light a cigarette before he conceded, "All right, Mr. Dix. This round is yours."

Dix hesitated at that capitulation, apparently a little surprised, then shifted to a conciliatory stance.

"Surely we shouldn't be contenders in that sense, Mr. Flagg. I must, of course, adhere to certain principles and rules which aren't of my making, but I assure you—"

"No. You can't. At any rate, you obviously didn't come here to answer questions, so why *are* you here?"

"Oh. Well . . ." He didn't seem quite ready for that, but made the best of it. "As I said, I'm deeply involved in Eliot's death as a friend and as an official of the IRS. I am, of course, anxious to see this case brought to a satisfactory conclusion, and I'm happy to say that the police, both local and state, have been very sympathetic in offering their cooperation and in assuring me that I'll be kept up to date on the progress of the investigation.''

Conan waited for him to come to the point, but when he stopped and simply smiled expectantly, he realized the point had been reached. Dix expected *him* to follow the sterling example of the police.

He took a drag on his cigarette and smiled coolly into the smoke.

"Don't count on that kind of *sympathy* from me."

Dix stiffened into pink stoniness again.

"I'm sorry you're taking that attitude, Mr. Flagg."

"I'm sorry about *your* attitude, Mr. Dix."

Stalemate. Meanwhile, Meg had concluded her repast and sought a comfortable spot to carry out the ablutions repletion demanded. It was almost inevitable that she chose Luther Dix's lap, despite the fact that it was occupied with his hat. The choice was predicated on feline perversity. Dix didn't like cats; at least not cats who put themselves in his way and nearly piled him on the floor. If Dix didn't like her, then it followed automatically that Meg loved him.

She hopped into his lap, purring audibly.

Dix responded with a startled shout and a flailing of arms, and Meg made a yowling retreat to the top of Conan's desk, landing in an explosion of papers and ashes; her trajectory was on a direct line with the ashtray.

"My God!" Dix breathed, aghast, then when Griswold hastily retrieved his hat and tried to brush the debris of ashes and cat hair off his suit, "Never *mind*, Russell."

Conan got Meg under control along with his cigarette and the hot coals smoldering among the scattered papers, and said—sympathetically—"Mr. Dix, I'm . . . sorry about that."

"It's quite all right," he sniffed, recovering his equilibrium as he restored the crown of his hat to its proper shape. "Has the cat had rabies shots?"

Even Griswold had a hard time keeping a straight face, and Conan found it necessary to lean down to pick up the ashtray from the floor before he answered.

"Yes, she's thoroughly inoculated." He rubbed the potential health hazard behind her ears, offering words of soothing comfort, which she accepted ungraciously, tail twitching, but she consented to stay on his lap.

Dix made a point of checking his watch.

"Before I go, there's another matter I'd like to discuss with you, Mr. Flagg, and that is the missing Surf House records. Since they *were* in the possession of an IRS agent at the time of their disappearance . . . well, I'm sure you understand our concern about them."

Conan said casually, "Well, it might be a little difficult to substantiate the deficiency claim without them."

"Uh . . . yes, I suppose it would. Mr. Flagg, I'm sure you have no idea what happened to those records."

"I do not."

Dix was already nodding before the words were out.

"Well, I just wanted you to know that the IRS is very anxious to recover those records. So anxious we wouldn't be at all inclined to ask questions if they should be returned to us by any means whatever, even mailed in the proverbial plain brown wrapper"—he paused to chuckle at his little joke—"with no return address."

Conan felt a chill in his cheeks and clamped his teeth on his anger. Behind that oblique offer was the assumption that Brian Tally *had* stolen the records—and killed Nye—and that Conan, by virtue of his close relationship with him, was in a position to expedite their return.

Dix was getting uncomfortable with the silence.

"Of course, we realize the records may have been destroyed, but in the hope that they haven't been . . ."

Conan said levelly, "This is a criminal case, Mr. Dix, and the rules are a little different from those you've become accustomed to in the IRS. In a criminal case, a man is presumed innocent until *proven* guilty.''

Dix's face reddened again, and that, at least, Conan thought, was to his credit.

''Yes. Of course.'' He inspected the brim of his hat—for stray cat hairs, perhaps—then rose. ''Well, we must be on our way. Russell?''

He was already on his feet. ''Yes, sir.''

Conan didn't rise, and Meg, from the sanctuary of his lap, offered only a strabismic glare and a twitch of her tail in recognition of their leave-taking.

Conan started the coffee pot on its volcanic cycle and smoked a cigarette down to the filter while he paced the small room like a cage. When he reached the point where he could tell himself—and believe it—that Luther Dix was only doing his duty as he saw it, he moved Meg from his chair to the top of the desk and sat down to make a phone call. Again he found Steve Travers at the police station.

''I told you I'd call anyway, Steve.''

''Sure. Well, you must've at least found out why Dix wanted to talk to you.''

''Oh, yes, he made that clear enough.'' He related Dix's offer concerning the Surf House records, and Steve's colorful response took him back to his youth and some of the rawhide-tongued buckaroos who rode for the Ten-Mile.

In conclusion Steve sputtered, ''No questions asked! Damn it, didn't he think the *police* might have some questions if those records turned up?''

''He only speaks for the IRS, Steve. Anyway, the interview wasn't a total loss, but what I learned was mostly from what he *didn't* say. Except he admitted that Nye *asked* to do the second audit, and since he was so tenacious and conscientious—Dix didn't hold back there—maybe it was because something bothered him about the first; something that changed the picture. Also, I think we can safely assume that the first audit *was* prompted by an informer's tip.''

"That must've been one of the things he *didn't* say."

"Yes, and he was so careful about not saying it, I believe it."

"Conan, sometimes—never mind. You can enlighten me later. Right now, *you* might get some enlightenment if you get down here fast. Kleber's out, so you're safe."

"What kind of enlightenment are you offering?"

"You getting picky so early in the game? I'm offering Lorna Moody Nye and Luke Kautsky, present owner of a red Ferrari. They're here."

Conan jerked upright. "Where? At the station?"

"In person. She came to make arrangements about her husband's body, and I suggested maybe they should answer a few questions about the late unlamented."

Conan was on his feet. "I'll be there in ten—no, five minutes."

CHAPTER 10

Lorna Nye and Luke Kautsky were waiting in Kleber's office, which Steve had commandeered in his absence. Steve entered first and seated himself behind Kleber's desk.

"Sorry for the delay. Oh"—as if it were an afterthought—"this is Conan Flagg. He's working on the case, too. Mrs. Lorna Nye . . . Mr. Luke Kautsky."

Mrs. Lorna Nye said coolly, "I don't use that name anymore. I use my maiden name. Moody."

She was seated in front of the desk, her back straight, not touching the chair; in fact, she was so daintily petite, it seemed doubtful that she exerted any weight on the chair at all. Her hands were folded in her lap, gloved in blue-gray kid exactly the same shade as the suede coat with the clever gold buckles, which was open to reveal one of those *chic* little dresses of French wool whose subtleties only money could buy.

It was very becoming; anything she chose to wear would be becoming. This was the pretty girl in the graduation picture in Eliot Nye's wallet, and she had graduated into an extraordinarily beautiful woman. Here was a face to launch a flotilla or two; fair, flawless skin contrasting nicely with black hair in which blue highlights reflected the color of her eyes, and those eyes, large in her exquisitely modeled face, shadowed by dark lashes under finely arched brows, were mesmerizing in their living perfection.

Conan could understand Luke Kautsky's protective, even possessive, attitude. He had taken a stand at her side, and a sporty-looking feller he was, with curling jet hair and mustache complimenting his saturnine features. There was something about him that suggested a Renaissance lord; beneath the handsome, even elegant facade, the quiescent street-fighter lurked.

He studied Conan with dark, skeptical eyes.

"Are you with the police?"

"No. I'm a private investigator."

"Who hired you?"

"Why do you ask?"

He hesitated, then when he couldn't come up with an answer, said nothing at all, to Conan's amazement.

Steve began in his lulling drawl, "Well, I'm glad the two of you came down to Holliday Beach today, although I'm sorry about the circumstances, Mrs.—uh, Ms. Moody."

She said, "So am I, Mr. Travers."

Kautsky asked, "Why are you glad we came here today?"

"Because I wanted to talk to both of you."

"About what?"

Steve gave him his long-distance squint.

"Ms. Moody's husband was murdered Monday night. I can't really believe you're surprised the police would want to talk to her. Or to you."

Kautsky considered that, then went directly to the heart of the matter.

"Are Lorna and I under suspicion?"

"At this point, half a dozen people are under suspicion

just because we don't have enough information yet to mark any of them off the list.''

''If that list includes Lorna and me, I think we should have our lawyer here before we answer any questions.''

Steve sighed. ''You're not under arrest. Right now I'd just like to ask a few questions, although I will want a statement later.''

''And I'll give you one—in my lawyer's presence.''

Lorna reached into the blue leather purse by her chair, extricated a compact, and gilded the lily of her perfect nose with a pat of powder.

''Oh, really, Luke, we have nothing to hide. If they *must* have a statement, let's get it over with.''

''No, Lorna, I don't think so.''

She snapped the compact shut and put it away.

''You'll only make them more suspicious, you know. After all, I talked to the man at the motel; I gave him my name. They know we were there, so why try to hide it? We *didn't* kill Eliot.''

Conan wondered who she was trying to convince, and he had the uneasy feeling this dialogue had been rehearsed.

She turned to Steve. ''Isn't that what you wanted to ask us about? Luke and I going to Eliot's motel?''

''Yes. Why did you go there?''

Kautsky was on the verge of protesting again, but when he looked at Lorna the very sight of her seemed to rob him of resolve; he lapsed into dubious silence.

''Oh, it was stupid, really,'' she admitted, her Botticelli mouth almost less than beautiful for a moment. ''I mean, even if nothing had . . . happened to Eliot. I'm sure you know that I left my husband a year ago. Our marriage was hopeless, but he refused to agree to a divorce.''

Steve asked baldly, ''Why?''

''Religion,'' she pronounced sacrilegiously. ''He *believed* in that till death do us . . . oh—'' The color rushing to her cheeks was incredibly fetching. ''I didn't mean . . .''

Kautsky had stiffened, but Steve only assured her amiably, "I'm sure you didn't, Ms. Moody, and not many people, or the law, take that part of the marriage vow literally."

She smiled gratefully and pulled in a quick breath.

"But Eliot did, and I was helpless against that as long as he was determined to contest any complaint I filed. You see, I—well, I'm afraid most judges wouldn't understand my situation."

"You mean in regard to Mr. Kautsky?"

The dark lashes swept down demurely. "Yes."

Kautsky said coldly, "Lorna and I aren't married at this moment *only* because of Eliot's medieval morals."

Steve replied indifferently, "Mr. Kautsky, I'm sure your intentions are honorable. I just—"

"You're just looking for a motive against Eliot in our relationship, aren't you?"

"Is there one?"

The Medici eyes flashed, then abruptly hooded themselves.

"No."

"What I'm trying to find out"—he turned to Lorna—"is why you came to see Nye Monday night. Anything incriminating in that?"

"Of course not," she replied, as if to a patent absurdity. "Actually, it was just—well, a whim. I'd filed another complaint, but Eliot hadn't made any response at all. I thought if I could—if Luke and I could talk to him face to face, maybe he'd *finally* understand. . . ."

"Did he?"

"I don't know. I mean, we didn't get a chance to talk to him. Actually, I was a little relieved. It seemed like a good idea when we left Portland, but by the time we got to Holliday Beach . . . well, I wasn't so sure."

Steve tilted back his chair to cross his legs.

"You *didn't* talk to him?"

"No. He wasn't in his room. I knocked and knocked, but there was no answer. And it was so late—after midnight. The curtains were drawn and there weren't any lights, but his car was there, one of the government cars he uses when he's on a field audit."

"Was he a heavy sleeper?"

"No. In fact, he was always a very light sleeper."

"Do you think maybe he just decided he didn't want to open the door for you and Mr. Kautsky?"

She pondered that briefly, then shrugged.

"I don't know. I wouldn't have thought so."

"What did you do when you didn't get any response from him?"

"We went back to Portland. What else was there to do?"

Steve let that pass. "What time was it when you left the motel?"

"Oh . . ." She looked up at Kautsky, but seemed oblivious to his growing restiveness. "It was about twelve-thirty. No later than that, I'm sure."

"When did you get back to Portland?"

"Well, about two-thirty. It's a two-hour drive."

"Do both of you live alone?"

Her piquant chin came up. "Yes. And separately. I've worked and paid my own way since I left Eliot."

Conan wondered who paid for that *chic* outfit, and a flickering movement in Steve's eyes suggested he was wondering the same thing.

"The reason I asked if both of you live alone is that I was hoping somebody could verify your arrival in Portland at two-thirty."

"Oh. Well, no, there wouldn't be anybody . . . but we can *both* testify to that."

Steve didn't comment on the value of that testimony.

"How did you know your husband was here working on the Surf House Restaurant audit? Did he tell you?"

She didn't even blink at that barbed query.

"I haven't seen Eliot for six months, but when I decided to talk to him Monday night, I called our—his house. I got no answer, so I called an old friend, another IRS auditor. He told me Eliot was here and staying at the Seafarer, but he didn't know which room. That's why I had to ask the man at the motel."

"And your friend told you about the Surf House audit?"

She hesitated, then answered cautiously, "Well, he said Eliot was here to do an audit."

"Of the Surf House?"

"What? Well, I don't . . . remember . . ."

Steve frowned slightly. "But you said—"

"Oh, all right. Yes, I knew he was auditing the Surf House, but I *won't* give you the name of the person who told me. That would only get him in trouble with Daddy Di—I mean, Mr. Dix."

Steve laughed. "I, uh, met *Mister* Dix."

She laughed, too, with a shared understanding, but Luke Kautsky wasn't amused.

"Lorna, you've said enough." His lordly displeasure was focused on Steve, but at his sharp tone, Lorna looked up at him like a child who had just been slapped.

"But, Luke, what did I say?"

"Nothing, darling." Even a *condottiere* lord wasn't proof against those eyes. "I just think Jacobs should be here before we answer any more questions."

Steve made a palm-up gesture toward the phone.

"You can use this one, or I'll try to find you a more private one."

"You want me to call my lawyer *now*?"

"I need your statements, Mr. Kautsky."

He frowned irritably. "You mean he has to come here?"

"Considering it's a murder case, he should be willing to make the trip for his clients."

"Damn. All right." He picked up the phone, and while he was occupied with the call, Steve leaned toward Conan.

"I have the lab reports—thank God Kleber has a Telex— and a prelim from Dan Reuben. Maybe we can mix business with lunch. 'The best' is open today, incidentally; I gave Tally the go-ahead this morning."

Conan nodded. "Good. By the way, where's Kleber?"

"He's in Westport." The flicker of tension around his eyes was at odds with his casual tone. "Left about an hour ago."

Conan made no response to that. Westport was the county seat, and it was there the grand jury met and there the circuit judge would act on their indictment and issue a warrant for the arrest of Brian Tally. The law would offer no delays; not in this case. Culpepper would see to that.

Lorna was watching Conan with unabashed curiosity. He made a tentative overture with a friendly smile and was a little surprised when she returned it. He decided to see how far friendliness would get him.

"Ms. Moody, I'd like to ask you a few questions, but they have nothing to do with—"

That was as far as he got on his first try; at that moment Kautsky cradled the phone and said coolly, "Lorna's answered enough questions."

Conan started to argue, then tried another approach, displaying an approximation of that slapped-child look for Lorna, then averting his eyes in embarrassed hopelessness.

"Yes, of course. I . . . understand."

It worked. Her voice floated out to him plaintively.

"Mr. Flagg, who *are* you working for?"

"For a man Eliot Nye was on the verge of bankrupting, a man who will without a doubt be arrested for his murder." He saw Steve's blinking look of inquiry, but ignored it. "I know he's innocent, but I can't prove it. Still, it doesn't seem fair that alive Nye could break him financially, and now . . . well, at least we don't have the death penalty in Oregon."

Her blue eyes burned hot at her husband's name, and despite Kautsky's warning frown, she asked, "What did you want to ask me? I mean, what could *I* tell you?"

"Lorna—"

"Oh, Luke, at least let him tell me what he wants to know. I don't have to answer his questions."

Conan grasped his advantage before Kautsky could offer further protest.

"I just want to know something about your husband; the kind of man he was. Especially how he approached his work. Luther Dix tells me he was conscientious, tenacious, and all those good IRS virtues, but virtues carried to excess become vices. I want to know how far he carried his virtues."

Now her eyes turned icy. "To the limit, Mr. Flagg. He was puritanical, dogmatic, moralistic—" She caught herself, perhaps feeling Kautsky's disapproving gaze. "Well, the very fact that I left him tells you I didn't see eye to eye with him on many things."

Conan sat down on the edge of the desk, arms folded.

"Why did he choose to work for the IRS?"

Her mouth *did* manage to achieve unattractiveness then.

"He saw it as his moral and patriotic duty to put all those tax evaders behind bars, even widows and children."

Conan demurred mildly, "Well, some tax evaders deserve to be behind bars, I suppose."

"Yes, of course." She restored her mouth with a pretty smile. "And I guess it's a good thing *somebody* feels the way he did about it."

"Was he so zealous in punishing tax evaders that he'd . . . bend the facts, shall we say?"

She considered that and finally gave the dead its due.

"I doubt it. He was such a—well, I'm sure he never railroaded anyone, if that's what you mean."

"That's what I mean. Was he capable of admitting error? His own or the IRS's?"

"Oh, yes. Errors—of any kind—upset him. I remember one case where something about the first audit bothered him, so he did a second audit on his own time, and then told Dix to drop the case. He nearly lost his job over that one."

Conan frowned. "He risked his job because a taxpayer was right and the IRS wrong?"

"Yes, but not because the taxpayer was right. He just

couldn't stand it if everything didn't balance out to the last penny.''

"How did he feel about working on informers' tips?''

"Well, he didn't like it. He said it was usually a matter of casting the first stone.'' Then she smiled capriciously. "He always audited the informer *too*. Just a random audit, of course.''

Conan looked at her so intently her smile faded.

"He audited the *informer*? Did he always do that?''

She shrugged. "I don't know if he made it an absolute rule, but he did it quite a lot. I'm sure of that.''

Conan glanced at Steve, and the slight lift of one eyebrow told him the significance of the Van Roon file in Nye's attaché case hadn't been lost on him.

Conan returned to Lorna, giving some thought to the wording of his next question.

"Your husband took a highly moralistic attitude toward tax evaders. Did he—well, hold a grudge against any of the people whose cases he handled?''

She laughed caustically. "No. All he cared about was setting the books right. You know what I mean? He'd be more likely to know their Social Security numbers than their names. A grudge? Never. That would be an emotional thing. Eliot never got that emotional about *anything*.''

With that acrimonious appraisal, she closed and locked a door with a finality that reverberated in Conan's mind.

As Steve had observed, it would take a hell of a grudge to make a man accuse another of his murder if he really wasn't sure he was guilty. That *would* be an emotional thing.

If the initials pointing that incarnadined finger at Brian couldn't be explained as a mental quirk on Nye's part, there was only one other possibility: the killer had made them, drawn them in the blood of one victim to incriminate another.

He said absently, "Thank you, Ms. Moody.''

"Is that all?'' She seemed a little disappointed.

"Yes. That's all.''

A few minutes later Conan stood at the window and watched Lorna and Kautsky departing in the red Ferrari. They would be back at three o'clock, armed with counsel.

"Steve, you didn't mention Nye's insurance policies."

"No. Thought I should keep something in reserve." He had his feet propped on a corner of the desk, hands cupped around the match held to his cigarette. "Sounds like Van Roon ought to have more to offer than he put in his statement."

"About playing Judas to the IRS? Yes. Let me talk to him first."

"You're welcome to him."

"Don't say that as if it were a gift." He looked up at the sky; a curdled overcast had moved in, but there was no wind. "What do you think?"

"Of the young lovers? Well, if Nye had died of cyanide poisoning, I wouldn't have a doubt in the world that Lorna fed it to him. My God, she's a pretty little thing, isn't she?"

Conan laughed and put his back to the window.

"Enchanting. By the way, that was very neat about the Surf House audit. Now all you have to do is find out if she *did* learn about it from this anonymous auditor friend, or if she saw the records in Nye's motel room."

"Yes, well, if the case depended on finding that out, forget it." He assayed a smoke ring, but it didn't hold together.

"You know, there's something about those two that makes me want to doubt every word they say." Conan went to the chair Lorna had vacated and crossed his feet on another corner of the desk while he lit a cigarette. "But maybe I'm just envious of Kautsky. He's such a sporty-looking feller."

"And she might be damned sporty, too, on occasion."

"Well, you and I will never know. But I have this funny gut feeling they're telling the truth."

"Maybe you're just hungry. It's nearly noon."

"If they *are* telling the truth, and if Nye wasn't just snubbing them, then that means he hadn't returned to the Seafarer by twelve-thirty, but Beryl said she saw him heading for the door at the restaurant at five after twelve. It shouldn't take more than ten minutes to walk that distance.''

"Maybe he stopped for a drink." When that elicited only a musing puff of smoke, he added, "Little joke, there.''

Conan's eyes came into focus on him. "You said you have the lab reports and a prelim from Reuben.''

"Yes, but you're not going to like some of it.''

"Then you'd better give me the bad news first.''

He shrugged uneasily. "Okay. The bad news is about the initials. Conan, Nye did make them. There were three good prints where he started or stopped a line, all of them Eliot Nye's right index finger. And he *was* right-handed.''

Conan felt an aching hollow forming in his solar plexus. He asked tightly, "Can you be sure the killer didn't use Nye's finger to make the letters—and the prints?''

"Yes. I asked Harry Quincy—he's our handwriting expert. He said the angles and weight of the lines, the fade at the bottom of the verticals—it's all consistent with the position Nye was in. If somebody else made those letters using his finger, they'd be working above him, and the angle and set would be different. And the prints would be from the end of the finger, and there'd be some nail marks. But these prints are the flat of the fingertip—and no nail marks. Harry's willing to swear Nye made those initials.''

Conan's feet slammed down to the floor.

"But he couldn't have!''

Steve didn't argue; he didn't need to. Conan knew he was still faced with that sardonic enigma, and the two answers he had regarded as the only rational alternatives to both, within a few minutes, dissolved into meaninglessness like smoke in his hands.

"Damn it, Steve, it doesn't make sense.''

"No. Not if Tally didn't kill him.''

That was only a statement of fact, devoid of inflection. Conan discovered his cigarette still in his hand, took a puff and found it searingly bitter, then put it out before he reached for the phone.

Steve asked, "Who are you calling?"

"A lawyer—who else?"

CHAPTER 11

Steve Travers was smiling as they left the station.

"Marcus Fitch. Damn, Kleber'll drop his uppers."

"You don't think there's prejudice in Holliday Beach, do you?"

"I don't know about Holliday Beach, but I have a good idea how Earl's going to take it."

Conan was smiling a little himself at that. Marcus Fitch was one of Portland's top lawyers; he was also black. Not that Holliday Beach was consciously bigoted. The fact that there wasn't a single black among its twelve hundred inhabitants was an accident of economics and geography more than purposeful exclusion. But unfamiliarity inevitably breeds distrust.

"Marc is one of the best criminal lawyers I know, and he owes me a favor; otherwise I wouldn't expose him to Earl."

"He must owe you a *big* favor. Want to take my car?"

"Let's take mine. I like to have wheels handy, and you can always call the state patrol. My only alternative is the local taxi. You want to drive?"

"Sure. This is the only way *I'll* ever get to drive a twelve-thousand-dollar car. That hand bothering you?"

Conan surrendered the keys to him when they reached the Jaguar, then went around to the passenger side.

"Not really, but I have to think harder when I drive. Just remember, it doesn't have an automatic shift."

"Relax. After all, I learned to drive on a ten-gear cattle truck."

"I remember. What about the rest of the lab reports?"

"You can boil it all down to one word: nothing. At least, nothing Hancock didn't mop or disinfect out of existence. The only clear prints Jeff pulled belonged to Hancock, Jastrow, Bliss, or Tally, which figures since they're in the kitchen every day. Yes, we checked the mop. Smudge."

Conan nodded and waited until Steve turned onto the highway and passed a braying log truck.

"What did Dan Reuben have to say?"

"Hypothermia. Nye froze to death. No alcohol or other extraneous ingredients in the stomach or blood. No contusions, abrasions, fractures, et cetera, other than the head wound. Time of death is hopeless. Circumstantial evidence tells us more about that than Dan could."

"What about the head wound?"

"Inflicted by an unidentified blunt instrument. Not so blunt, really. Dan said the wound seemed to be made by something with three sides coming to a point at right angles. You know anything that would fit that description around the kitchen?"

"I was in that kitchen only twice before yesterday, and cooking utensils are one of the eternal mysteries to me." He gave the bookshop the usual survey as they passed; business was a little better today. Then he looked to the other side of the highway and Driskoll's Garage. Beryl's Mercedes was absent from the ranks of the disabled.

"Steve, what about Beryl's car? Did you see any of the reports on that?"

"Yes. It was clean. I guess somebody was smart enough to wear gloves."

"But not smart enough to get farther out of town before they stopped to enjoy the view. Or whatever."

"What do you mean?"

"Never mind; it's not important. What about those drugs Jeff found in the cooler?"

"Oh, damn, I almost forgot. We got some nice clear prints, all belonging to Johnny Hancock. We put out an APB on him this morning. He lives in a trailer park in the north end of town, but he wasn't home last I heard."

"He may never be. Take the next turn to the right."

"Already? Funny how the miles fly when you're driving a twelve-thousand—"

"Yes, Steve, I know the price tag. I wrote the check."

The Surf House parking lot was full, so Steve nonchalantly left the XK-E in a loading zone. When they reached the restaurant door, they encountered a contingent of elderly ladies on their way out. Steve gallantly held the door for them and pretended not to notice their meaningful looks and *sotto voce* comments.

". . . detective . . . the *state* police . . . well! Didn't I tell you . . ."

Inside the entry hall, he shook his head ruefully.

"Word sure gets around, doesn't it?"

"Apparently. Seems to be good for business, though."

The dining room was crowded, which was a phenomenon at this time of year, but the diners were nearly all locals. Tilda Capek was at the counter behind the cash register ringing up a guest check and trying to ignore Claude Jastrow, who was leaning close to her, speaking in low, taut tones.

". . . doesn't mean anything to you, I suppose? Oh, Til, you're making a terrible mistake. Don't you know that?"

She counted out the change onto a small tray and handed it to a passing waitress.

"For A-2, Kay. No, Claude, I don't know it. Now,

please—'' She stopped when she saw Conan and Steve; Jastrow turned, head tilted back, eyes hooded.

"Ah, the fell sergeant, so strict in his arrest." That was for Steve, who only looked at him blankly.

Conan said, "Bad casting, Claude. Steve would never play as Death."

He laughed. "True. Horatio, perhaps. *Give me that man that is not passion's slave . . .*" He paused as a couple came down the steps, and Tilda took menus and went out to greet and seat them. She was wearing a rose-beige pantsuit of a soft material that clung nicely exactly where it should.

Conan reluctantly turned his attention to Jastrow, and his effort was rewarded. In that unguarded moment, Jastrow's face was a revelation. He *was* passion's slave, and Tilda Capek was his passion.

Then he seemed to catch himself and displayed a smile.

"Gentlemen, you'll excuse me if I make my exit now. . . . *a poor player that struts and frets his hour upon the stage . . . And then is heard no more.*" He executed a mocking bow with his exit, while Steve delivered a sigh.

"I guess I should brush up on my Shakespeare."

Conan laughed. "At least *Hamlet* and *Macbeth*, and what could be more appropriate? They're both about murders."

Tilda paused to give orders to a busboy on her way back to the counter.

"Water B-7, Ken. Oh—next time I pass C-4, I want to see the silver placed properly. You should know better by now. Jenny . . ." This to a waitress sailing past under a loaded tray a yard in diameter. "Cocktail B-7 for me, please, when you get your table served." She didn't mention Jastrow when she reached the counter.

"Conan, is something wrong?" Then she added bitterly, "Or should I ask, is anything right?"

He shrugged. "Everything and nothing. We're just here for lunch, Tilda. Looks like you have a full house."

"The smell of disaster. We haven't had so much lunch business since summer." She assessed the seating possibilities in a sweeping glance. "In about ten minutes I can give you a window table."

"That's worth waiting for. Where's Brian?"

"At his apartment. At least, he said he was going there. He couldn't stand it here. All the people. Conan, is . . ." Her gray eyes were so full of aching appeal, it was all he could do not to turn away.

"I don't have any good news, Tilda. In fact, Kleber's in Westport now, and when he returns he'll have a warrant for Brian's arrest."

"Oh, dear God . . ." For a moment it seemed she might faint, then she turned her look of stunned appeal on Steve. He couldn't meet it.

"Miss Capek, I'm sorry, but there's nothing I can do."

"No . . . no, of course not. I understand that." She took a deep breath to compose herself. "Conan?"

The real question was in her eyes; she couldn't seem to reduce it to words.

"I have nothing but bits and pieces, Tilda, a maze of maybes. But I'll put it together somehow." It seemed a pitifully inadequate assurance.

She nodded, apparently satisfied with it, but a moment later her eyes seemed to slip out of focus.

She said softly, "But who will put Brian together again after . . ."

There was fear in that, and something very near grief.

CHAPTER 12

After a lunch protracted by the unanticipated pressure of in-season business on an off-season staff, Conan drove Steve back to the police station, went in long enough to find out that Kleber was still in Westport, then departed, offering Steve the vague assurance that he would return sooner or later.

A rising wind flung desultory sprinkles of rain that demanded windshield wipers, but after a few strokes left them squeaking like fingernails on a blackboard. Conan winced and flipped them off to wait for the droplets to collect, finding in that a bent metaphor for his present situation.

When he reached the highway, he turned south and after a few blocks gave the wipers another chance just before he turned into the empty parking lot beside a forlorn prefab building where a miniature marquee announced, "BCH FRT 3 BDRMS IDEAL INV PROP." A sign in the door assured the world that F. Conrad Van Roon was open for business.

As Conan walked to the door, he looked in through the expanses of dirty glass and saw Conny Van Roon hurriedly preparing for his arrival. His preparations consisted of snatching the pint of whiskey from the top of his desk and secreting it in a drawer. When Conan opened the door, Van Roon was on his feet and ready with a welcoming smile.

"Mr. Flagg—come in, come in!"

He was already in. He looked around, noting the tracked, unwaxed floor, the faded photographs of real estate bonanzas decorating the walls, and the three empty desks, none of which showed recent signs of occupancy.

"Well, Mr. Flagg, this is a real pleasure. You're probably thinking of some investment property, I'll bet, and there's no sounder place to put your money than beach property. No, sir, not these days. You just have a seat. I've got some listings here. . . ." He shuffled through the piles on his desk with shaking hands. "I know you're going to find just the thing you're looking for . . . if I can just find the—heh-heh—listings. . . ."

"Conny, I'm not here to look at property."

Van Roon slowly collapsed into his chair, which, luckily, was right behind him.

"Oh."

"I'm sorry." And he was; Van Roon was such a sorry human being. Conan sat down in one of the chairs waiting hopefully in front of the desk. "I'm investigating Eliot Nye's murder, and I'd like to ask you some questions."

"Nye? But I thought . . ."

Conan waited, then asked, "You thought what?"

"Well, I . . . uh, heard Brian Tally was . . ." He stopped, then made a hasty retreat. "Well, nothing, really. Just talk, you know."

"Sure. Monday night after Brian floored me, you followed Nye into the hall to ask him about Brian's tax case."

Van Roon treated that as a question, or even an accusation.

"I was interested, that's all. I mean, Brian was always a good friend to me."

"How did you know about his problems with the IRS?"

"Well, he . . . he told me about it. That's right, he told me."

Conan gave him a direct look, waiting until his eyes dropped, which took about three seconds.

"Okay. Now, you tell me about the Nevada backers you had lined up to buy the restaurant."

Van Roon flared, "I *do* have backers lined up. They're ready to lay out half a million just like *that*!" He meant to snap his fingers, but got no snap out of it. "They're *still* ready, and Brian's a fool not to take it. Hell, he could build two restaurants for half a mil, or spend the rest of his life soaking up the sun in Acapulco."

"Or in Vegas or Reno?"

Van Roon's eyes wavered. "Well, sure. Anywhere he wanted."

"*You* seem to enjoy the sun in Nevada."

"Me? Well, why not? Lots of people do."

"And lots of people gamble, but not many quit winners. The house always wins in the long run, right, Conny?"

His shoulders twitched in a shrug.

"That's . . . what they say."

"And the house always collects its IOUs—one way or another. The trouble with some houses is their collection methods are rather crude."

At that, Van Roon's thin face went gray.

"Listen, Mr. Flagg, I . . . I don't know what you're getting at, but I don't think I like what you're insinuating."

"Insinuating? I'll spell it out for you. It's no great secret that certain Nevada interests have been trying to get a toe hold on the Oregon coast for years; it's relatively virgin territory. However, Oregonians are an independent lot, and they haven't offered the Nevada interests much of a welcome. But they keep trying. Now, Brian has made an impressive success of the Surf House Restaurant; impressive enough to entice *any* potential investor in resort property, and it hasn't escaped the attention of those Nevada interests. And conveniently for them they have a local real estate dealer under their thumb.''

"What do you mean by that?" His attempt at indignation only produced a squeaking admission of fear.

Conan turned hard black eyes on him.

"How much do you owe them, Conny?"

"Owe—what do you . . . now, wait a minute!''

"Will your commission on the sale of the restaurant cover it, or is that just earnest money?''

"You—you got no right—what do you mean, coming in here and saying—''

"And what's the alternative if you *don't* come through with the restaurant sale? A place in the Nevada sun—six feet under?''

"*No!* Damn you, stop it! Get out! Get out and—and leave me . . . alone. . . .'' He had a handkerchief out to wipe his sweating forehead and finally buried his face in it.

Conan waited and again felt sorry for him, but he was reminded of one of his father's maxims: *Even a rabbit'll fight like hell if it's cornered.*

At length, Van Roon composed himself, and if he was surprised that Conan hadn't obeyed his summons to leave, he gave no hint of it.

"Mr. Flagg, I fail to see,'' he began with some dignity, "what all this has to do with the murder of—of Eliot Nye.''

"Do you? Well, there's usually more than one road to the top of the mountain. The trouble with Brian is he didn't want to sell the restaurant at all; it's his pride and joy, his life's blood. At least, it used to be. And you made an error when you told him your moneyed backers hailed from Nevada. That settled it for him. He said no deal, no way. So you had to find that other road. A letter to the IRS; that's all it took. Then you had two possibilities: once they put the screws on him, he might change his mind and decide to sell after all, but even if he didn't, the chances were good that you could pick up the restaurant for a fraction of its value at a tax sale.''

Van Roon came erect with a jerking wrench.

"What did you—what's this about the IRS?"

"I talked to Luther Dix this morning, Conny. The assistant district director."

"But they—they wouldn't . . . they *promised* me . . ." He was too stunned to be aware of the admission implicit in that.

"Nye is dead. Murdered. That . . . changes the picture."

At those words, Van Roon hunched back in his chair, eyes narrowed warily.

"I was only doing my duty. I pay taxes, too, and it's not right when somebody else gets by without paying what they owe. That's a *crime*, you know."

Conan's sympathy was evaporating rapidly.

"What made you think he wasn't paying what he owed?"

"Well, I . . . I keep my ears open."

"What did your open ears garner that made you think the IRS might have a case against Brian?" Then, when Van Roon puffed himself up for another display of righteousness, "Brian has retained Marcus Fitch to defend him, and don't kid yourself that he won't subpoena you just for the hell of it. I doubt your Nevada backers want to see you in any court of law."

He deflated suddenly. "In court? But—but you can't—"

"You'd only be doing your *duty*, Conny, if you have information bearing on a crime—and murder is also a crime. But all I want is information. I'm not interested in putting you on the witness stand."

He grasped at the straw of the unmade promise. "Okay! I'll tell you. I mean, it's no big thing. Nothing wrong about it. I was having a few drinks in the Tides Room one night and happened to be talking to a couple of the people who work there. It wasn't anything solid, you understand, just they thought something fishy was going on." He laughed nervously. "Fishy. That's funny."

"Hilarious. But explain it to me."

"Well, it's just that they thought there was some funny business going on with the suppliers' accounts, especially the gypo wholesalers who come through maybe once or twice with a load of goods, then just disappear. One of the dealers was a *fish* supplier.''

''The humor is beginning to reach me.''

''The guys I was talking to—well, one of them—saw some of the invoices. That's where the . . . fishy part comes. He said the invoices didn't match up with what was delivered.''

''Names, Conny. I want your drinking buddies' names.''

He supplied them willingly. ''Claude Jastrow and Howie Bliss, and *they* should know what goes on in that kitchen.''

Conan leaned back, eyes slanting as he considered that. The source wasn't as surprising as the information, and he wondered if there was any truth to it. Apparently, the IRS case against Brian was based on the discrepancy between the restaurant's reported profit and the expected averages compiled by the IRS—not on the kind of outright fraud Van Roon had implied.

But Conan reminded himself that he had very little information on the IRS's case. He only knew Howie Bliss to be unstable, unpredictable, and generally unsober, while Jastrow's arrogance hinted at a fragile ego which would make him vulnerable to jealousy, and he was still in love with Tilda. And she was in love with Brian.

At any rate, the truth behind the fishy rumors was irrelevant. The IRS had made its case and served Van Roon's purpose.

Conan studied him, noting the glint of furtive wiliness behind the fear in his eyes.

''Conny, did you discuss your plans to betray Brian to the IRS with Howie or Claude?''

He licked his lips. ''I . . . don't remember.''

''Don't you?''

''I *said* I don't *remember*!''

Conan nodded indifferently. ''So, you did your duty and reported Brian to the IRS, and whether he finally gave in and sold the restaurant, or you picked it up in a tax sale, your Nevada backers would be satisfied. Besides, the informer's fee on the deficiency Nye turned up would finance another trip to Vegas. Things were looking good, weren't they—until Nye came into the bar Monday night with the news that something had changed the picture.''

Van Roon asked cautiously, ''What's that supposed to mean?''

''Disaster for you if it meant a reprieve from ruin for Brian. And it's interesting that you left the restaurant within minutes of the time Beryl said she saw Nye leaving, yet according to your statement, you didn't see him at all after your departure.''

''Well, I didn't! I didn't see *anybody*!''

''You were faced with potential disaster, yet you just shrugged it off and went home without making any further effort to talk to Nye? Conny, I don't believe that.''

He crouched, hands clenched on the edge of the desk.

''I went straight home! Ask my wife. She can tell you when I got home. She bitched enough about it. Damn it, I went *home*!''

''But was Eliot Nye alive then?''

He seemed to quiver in the backwash of that question, and at first he didn't move a muscle. Then suddenly he began scrabbling at the top drawer, his shaking hands defying him, then jerking up, locked around the butt of a fist-sized automatic.

''*Get out!*'' he shrieked. ''Just get *out* of here!''

Conan did, but slowly; no sudden movements to make the trembling finger on that trigger jerk.

It was a long way to the door.

CHAPTER 13

Having a gun pointed at him was an unnerving experience under any circumstances, and all the more so when the pointer was a desperate drunk, but when Conan arrived at the police station, he didn't report his experience to Steve. It would keep, and there were other things to occupy his mind. Like Kleber.

The chief, Steve informed him, hadn't yet returned from Westport.

Conan scowled at the clock on Kleber's wall. Three-thirty. The Damoclean sword still hovered.

"What about Hancock, Steve? Anyone found him yet?"

"Mm?" Steve was pecking out a report on an electric typewriter that seemed to get away from him occasionally, stuttering out half a line before he could restrain it. "No, he's still at large." While Steve continued his contest with the typewriter, Conan availed himself of one of the phones on the desk and called the Surf House. Tilda told him in a constrained tone that Brian had returned; he was working in the kitchen.

133

When Conan hung up, he relayed that information to Steve and added, "I'm going down to talk to him."

"What about?"

"The weather. I don't know. At least I think he should be prepared for Kleber."

Steve glowered at the sheet emerging from the typewriter, then ripped it out and rose.

"I'll go with you." Then as if Conan had questioned that, "Maybe I can look around for a likely not-so-blunt instrument."

Business was still good at the restaurant, and when they arrived they had to wait for Tilda to seat a bevy of local ladies, a task she executed with unflagging grace and efficiency. It was only when she approached Conan and Steve that she let her guard down and her smile slip.

She didn't waste words on amenities. "Conan, Brian is in the kitchen. I . . . I'm glad you're here."

She didn't have time to explain that—a new customer appeared—and perhaps it didn't need explaining. Conan led the way through the pantry, sidling cautiously down the middle after nearly being decapitated by a passing tray, wondering through every foot of the crowded gauntlet whether he was supposed to dodge or simply drop to the floor when someone shouted, "Behind you!" The waitresses and busboys seemed engaged in a hectic quadrille, which they managed without a missed step, their exchanges spiced with a casually foul vocabulary that would call forth blushes in the dining room, but here the roar of the exhaust fans acted as a damper.

Brian was at the cutting table by the side entrance reducing a slab of beef to steaks, each perfectly consistent in thickness, a succulent two inches of prime filet. The foot-long blade of the knife was as red with blood as his hands, and he wielded it with violent finesse.

"Brian?" Conan had to shout over the general uproar.

Thunk. The blade slipped at an errant angle and struck the table.

"Hell." He turned to glare at the source of the distraction, then the corded tension in his features relaxed.

"Conan—well, I was wondering . . . Hello, Mr. Travers."

Steve touched his finger to a nonexistent hat brim, a gesture that was a holdover from his youth.

"Mr. Tally. Mind if I look around the kitchen a little? I'll stay out of the way." He ducked as a busboy sailed a tray of dirty dishes past. "At least, I'll try."

Brian laughed. "Go ahead, but it's at your own risk." When Steve had wandered off toward the dishwashing assemblage, he asked with forced lightness, "Well, Conan, what's the good news?"

While Conan gave him the news of his impending arrest, tempering it with the assurance that Marcus Fitch was on stand-by, Brian took up the knife again, his big hands seemingly functioning independently of his thoughts. The surface of the table was soaked red.

But when Conan finished, the deft movements of the knife stopped, Brian stood for a moment with his eyes shut, the muscles of his jaw flexing spasmodically.

"Oh, God, Conan, I can't . . . I can't *take* much more."

"You can take more. I don't know how much." His tone was detached, almost cold, and served its purpose; Brian pulled in a long breath and finally nodded.

"Sure. But about this lawyer—look, I can't afford any high-class city lawyers. Hell, I still owe Herb Latimer."

"Don't waste any worry on that. Marc owes me a favor, and this seemed like a good time to call him on it."

Brian reached for a damp rag to wipe his hands.

"But what'll you do next time *you* land in jail?"

Conan laughed with him. "Well, I guess I'll have to do him another favor before it comes to that." His laughter faded as quickly as Brian's. "I'm sorry I can't offer much in the way of encouragement now. All I can say is I have some leads, but I don't know where they'll take me.''

"Just knowing you're working on it is encouraging. It's about the only thing I've got going for me right now.'' His jaw was tightening again as he began mopping the blood from the table. "You know, it wouldn't get to me so much if I just understood about Nye. I mean . . .'' His fist doubled in the rag. "For God's sake, why? He nailed me to the cross with those damned initials! *Why!*''

Conan stared down at the table, at the smeared patterns left by the rag, and perhaps it was his recent encounter with Jastrow that brought the words to mind: *Yet who would have thought the old man to have so much blood in him?*

"Sorry, Conan.'' Brian had himself under control again. "I guess I better pull myself together before Kleber comes.''

Conan didn't seem to hear that, nor did he look up from the table, rather, from the corner where the layered wood made a sharp angle barely softened by years of wear and scrubbing. His intent gaze dropped to the floor, tracing lines that Jastrow had created in his imagination.

"Conan? What's wrong?''

He looked up at Brian, but didn't answer the question. He'd just answered another.

"Steve! Where the hell did he—*Steve*!''

That shout turned heads in the pantry and brought Steve at a run from the back of the kitchen.

"Holy mud, Conan, what's going—''

"Steve! I found your not-so-blunt instrument!'' He pointed to the corner of the table. "Something with three sides coming together at right angles. And the scuff marks—no one makes scuff marks as long as Jastrow described them in normal walking, and not two parallel. That would happen if someone *slipped*. For instance, if they slipped on a wet, freshly mopped floor. Maybe Nye was pushed or hit first, but one way or another, he slipped and fell—fell against this poised not-so-blunt instrument.''

Brian stared in bewilderment at Conan, the table, then at

Steve, who leaned down to examine the corner from a distance of six inches.

"Well, it's possible. Maybe the lab can pick up a blood stain; a *human* blood stain." He straightened, eyes set in a tight squint. "Mr. Tally, how often is this table cleaned?"

"Every night."

"I suppose Hancock does that?"

"Yes."

"Do you know when? I mean, does he have a routine? Would this come before or after mopping the floor, say?"

"If he sticks to the routine I laid out for him, it comes sort of in between. The table is soaked with chlorine bleach for at least an hour, then scrubbed with a brush, so he starts the soaking early while he takes care of the garbage and the floor, then goes back for the scrubbing."

Steve winced. "Chlorine bleach?"

"Well, it's about the best disinfectant there is."

"I wonder what it'll do for chemical analysis. Well, we can try it." He delved into various pockets until he came up with a jackknife and an evidence bag. "Mind if I carve out a piece?"

Brian's jaw dropped. "Carve out—do you know what a table like this costs?" Then he seemed to hear himself and found it bitterly amusing. "Well, it doesn't look like replacing it will be *my* problem, so carve away."

"I only need a few shavings; I don't think you'll have to replace it." He leaned down to procure his shavings. "You know, Conan, if you're right about this—"

"It means Nye never left this building Monday night."

Brian shook his head as if to clear it.

"It means what?"

"We know when the scuff marks were made," Conan explained. "Jastrow discovered them at about twelve-fifteen, and Hancock insisted they weren't there when he mopped, which was only a short time before. If Nye made them while slipping on the wet floor and colliding with this corner, then it had to be before Jastrow found them, and after Nye was last seen alive, which was about five minutes after twelve. And he must have been put in the freezer immediately after he knocked himself unconscious, or Jastrow would've found *him* with the scuff marks. He didn't get up and walk out on his own after taking a blow like that—nor clean up his own blood.''

Steve sealed and marked the bag. ''So, Lorna and Luke were telling the truth. Nye *wasn't* at home when they knocked. Damn; makes you wonder. I'd have sworn they were lying in their teeth. But don't pin too much hope on the lab turning up traces of human blood on this, Conan; not when it's been soaked with bleach.'' While he looked for a pocket for the bag, he asked Brian, ''Is Mrs. Randall around today?''

''She's down in her office. Why?''

''She was the one who said Nye left the restaurant at five after twelve.''

''No,'' Conan demurred, ''she said she saw him walk *to* the door while she was on her way to the ladies' room. Once in there she wouldn't see him if he came back in. Or he might have gone out and entered the kitchen through the back door.''

''Hancock.'' Steve's mouth pulled tight. ''Well, I hope we pick him up before he gets out of the country. I have a few questions to ask him.'' Then he turned, frowning into the pantry. In the confusion of noise, Tilda's voice was almost lost, but it was Steve's name she was calling.

''Mr. Travers, there is . . . someone out here to see you.''

Her face was pale and tautly expressionless, and Conan could all but read the name of that ''someone.'' Earl Kleber.

Steve hunched his shoulders and pushed his way through the pantry, while Brian took up the knife and began hacking at the meat. There was no finesse in it now, and Conan was on the verge of stopping him before a finger fell under that scimitar blade.

But within a minute, Steve reappeared, his face as eloquently expressionless as Tilda's had been; Earl Kleber was only a pace behind him. A busboy pirouetted to keep his laden tray balanced while avoiding a collision, but neither of them seemed to notice him. Brian stared at the folded document in Steve's hand, then looked up past him to Kleber, and the meeting of their eyes was a silent explosion.

Steve stopped a pace from the table and said in level, clipped tones, "Brian Tally, I have a warrant for your arrest on the charge of murder in the first degree. You have the right to remain silent, the right to . . ."

Conan didn't hear the rest of the litany; he was watching Brian, reading in the deathly stillness of his face a man on the fine edge, every muscle strained to immobility.

"Do you understand your rights?" Steve asked in conclusion.

"No!"

That wasn't a response to the question, but to Kleber's movement; he had pulled out a pair of handcuffs.

Brian dropped the knife, tossed it away from him, and his right hand closed into a fist. Kleber let out a hoarse shout as that pile driver came at him; there were shrieks from the pantry, a resounding crash as a tray hit the floor. But Conan had the arm behind the fist and used its momentum to twist it under and behind Brian's back.

"Brian! Damn it, you want him to put a bullet in your guts?"

Kleber had his gun out ready to do just that, but Conan doubted that threat was what made Brian sag against him in sudden submission.

As the tension ebbed in sighs of relief, Steve said irritably, "Earl, put that thing away. You'll blow a hole in somebody's steak." He looked at Brian, who stood rubbing his shoulder, his gaze fixed blindly on the floor.

"Mr. Tally, do you understand your rights?"

He only nodded mutely, understanding nothing.

Steve said to Kleber, "You can put the cuffs away, too." Then he took Brian's arm and led him, numbly docile, to the side entrance. "Come on, let's get this over with."

CHAPTER 14

At seven o'clock Conan was driving south on 101 through a dense, fine rain that seemed to swallow the light of his headlights and make the reflections of billboards, shops, and streetlights seem wan and forlorn.

The last three hours he regarded as not only painful—Brian had suffered his incarceration with such hopeless stoicism—but a total waste of time, most of it spent in the outer room of the police station waiting for Marcus Fitch to arrive from Portland.

Still, he could look back with some satisfaction on the initial meeting of Fitch and Kleber.

Marcus Fitch arrived in his silver Continental Mark IV dressed like a model for *Gentlemen's Quarterly*, his bearing as commanding as a Benin prince. Kleber's back went stiff from the outset, but Fitch was ghetto-bred and immune to intimidation, and he had the psychological advantage of nearly a foot in height. Within ten minutes Kleber was calling him "sir," which Conan decided spoke well of both of them.

He gave the bookshop a perfunctory glance in passing; it

looked particularly bleak in the sodden darkness with only the night lights glimmering in its windows. His immediate destination was Tilda Capek's apartment. She was expecting him; they had talked briefly at the station an hour earlier. That was after she had spent herself futilely against the stone wall of Kleber's refusal to let her see Brian, a blanket exclusion that included Conan. She'd been close to weeping when she departed, although she didn't concede Kleber one tear.

Conan found her apartment—after an abortive detour up the wrong dead end—on a wooded hill overlooking Holliday Bay. The view was undoubtedly magnificent on a clear day, but tonight the Bay was only a distant, misty circle of lights around a deeper darkness.

She came to the door in a breath of Je Reviens and a full-length skirt of umber velvet with a satin blouse the color of her champagne hair. But she only had on one earring, a big gold loop to go with the chains at her neck.

"Oh, Conan, I'm so glad to see you." She had recovered her composure since her encounter with Kleber. At least outwardly. The other earring was in her hand; she hurriedly put it on as she stepped away from the door. "I'm on duty soon at the restaurant, but there's no hurry. Business will be slow tonight. Did you ever get to see Brian?"

"No, but Marc Fitch did, and that's more important."

"Fitch? Oh—the lawyer you told me about. Thank goodness for that. But let me fix you a drink." She went to the kitchen, an alcove separated from the living room by a low counter. "Bourbon, isn't it—on the rocks?"

"You have a bartender's memory. Yes, thank you."

He looked around the living room while he waited. No doubt the apartment was rented furnished, but there were a few personal touches: a stitchery wall-hanging in yellows and oranges, pots of ferns and fuschias, bright colored pillows on the couch.

On the top shelf of a modular bookcase he found two framed photographs, one of an elderly couple—her parents, he guessed from the close resemblance between the woman and Tilda—the other a studio portrait of a child of four or five, and again family resemblance suggested identity. This must be the daughter Beryl had mentioned.

When Tilda came out of the kitchen, he asked her.

"Is this your daughter?"

She stopped short and looked toward the photograph.

"Yes. Bettina. I . . . called her Tina."

"She favors you, to her good fortune. How old is she now?"

That polite inquiry evoked a shocked stare before she turned and put the glasses she was carrying on the coffee table.

"Tina isn't . . . she died. That was the last picture ever taken of her."

Conan felt his cheeks go hot, and it was anger as well as embarrassment. That was a coldly feline lie Beryl told him when she said Tilda had left her daughter with her parents. But perhaps Beryl believed it.

"I'm sorry," he said lamely.

"You couldn't know, and I'm past the grieving, really. That was five years ago. Won't you sit down? This is a good man's chair, so Brian tells me."

Conan went to the big armchair at the end of the coffee table while she handed him one of the glasses and sat down on the couch with the other. He offered her a cigarette, which she declined, but she rose to bring an ashtray within his reach while he lit one for himself.

"Tilda, do you know anything about the IRS case against Brian?"

At that, her gray eyes turned frigid as a winter sky.

"No, not the accounting part of it. I only know what it's done to Brian. And I know he never purposely cheated the government of a cent. My God, the money he gives to the government—federal taxes, state taxes, property taxes, licenses, permits, state accident insurance for the employees, and their Social Security. I have never understood why anyone should be forced to pay someone *else's* taxes, yet he pays half of every employee's Social Security. And what he pays directly to the government doesn't include what it costs him to pay it. The number of forms that must be made out simply to keep one employee on the payroll is incredible. A business can't survive without a bookkeeper, and think what *they* cost.'' Then she sighed and raised her glass, which Conan suspected contained nothing stronger than ginger ale. "I'm sorry. I didn't mean to begin a speech."

He laughed. "I could give you a speech or two on that myself. What about Beryl? I mean, as a bookkeeper?"

She smiled equivocally and paused to choose her words.

"As a bookkeeper she is excellent, and I'm sure she's been more than worth her salary to Brian, and actually, I don't think it's so high. She's never been demanding of him in that way.''

"He's entirely satisfied with her work, then?"

"Yes, and he should be. When it comes to her books, Beryl is a perfectionist. I've known her to spend a full day tracking down a ten-cent error, and she never lets a single dollar out of her office without a proper receipt or invoice. Even Brian can't take change from the registers for cigarettes. And that's as it should be, as it must be.''

That defense was almost passionate, and Conan couldn't avoid the comparison with Beryl's damning words of faint praise for Tilda. ''. . . a lovely young woman, of course, but . . .''

Yet Tilda didn't like Beryl personally any more than Beryl liked her; that was there to be read between the lines.

He asked, "Is Beryl as honest as she is conscientious?"

"Yes, I'm sure she is. Why?"

He frowned as he tapped the ash from his cigarette.

"Oh, I was just wondering why Eliot Nye, who was equally conscientious from all reports, seemed so sure he had a fifty-thousand-dollar case against Brian.''

"But *was* he so sure? You heard what he said Monday night.''

"Yes, and I'm convinced he wasn't so sure of his case then, but I was thinking of the first audit."

"As I understand, it wasn't so much a question of juggling books, but that the IRS thought Brian *should* have shown more profit."

"Yes, that's what both Brian and Beryl told me."

"If Nye found an error in his first audit, I think it must have been his own. Oh, if *only* he had lived!" Her mouth compressed brutally. "I think if I knew who killed Nye, I would kill them for what they've done to Brian. Now everything is even worse than before for him."

Conan stared down into his glass glumly.

"I know, Tilda. But let's get back to Beryl. What do you know about her past or her life outside the restaurant?"

"Only what's said in the kitchen; just gossip."

"What *is* said?"

"Oh, that she's twenty years older than she admits, and she wears a wig." Tilda laughed as she repeated that. "She does wear a wig, but since she says she's forty-eight, I don't believe the other. *Ten* years, perhaps, but no woman would begrudge another woman that. And I've heard that she came of a very wealthy family that lost its wealth somehow, but when she married, it was to a man of wealth."

"A distaff Midas touch," Conan commented dryly. "Have you ever seen her house?"

"Beryl's?" That he should ask seemed to surprise her. "No. She doesn't . . . socialize with the help."

"Who *does* she socialize with?"

"I don't know. She doesn't discuss her personal life with me."

"No, I'm sure she doesn't. Would you mind discussing part of *your* personal life with me?"

She eyed him curiously. "No, not if it's important to you—to Brian."

"It may be. I'd like to know about your relationship with Claude Jastrow, past and present."

"Ah. What did Beryl tell you about it?"

"That you were friends before you came to Holliday Beach."

"Friends? Yes, I can imagine how she said that." Then she dismissed Beryl with an indifferent shrug. "We lived together, Claude and I, for about a year. I moved to San Francisco after"—her eyes strayed to the child's portrait—"after my divorce, and got a job at Tarantino's waiting tables. Claude was meat chef there. Actually, we knew each other for a long time before we became close, and I'm afraid his feelings for me were always stronger than mine for him. When he accepted the job here, I was a little relieved. He asked me to come with him, but I refused. I thought he accepted that as the end of it; I mean, of what was between us."

"Were you surprised when you were offered a job here?"

"Yes, and I knew it was Claude who recommended me for it." She averted her eyes uncomfortably. "But it was a very attractive offer. I would be hostess and dining room manager, and the salary was more than I was making at Tarantino's even with tips. And . . . I had had too much of the city. Cities aren't good places for a woman alone."

Her narrative lapsed briefly, but Conan's movement in lifting his glass to his lips was enough to rouse her to continue.

"I called Claude before I made my decision. I wanted him to understand that it was the job that attracted me, not him, and I thought he understood. But he didn't. In that sense it was a mistake to come here, and I considered leaving on his account, but . . ." Her mouth curved in a wistful smile. "I'd met Brian by then, and I couldn't bring myself to leave him for Claude's sake, and I'm sorry about that; I didn't want to hurt him. I was always very fond of Claude."

Conan thought that if a woman he loved ever said that about him in that way, his love could only turn sere and die. Yet Jastrow still loved her; he was still passion's slave. Where did he turn the pain inflicted by that tantalizing fondness?

Tilda lifted her chin and looked directly at Conan.

"I never did or said anything to lead him on, but when he

decides he wants something, he'll stop at nothing, and nothing will stop him. You heard him today, telling me I'm making a terrible mistake. It's *my* life and I know what's right for me. He had *no* claim on me and no—''

She stopped to get herself under control, and Conan asked, ''What terrible mistake did he mean?''

''He . . . he meant my marrying Brian.''

At that, Conan's eyes narrowed. ''Well, I guess congratulations and good wishes are in order.''

Her responding smile was oddly tenuous.

''We decided to get married two months ago, but Brian wanted to wait until—well, as he put it, until the IRS is through with him, one way or another. He didn't want to tell anyone about it yet, and I wouldn't have told Claude except I thought it might make him realize, finally, that it was all over between us.''

Conan had to make a conscious effort to keep his voice from betraying the alarm those words triggered in his mind.

''When did you tell Claude about your marriage plans?''

''When?'' She frowned after an answer. ''These last few days have been so confused. So long. I think . . . yes, it was Sunday evening. Business was very slow, and between orders he came out into the dining room to talk to me.''

''Sunday? You mean this last Sunday?''

''Yes.''

The day before Eliot Nye's murder.

''Conan? Did I do the wrong thing to tell Claude?''

''What? Oh—no, Tilda. You did what you thought you must.''

''Yes. But in a way I wish I hadn't told him.'' She turned away, pent tears glistening under her lashes. ''Because now I'm not sure it's . . . really true.''

He leaned forward to put out his cigarette, watching her closely.

''What do you mean?''

''I'm not sure it will ever happen.''

''Because Brian might be convicted of Nye's murder?''

"If he's convicted I *know* he won't go through with it, but even if he isn't, I'm not sure he can . . . Oh, Conan, it's not just being accused of the murder. It's all the months that went before. The IRS—it's like a Chinese water torture, you know. Day after day living under the threat of losing everything important to him, being treated like a number that had somehow gotten out of place, and it was all his fault. Or even like a cheap criminal. I saw that. Those Collection Division men. That . . . smug, cynical, *knowing* look. Nothing he did or said made any difference or changed anything. And yet he is innocent. He is *innocent*."

Abruptly she rose to go to a window, standing tensely there with her back to him. He said nothing, waiting for her to go on if she chose to, or could.

And at length she did. "It changed him, Conan. It destroyed something in him. Faith, perhaps. Faith in honesty, in justice, and even in . . . in God. And this last month . . . well, I'm not sure the damage can be undone now. It's like a bad burn; it may heal on the surface, but the nerves never recover. He'll never be able to . . . feel as he once did; to feel anything. And to be accused of Nye's murder—that's the final straw. He is *still* innocent, yet it makes no difference. No difference to the law—no difference to anyone!"

Conan went to her and took her hand.

"That's not quite true, is it, Tilda?"

After a moment, she shook her head, but didn't look up at him; perhaps because the tears were slipping out of control down her cheeks.

"No, it's not quite true. It still makes a difference to me. And to you. I'm very grateful for that."

"Perhaps the damage isn't permanent, and I hope . . ."

What? That he could *force* the law to take cognizance of Brian's innocence? And even if he succeeded in that—

Tilda had already said it: Who will put Brian together again?

Tilda, perhaps. Not Conan Flagg. All he could put together was answers, and so far he hadn't been notably successful at that.

He withdrew his hand from hers and checked his watch.

"It's getting late. Can I drive you to the Surf House?"

She looked at her own watch and mustered a smile.

"Thank you, but I have my own car, and it will be well after midnight before I come home."

As she accompanied him to the door, he said, "I'll probably see you later this evening. Steve and I will be down at the restaurant, but it will be purely for the pleasure of your cuisine."

She opened the door for him, her smile on more solid ground now.

"I'll reserve a table for you, a window table."

When Conan reached his house, he found Steve in the kitchen staving off hunger with peanut butter and crackers.

"Marc Fitch left," he mumbled around a mouthful. "He's got a court appearance in Portland in the morning, but he'll be back tomorrow afternoon. He told me to give you this."

"This" was a note on creamy bond written with dashing flair in brown ink.

Conan— You can now consider yourself a hireling of Marcus Fitch and Associates. That makes you my agent and means Earl-baby can't lock you out when you want to see your/my/our client. I guess you know said client is in a hell of a hole, and there isn't much I can do for him now. By the way, I *believe* he's innocent, but you've got to give me something to work with, brother.

                                                                    Marcus F.

CHAPTER 15

The window table was waiting for Conan and Steve at the Surf House; the service was elegant, and the Sebastiani Pinot Noir—compliments of the house—was exquisite. Their steaks were a little overdone, however; apparently Chef Claude wasn't at his best tonight.

By the time they had consumed the baba au rhum, Conan had finished recounting his interviews with Van Roon and Tilda, and they had chewed over the implications in Jastrow's stubborn pursuit of his passion running aground on the rock of Tilda's acceptance of Brian's marriage proposal, and in Van Roon's tacit admissions that he was the informer and that he was in debt to the Nevada interests so interested in buying the restaurant.

With his Courvoisier, Conan was served the lab findings on the shavings from the cutting table.

"Zero," Steve pronounced sourly. "After the cleaning Hancock gave that table, chemical analysis was hopeless."

Conan consoled himself with a savored sip of cognac and

the assertion, "Well, I can still use those scuff marks hypothetically, even if I can't prove Nye made them."

"Sure. Hypothetically it's a free country."

"I won't go into that. But *if* Nye cracked his head on that table at that time—which would be just after midnight—then at least we can eliminate three suspects."

"Lorna and lover and who else?"

"Howie Bliss. No one saw him leave the bar until one-thirty when he left the premises altogether."

"So, who does that leave you with?"

"Van Roon, Jastrow, Hancock, and Beryl."

"In that order? Wait a minute, you just *added* a suspect. I thought you eliminated Beryl because of loyalty above and beyond."

Conan looked out at the spotlighted surf breaking almost beneath the window.

"I guess I just don't trust people who collect Victoriana; it suggests a convoluted mentality. But she probably doesn't belong on the list if Brian is the real victim in this thing. She's in love with him, you know, in her own peculiar way. What about Hancock? Another zero?"

"So far. We've got a state-wide alert out for him."

Conan didn't go into that, either; he could muster no more optimism about Hancock's apprehension than Steve did.

"What about Luther Dix?"

At that, Steve smiled serenely over his cognac.

"Well, he had to go back to Portland this afternoon. Didn't seem too happy, all in all, but he's got a pile of fresh audits on his desk. Something like that. I guess we'll manage without him somehow."

Conan drank to that. "As well as we did with him, at least. Before we go home, I'd like to stop by the police station to see Brian."

Steve eyed him through a doubtful squint. "Why?"

"Nothing ulterior. I just thought he might like a little company."

Conan brought some magazines and a deck of cards to

Brian, and they seemed more welcome than the company, but that was only because it was such an obvious effort to keep up the front of ironic stoicism.

It was perhaps fortunate that the detention facilities in the station weren't designed for long occupancy or full security; only six cells separated by open walls of bars. Solid walls would be unbearably confining. On the other hand, privacy was precluded, but at the present time the only other law-breaker confined here was Percy Dent, to whom this was a second home. His snores emanated from a corner cell with the lulling regularity of the surf.

The guard who let Conan into the cell took a tray with the remains of Brian's supper on it as he left.

Conan asked, "How's the food?"

Brian laughed a little too hard at that.

"Great. Damn, Claude couldn't do better. Filet de boeuf au Château."

"Locally known as roast beef à la steamtable?"

Brian kept up the stoic front while Conan outlined his progress on the case, which didn't ask much of the front; it didn't take long. And Brian didn't seem particularly interested. Rather, he couldn't seem to concentrate long enough to make sense of it. Perhaps that distraction explained his apparent absence of concern or even curiosity about Tilda. Even when Conan told him that she had tried to see him, but been turned away, he only nodded vaguely. Finally, Conan answered the question he didn't ask.

"She's holding up very well; beautifully, as always."

He turned away to look up at the barred window.

"Tell her . . . I don't know. Tell her I miss her."

Conan promised that, then called for the guard and left Brian to his first night in a jail cell. The first night was the worst, so they said, but he couldn't believe the second or tenth or hundredth would be any easier.

At the front desk, he found Steve conferring with Earl Kleber, but at first Conan didn't recognize the chief; he was out of uniform and in loose slacks and a khaki shirt. Steve explained Kleber's dishabille as Conan approached.

"A call came in from the state patrol a few minutes ago. They picked up Hancock just outside Westport. They're bringing him in now."

Kleber seemed too pleased at the news to remember to be rude to Conan.

"Evening, Mr. Flagg. Well, I guess we gotta get lucky once in a while. I figured Hancock'd be halfway to Mexico by now. By the way, Mr. Travers says Tally might have some information that could help make a case against Hancock for peddling along with possession."

Perhaps that explained his friendliness; he was hoping for Conan's good influence with Brian.

"I don't know how useful his testimony would be, Chief." He smiled and didn't add that Kleber had made his potential witness an accused killer. "But he'd probably give you a statement if you asked him." Nor did he add, *nicely*.

The dispatcher opportunely required Kleber's attention at that point, and a radio discussion with one of his officers on the fine points of breaking up a marital donnybrook occurring in a locked bathroom occupied him fully for ten minutes, and by then the state patrol car had arrived.

Hancock was wearing the same sweatshirt and patched Levis Conan had last seen him in, but the dark glasses were missing, and his glazed, dilated eyes suggested an explanation for the fact that he'd gotten no farther toward Mexico. But he was fully aware of his surroundings and situation, and treated his captors, Kleber, and anyone within range, to a foul but unimaginative commentary on social injustice.

Kleber smiled acidly through the tirade, then turned to Sergeant Billy Todd, who was standing by for the order.

"Book him. Possession of narcotics and—well, we'll hold off awhile on drug peddling."

Hancock predictably protested, but Conan suddenly ceased hearing him. But not seeing him. Rather, seeing what he was using now to restrain his straggling locks.

"Wait a minute!" At Conan's shout, Sergeant Todd turned, and Hancock stopped with his mouth open, mid-epithet. "That hat! Where did you get that hat?"

Hancock looked around as if someone might explain Conan as a phenomenon, but everyone else seemed equally puzzled. Except Steve Travers.

"Is that *Nye's* hat?"

"Yes. It must be." Conan was close enough to take it from Hancock's head, but Kleber reached it first, gave it a brief inspection, then squinted at Conan.

"You say this hat belonged to Eliot Nye?"

"Yes. He was wearing it when he came into the bar Monday night."

Kleber didn't question that; his cold query was directed to Hancock.

"Where'd you get this thing, Johnny?"

"I bought it. Any law against possessing a *hat*?"

"Where'd you buy it?" He made a show of studying a label inside the hat. "Some store with the initials E. N.?"

Hancock turned gray, the arrogance slipping out of his slouch.

"Okay! Okay, so I—I *found* it."

Conan demanded impatiently, "Where did you find it?"

"Well, I . . . ." He glanced at Kleber, who offered nothing; he was too busy reining his indignation at Conan's assumption of the interrogation. But Conan threw caution to the winds to risk his further displeasure by repeating the question and amplifying it.

"Where did you find it, and when?"

"What the hell is it to—okay! I'll tell you. In the kitchen. I found it in the kitchen."

"At the Surf House?"

"Well, where'd you *think*?"

"When, Johnny?" He waited tensely for the answer and found it too slow in coming. *"When?"*

"Damn it, I don't know!" Then seeing both Kleber and

Steve regarding him with the same demanding impatience, he reconsidered. "Well, it was Monday night."

"Monday?" Conan didn't let himself relax yet. "What time Monday night? Early, late, what?"

"Early. I mean, early for me. Hell, it was right after Claude come in to bitch at me about the floor. I told you about that, remember?"

Conan took a deep breath. He remembered.

"Exactly where in the kitchen did you find it?"

"Under the meat-cutting table. There's a shelf under it, so I never saw the thing till I was mopping the floor again. I flipped it out with the mop, and I figured, you know, like they say, finders keepers."

Conan only nodded and Kleber reassumed his prerogatives, repeating his order to Todd. "Book him." Then when Hancock had been taken away, complaining churlishly all the while, Kleber turned on Conan.

"All right, Flagg, what was *that* all about?"

Conan looked at him blankly; Kleber still had the hat in his hand.

"Don't you see? That hat clears Brian."

He didn't see. "Guess that's what you call a hat trick, right? Just reach in and pull out an innocent man."

"Yes! The time, damn it! That hat was under the cutting table near those scuff marks. That supports the theory that Nye was in the kitchen before twelve-fifteen and that he made those marks. The hat was probably knocked off his head and rolled under the table when he fell against the corner."

"Didn't Mr. Travers tell you about the lab tests on the wood from that table?"

"The tests didn't say there *couldn't* have been human blood on those shavings."

"But they sure as hell didn't say there *was* any."

Conan said tightly, every word spaced, "You're missing the point. That hat is evidence that Nye was in the kitchen *before* twelve-fifteen, when Jastrow came in to complain about the scuff marks—the marks Johnny says weren't there when he first mopped the floor. Add to that the testimony from Lorna and Kavtsky that Nye hadn't returned to his motel by twelve-thirty—''

''He didn't answer when they knocked, you mean.''

''—plus the fact that his bed hadn't been slept in. Chief, Nye never left the restaurant. He went into the kitchen where he slipped, or was pushed, and hit his head against the table, inflicting that three-cornered wound and knocking himself unconscious. The killer either thought he was dead or saw an opportunity to make sure of it, and the freezer was handy. It was also the nearest hiding place for a body, and the killer didn't have much time—not when Hancock might come in from the back door at any second, or someone else might come in from the bar.''

Kleber stood his ground, hands on his hips.

''So, who d'you think put Nye in this handy hiding place?''

''I don't know. It could've been Hancock, or Van Roon, or Jastrow, or even Beryl; they were all either in the kitchen just after midnight, or out of sight of the others long enough to go into the kitchen with Nye without anyone else seeing them. But the point is, Brian *wasn't* in the kitchen, nor was he alone at any time until after he returned from the hospital, and it was all over by then. Brian *couldn't* have killed Nye.''

''Uh-huh. Well, there might be something to that—*if* you had any way of proving this is Eliot Nye's hat.''

Conan stared first at him, then at the hat.

''But you said—the initials E N. Isn't that proof?''

Kleber thrust the hat out, upside down, for Conan to see. There was no label, no initials; nothing.

''I never said there was initials in here,'' Kleber noted. ''Just sort of suggested it to see what Johnny would say. It worked, too.''

Conan stood a pillar of tension, every muscle in his body crying to be unleashed. It worked. It worked on Johnny Hancock, and it worked on Conan Flagg.

Yet that tweedy, shapeless piece of haberdashery *was* Nye's; it asked too much of coincidence that Hancock would find another identical to it only a few feet from the icy tomb where Nye's body was found.

Conan didn't trust himself to speak, and Kleber's satisfaction gave way to frowning preoccupation.

"Look, I got nothing against Brian Tally personally, but we have to look at this thing from behind a badge. Right, Mr. Travers?" He paused to get a desultory nod from Steve. "We'll tag this hat as evidence, but it's not going to make any difference to anybody. Trouble is, the D.A. could go into court on this case with only one piece of evidence and get a conviction: the initials Nye left in the freezer. There's just no way around them. No way at all."

Conan felt Steve's hand on his arm.

"Come on, Conan. Your bar's open. I'll buy you a drink."

He turned for the door. He didn't need a drink; more than anything, he needed to be outside that door.

CHAPTER 16

It didn't surprise Mrs. Early when she arrived at Conan Flagg's house Thursday morning that no one opened the door for her. Her employer was often absent when she came, and she had a key.

It did, however, surprise her when she went into the library to find Mr. Flagg, outfitted in a bathrobe and sound asleep, sprawled in that metal and leather contraption he called a lounge chair. *Eames*, always, whatever *that* meant. The television was chattering away—some cartoon show— and the ashtray on the table beside him was overflowing. She sighed gustily. He'd burn the house down one of these days.

Then her eyes narrowed. Sure enough, he *did* have a cast on his hand. Well, that would take some looking into. She turned off the television, and he came awake abruptly, staring around him as if he had no idea where he was.

Mrs. Early clucked her tongue at him.

"I swear, Mr. Flagg, you'll put a permanent crick in your neck sleepin' on that chair thing."

"Mrs. Early? What *time* is it?"

"Well, it's just nine-thirty."

At that, he bounded out of the chair and succeeded in knocking the ashtray to the floor.

"Oh, God, the rug!"

She shook her pink head, misted in a fluff of white. The rug, indeed. As if those old Injun rugs were the most precious things in this house.

"I'll take care of it proper with the vacuum. You just go on, now. Oh—you want me to fix you some breakfast?"

"Just coffee."

She wheezed another sigh. "Just coffee. I swear, Mr. Flagg . . ." But he was out of range of her swearing.

He was doing some swearing of his own as he climbed the stairs. It had been another bad night, and only the late *late* show had proved soporific enough finally to put him to sleep. And now he was suffering most of the symptoms of a hangover without having had the pleasure of the binge.

Steve was gone, he noted grumpily, and he had specifically asked him to wake him before he left.

But after five minutes in the shower alternating the water temperature from hot to take out the "cricks," to ice cold to get his mind and eyes in focus, it came through to him that Steve undoubtedly would have wakened him if he'd known he was asleep behind the closed—and virtually soundproof—library door. Steve had probably looked at his empty bed and assumed he'd risen unusually early and gone out for a walk on the beach.

By the time he finished dressing, Conan was beginning to feel less hung over, although he put on a pair of sunglasses. This promised to be another bright, vernal day, and his eyes weren't up to the raw sunshine.

He found Mrs. Early in the entry hall in command of the roaring dragonhead of the vacuum cleaner.

"*I have a guest,*" he shouted. "*Why don't you—*"

She screwed up her face and tamed the dragon with a stamp of her foot on the switch.

"Yes, I know you have a guest. I saw the bed."

"It's Steve Travers. You remember him." He took out his wallet and extricated two twenties. "Why don't you go light on the cleaning today. I'm more in need of your culinary talents. Here—I'm afraid the larder's in need of replenishing." He handed her the money, adding, "The first thing Steve asked was if I had any of your lemon pie stashed away. And that salmon loaf with the egg sauce—he hasn't forgotten that, either."

She twinkled, cheeks puffed and pink.

"He remembered that thing? Well, I'll see what I can cook up for you. How long's he plannin' on stayin'?"

"Oh, three or four days. I'm not sure." He started down the hall and turned into the utility room. "Thanks, Mrs. Early. You're a doll."

"Oh, Mr. Flagg! But wait—don't you want some coffee?"

He shrugged on his jacket and went out the door into the garage as she reached the utility room door.

"I'm running late. Sorry."

"But I heard you was . . ." Whatever she heard was drowned as the Jaguar roared to life and the garage door rumbled up at his electronic command. He waved as he backed out into the street, then the door rumbled down again.

"Tarnation!" she snapped irritably. Now he'd gotten away from her, and she never had a chance to find out about the goings-on at the Surf House.

On his way to the police station, Conan noted that Miss Dobie was dutifully on duty at the bookshop. That was nearly as inevitable as the tides, but it never ceased to amaze him.

The second thing he noted in passing was that F. Conrad Van Roon was *not* open for business today.

At the station he found Steve in Kleber's office, but not in his chair; Kleber occupied it this morning. Steve was sitting in one of the chairs in front of the desk, laying claim to a corner of it with his feet. He was on the phone, but concluded the call and proffered a white pasteboard box as Conan entered.

"You had breakfast? Here. Local bakery. Damn, I'm going to take a couple of dozen of these home. *If* I ever go home."

Conan accepted a buttery cruller gratefully.

"Thanks. By the way, you'll be relieved to know that this is Mrs. Early's cleaning day. There *will* be a Care package in the refrigerator tonight."

While Steve nodded satisfaction at that news—his mouth was too full for verbal response—Conan tried a friendly greeting on Kleber.

"Good morning, Chief."

"Morning. There's coffee over there in the pot."

Had he been allergic to coffee, Conan would have turned down that unexpectedly magnanimous gesture. The percolator was mumbling on a file cabinet; he filled a Styrofoam cup, then sat down in another of the chairs in front of the desk.

"I was wondering if I could have a few minutes with Johnny Hancock, Chief."

Perhaps that was asking too much of his magnanimity. Kleber turned a cold eye on him that suggested he might take his coffee back.

"You're a little late for that."

"What do you mean?"

"He's gone. Herb Latimer came in an hour ago and bailed him out."

"Damn." Conan munched at his cruller, but its refinements were lost on him. "Where did Johnny get the money to put up a bail bond? Or to pay Herb Latimer?"

Steve answered that; it seemed too painful for Kleber.

"Somebody put up the bond—and I'm sure paid Mr. Latimer—*for* Johnny, but Latimer isn't saying who. He's acting for 'an undisclosed principal.' "

"Is Johnny under surveillance?"

Apparently, that was a sore subject. Kleber slapped a file folder down on his desk and burst out, "Damn it, I got ten people on my staff, including my secretary and the janitor, and since eight this morning, we've had *eleven* calls.''

Steve put in sympathetically, ''Been one of those days. I tried calling in some of my men, but it's one of those days all around. I've been on the phone for half an hour trying to untangle some of the knots in Salem.''

Conan nodded bleakly and asked, ''Did Johnny make any phone calls last night?''

Kleber replied curtly, ''He gets one call. That's the law and you know it.''

''I just wondered whether he took advantage of it or his angel learned about his arrest from another source.''

''He made his call right after he was booked last night. Sergeant Todd was there. Maybe he heard enough to tell us who Johnny called. I'll ask him when he reports in. Probably just another hophead or peddler.''

Conan finished his cruller without commenting on that.

''Maybe I should talk to Brian.'' Then when Kleber's eyes narrowed suspiciously, he explained, ''Johnny knows him, and they spent the night in close proximity. Maybe Johnny said something to Brian that would lead us to his benefactor.''

''Oh.'' Kleber shrugged indifferently and conceded with no real conviction, ''Well, it's worth a try.''

At this point, Conan thought, what *wasn't* worth a try?

In the windowless back corridors of the station, Conan found a guard by the jail-ward door perusing a copy of *True Detective*. He consented to put aside his magazine long enough to escort Conan into the ward and lock him into the cell with his client.

Brian was sitting on the wooden stool with a solitaire game spread on the bunk, but he swept the cards aside, apparently grateful for Conan's presence, yet still plagued with the tense distraction that seemed to make it an effort to bear. Conan hurried through the amenities and got to the point.

''Johnny Hancock was bailed out, Brian, and I'd like to find out who put up the bond for him.''

He laughed mirthlessly. "Well, I damn sure didn't; not this time. I couldn't make bail for myself now—if they'd let me make bail. Did Fitch tell you? They won't even set a figure on me. Well, what the hell. Uh, what did you . . ." He frowned, blinking rapidly. "Oh. Johnny."

"Yes. And his anonymous benefactor."

"I don't know, Conan. I don't even know who his friends are. He brought in a couple of scruffy kids to *help* him one night, and I found all three of them in the garbage alley passing around a roach. That's the last time any of his buddies set foot anywhere near the restaurant."

Conan offered a cigarette, then lit it for him when he couldn't seem to find his matches.

"Do you need cigarettes, Brian?"

"What? Oh . . . yes. I guess I'm out."

"Here, take these. I'll bring more next time I come. I thought maybe Johnny might've said something last night that would give me a hint, at least."

"A hint?" He took a long drag as if it had been weeks since he'd had a cigarette. "Oh, about who bailed him out? Well, he talked enough. Kleber put him in the next cell. Six cells to pick from, and he puts Johnny in the one next to mine. Well, maybe it wasn't Kleber. I don't know."

"What did Johnny talk about?"

"Mostly about what a kick it was, the two of us being practically cell mates. Funny. He thought that was really funny. He let me get too close once. I got hold of him through the bars, and I thought, why not? I'm already under arrest for murder one. Why not clean up the world a little before . . ." He seemed to run out of steam or lose track of his destination. "Anyway, it shut him up for a while."

"If he thought being virtual cell mates was such a kick, it must've been a bigger kick knowing he'd be out on the street by morning, while you were still sitting here."

"Oh, he loved that, but he didn't tell me who was putting up his bail. He kept saying you have to know who your friends are, things like that."

"Nothing to suggest who *his* friends are?"

"No. It was all just . . . just noise, Conan."

"But in all that noise, wasn't there something . . . well, something that caught your attention; that made you wonder?"

He considered that through a slow puff, and finally his eyes narrowed on a flash of remembrance.

"Well, there *was* something. Let's see, it was paying attention to . . . No—he said, *it paid to tend to other people's business*. That was it."

"To other people's—well, that's interesting."

"Is it? Why?"

"It suggests blackmail."

He shrugged. "Well, that's about Johnny's speed."

"Yes, but I wonder who he's blackmailing, and why."

"Conan, he was in a dirty business; anybody he knew was bound to be ripe for blackmail."

"But how many would have the money to make it worthwhile?" He looked around as the ward door opened and the guard approached. "Here comes the keeper of the keys."

Brian laughed. "Be nice to Charlie. He's my poker-playing buddy. But don't tell Kleber."

Charlie was obviously relieved when Conan promised not to divulge that secret to the chief.

He had little enough to divulge when he returned to the office, and the one pertinent quote on Hancock's interest in other people's business was of no interest to Kleber.

Conan didn't press the point. He turned to Steve and announced, "I'm going to Hancock's trailer and see what I can find out about other people's business. If he's there."

Steve unfolded himself and came to his feet.

"I'll go with you."

CHAPTER 17

Steve Travers came as close to exploding as he ever did, but the Jaguar's transmission took the brunt of it. Conan gritted his teeth while Steve lurched around the trailer court's drive and out to the highway.

"Damn, I should've tailed him myself," he muttered. "I hate these damn assignments where you have to tiptoe around in somebody else's damn jurisdiction."

Conan checked his watch while Steve jerked into third and in a few seconds topped the speed limit by twenty miles an hour. Eleven-thirty. It had taken only fifteen minutes—questioning the court manager and examining the trailer Hancock rented from him—to determine that the game had flown.

Hancock had apparently gone directly to his trailer from the police station, thrown a suitcase into his old VW van, and departed, assuring the manager he would return to pay the back rent he owed. That promise hadn't impressed the manager, but as he bitterly asked Steve, "What could I do? Call the cops? They just let him *out* of jail."

Steve didn't get a speeding ticket before he reached the

station, which was probably due to the fact that it was a bad day for Holliday Beach's finest, and when he stalked into Kleber's office with the news of Hancock's departure, it promised to get worse.

Kleber shouted out to the dispatcher, "Get hold of Billy Todd. Tell him those broken windows can wait. It's not raining. Tell him to get his tail down here and *fast.*"

Conan stayed in the outer room while Kleber and Steve marshaled the forces of local and state law. He had some calls to make, and the phone on the front counter was at least out of the way, if not private.

The first call went to Van Roon's office. Conan didn't expect an answer and wasn't disappointed. He tried his home number and got no answer there, either.

He tried Claude Jastrow's home phone next with the same result, then sought him at the Surf House Restaurant. The lunch hostess informed him that Jastrow wasn't expected until three o'clock. Ditto for Tilda.

Yes, Beryl Randall would normally be in her office now, but she had called in sick this morning and wasn't expected until tomorrow.

Conan frowned at that, remembering various references to her heart condition, and tried her home phone. No answer.

He was beginning to think he was under some sort of communications jinx, but the last number broke it. Tilda Capek was at her apartment.

He scarcely had time to identify himself before she asked, "Have you seen Brian today?"

"Yes, but only briefly. He's all right, Tilda."

"Oh, Conan, couldn't your lawyer friend do something? Why won't Kleber let me see him?"

"Marc will be here this afternoon. I'll ask him if there's anything he can do."

"I'd be very grateful."

"So would Brian—if anything can be done." He wasn't actually that sure of Brian's gratitude, but she needed the benefit of the doubt. "Tilda, Johnny Hancock got out on bail this morning and he's disappeared. Kleber wants him back to stand trial for drug possession, but I want him because I think he knows more about Nye's murder than he put in his statement. Do you know if he has any friends at the restaurant he might touch for bail money?"

"No. I didn't know Johnny well—I didn't care to—and I haven't any idea who his friends might be."

"Okay, Tilda. Thanks. Oh"—he tried to make it seem an afterthought of trivial consequence—"do you remember taking a call for Claude last night?"

"No, but someone else might have answered the phone when I was busy with customers. I'll ask the waitresses this evening. Or I suppose I could just ask Claude." There was a questioning inflection in that.

"No, let me talk to him." Then to forestall further questions, "I have to hang up now; Steve is paging me."

Steve not only hadn't paged him, but when Conan went into Kleber's office, he seemed no more interested in seeing him than did the chief. But that was only preoccupation. Conan arrived on the heels of Sergeant Billy Todd.

Kleber was preoccupied, too; he didn't object, nor even seem to notice, when Conan used his windowsill for a bleacher.

"Billy, you know Mr. Travers, don't you?" Kleber asked.

"Yes, sir. How are you, sir?" He sent Conan a glance, but limited his salutation to a brief smile.

Steve said, "I'm fine, Sergeant," with no conviction, then waved at the chair next to his. "Have a seat. We want to ask you about the phone call Johnny Hancock made last night. He skipped bail, you know."

Todd frowned soberly. "No, sir, I didn't know."

"Well, we're trying to find out who put up the bail for him. That might give us a lead on where he'd go. Herb Latimer handled the legal work, but he wouldn't say who he was working for, except it *wasn't* Johnny. He must've called somebody else, and they went to Latimer, so tell us anything you can about that call."

"Yes, sir. Well, he made the call at about nine o'clock. It was a local call, and he asked for a directory first. I couldn't see what part of the book he was looking in, except it was in the white pages."

"What do you mean—what letter of the alphabet?"

"No, sir. What town. There are five small communities listed in the one book; they're strung out along the Coast Highway for thirty miles."

Steve nodded. "Okay, but you're sure he got the number out of the white pages?"

"Yes, sir, but then a lot of businesses have listings in the white pages, too. He didn't write the number down. I was hoping he would."

Kleber asked impatiently, "What'd he say when he *got* the number?"

"Well, I can't repeat it verbatim, Chief, but it was short; I think I can give you the gist of it. He told whoever he was calling that he was in jail here, and the charge was drug possession. Then he went on to say that jails make him— well, nervous. 'Hyped out,' I think is what he said. The idea was that if he was left in jail too long, he might get so hyped, he'd start talking to the, uh, police."

Steve smiled bitterly at that hesitation; it was highly unlikely that Hancock had actually used the word "police."

"Did that sound like a threat?"

"Yes, sir. No doubt about that. I think the guy on the other end gave him some back talk then. He got mad and told them he meant what he said, and they'd better get him out fast. And then—I think this is close to the exact words—he said, 'I was *there* the other night. You didn't see me, but I saw you. Why do you think I called *you*?' "

Conan risked reminding Kleber of his presence by asking, "Billy, are you sure he said, 'the other night'? He wasn't more specific?"

"Yes, I'm sure. For one thing, the pharmacy was robbed Tuesday night, and I thought it was the kind of thing Hancock might be in on, so I was hoping for something specific."

Steve lifted an approving eyebrow.

"The local pharmacy? What was taken?"

"Drugs. Morphine, amphetamines, and barbiturates. No cash; Morey banks every evening when he closes."

"Okay, what else did Hancock say?"

"Well, he started smiling then. I guess the other guy got the message. He ended up saying the sooner he was out of jail the better. That was all; he hung up. And he never once used a name. I was hoping for that, too."

Steve nodded. "A good report, Sergeant. Thanks." He glanced inquiringly at Kleber and Conan, then, "That's all for now. Let us know if you think of anything else."

"Yes, sir. I will."

He rose and turned to his chief, who absently waved him away.

"Thanks, Billy. You can get back to those windows now."

Todd exited, and the door closed on a dissatisfied silence, which Kleber finally broke.

"Well, that didn't tell us a hell of a lot."

Steve cast him a veiled glance, then pulled himself to his feet.

"I'm going to find myself some lunch before something else happens. Conan, you got anything better to do?"

"Unfortunately, no."

"Come on, then. Chief? Care to join us?"

That was adroitly managed, Conan thought; Kleber wasn't likely to accept an invitation that included Conan Flagg.

"Uh, no, thanks. I've got some things to tend to here."

Conan drove this time, although his mental state made him as wearing on the transmission as Steve had been. He turned south at the highway, mumbling about a restaurant specializing in clam chowder down on Holliday Bay, then without transition announced, "Johnny's a dead man, Steve, if we don't find him soon. You know that."

"I do?"

"I doubt he has the restraint to limit his extortion to the

money for his bail, and you know the odds on blackmailing a killer and living to brag about it.''

"Uh-huh, so that's who he called—Eliot Nye's killer.''

Conan replied caustically, "No, he called one of his confederates in that pharmacy robbery, any one of whom would only have to snap his fingers to come up with the ready cash to put up the bond *and* a retainer for Herb Latimer.''

"Mm. Well, that might be a little hard for Johnny's type of confederate.''

"Herb wouldn't let Johnny's type in his waiting room, but he accepted Johnny's benefactor as a client.''

"Okay, you have a point—unless Johnny was tied into some sort of organization, and I'm not talking about the local lodges.''

Conan gunned the Jaguar past a billboard of a camper.

"Around here, you *should* be talking about the local lodges, but if Johnny was an organization man, he wouldn't have to remind his benefactor that he had something on him; benefactor would be well aware of it. Anyway, he wasn't talking to a confederate—of any type.''

"How do you figure that? And why are we stopping here?''

They weren't stopping, only slowing to a crawl as they passed the Van Roon real estate office.

"I just wanted to see if it was still closed,'' Conan explained. He checked the rearview mirrors and re-entered the southbound lane. "And it is. Conny's not at home, either; at least no one answered the phone. Johnny told us—or rather, Billy—that he wasn't talking to a confederate. 'I was there the other night. *You didn't see me,* but I saw you.' A confederate would know he was there.''

Steve nodded numbly. "Right. Damn fool. He *will* get himself dead, Conan, but I don't know what we can do about it. We've got every cop in the state looking for him.''

"It may be too late already.''

He gave the bookshop the usual survey, but it didn't register. He was looking ahead to the junction of Laurel Road and remembering an address he'd just seen in a phone book.

He made a right turn, swearing when his encased left hand slipped on the steering wheel while his right was occupied with the gear shift, but he succeeded in avoiding a collision with a jack pine.

Steve, suddenly upright, braced a hand against the dashboard and demanded, "What's this? A shortcut?"

"A detour. Claude Jastrow lives up here somewhere. I noticed the address when I was looking up his phone number a while ago. It can't be more than four or five blocks from Beryl's house, and it struck me as odd that she didn't say anything about it Tuesday; we had to pass his house to get to hers." He geared down and searched for numbers on the houses. "Of course, with her maybe it isn't so odd. She doesn't socialize with the help."

"I'll tell you what's odd—no, never mind. I *know* you have a good reason for checking out the help's housing facilities. Or for calling them." Then he frowned. "*And* Van Roon. Okay. Did Jastrow answer when you called, and when was that?"

"Just a few minutes ago at the station, and no, Jastrow didn't answer, nor was he at the Surf House. Let's see . . . it should be the next one on the left."

It was a well-designed house making good use of the pine surrounding it and unusual for this neighborhood in its newness; the cedar shingles retained some of their raw, unweathered yellow. The door was open on an empty garage, and the shades were down on all the windows.

Steve said, "Nobody home. Might as well put out a sign."

Conan shifted into first and continued down the road.

"Well, he could be out buying groceries, or picking rocks on the beach, or having a beer at the Last Resort, or—you name it."

"Sure. Or keeping an appointment with Johnny Hancock. But I don't have any legally reasonable reason to put out an APB on Jastrow—*now* where are we going? I thought you said this chowder place is down on the Bay."

"It is." He had reached Front Street, but turned north instead of south. "Beryl's house is a few blocks up here."

"Well, I damn sure don't have a good reason to put out an APB on *her*."

Conan laughed, noting that Beryl's Mercedes was in the carport in front of her deceptively modest little bungalow.

"Steve, the lady called in sick this morning, and since she has some sort of heart condition, I thought someone should check on her. I'll just knock on her door and see if she's all right."

Steve only hunched down in the seat with an afflicted sigh, arms folded.

When Conan reached Beryl's door, he knocked a little hesitantly, thinking that if *he* wasn't feeling well, he wouldn't welcome even a well-meaning inquiry.

There was no response. He tried again, then stood undecided, frowning at the door, then at her car, and finally returned to his car, thinking that on the other hand, if he was lying alone in the grip of a heart attack, he'd welcome any inquiry.

"Hello there, Mr. Flagg."

He looked up and saw an elderly man tending his rock garden at the house across the street. A bookshop customer. After a moment the name came to mind, and he walked over to meet him.

"How are you, Mr. Barnstad?"

"Fine, real fine. Pretty day, isn't it? You looking for Mrs. Randall?"

"Yes. They told me at the restaurant she was ill, and I thought I should look in on her."

Barnstad nodded. "Guess she has a little trouble with the old ticker, but I don't think you need to worry. I saw her early this morning when she came out for her paper. Said she was feeling a little tired and thought she better rest up before she ran into a real problem. Takes good care of herself. But then a person has to when they're all alone." He concluded with a sigh that reminded Conan that Barnstad had become a widower only a year ago.

"Yes, I guess so. Well, she's probably all right now if she was up and about this morning."

"She might be taking a nap now. Tell you what, I'll check on her in an hour or so."

"Thanks, Mr. Barnstad." He retreated to the car a little hastily, and a little guiltily, knowing Barnstad would enjoy exchanging small talk with him. With anyone.

Steve waited until after Conan turned the car in Beryl's driveway, then commented, "Well, we're headed south. Does that mean lunch is the next stop, or do you have more good deeds lined up?"

"That's my next good deed, Steve. Lunch."

CHAPTER 18

While Steve went through two bowls of clam chowder and one of blackberry cobbler, Conan managed half a bowl of each and repeatedly reminded himself to enjoy the view of Holliday Bay, a spangle of reflected blue sky and white cloud with miniature peninsulas of docks jutting from its banks. Most of the fishing boats were out to sea on this fine day, but he did get to watch one late-departing vessel thread the needle of the narrow channel beneath the parabola of the Coast Highway bridge.

Finally, a little after two o'clock, Steve, happily replete, insisted on paying the check, then used a pay phone to call the police station. The results of that put a damper on his good spirits. Hancock was still among the missing.

Again Conan drove, and when he backed out of the parking space, made a U-turn, and headed south, Steve objected, "What happened to your genuine Indian pathfinder instincts? You're going the wrong way."

"Just another detour, Steve, and I know you miss Earl, so I'll get you back to the station as soon as possible."

Beyond the bridge, 101 shook off the last of the ticky-tack monuments of highway culture and cut through a thick stand of spruce and fir, but Conan didn't push the speedometer above forty; it would be a short drive.

"At least you could tell me where I'm going," Steve said peevishly.

"There." He pointed to a road sign. "Shag Point state wayside."

"Oh. Of course. Why didn't you say so before? We could've brought our chowder down here and had a picnic." Then he frowned as Conan geared down for a right turn. "Is this the wayside where Beryl's car was found?"

"The very one, and we have it all to ourselves except for the gulls." He idled halfway around the loop, past the picnic tables and restroom building to the parking area on the west side. A flock of gulls rose in screaming complaint from their resting place on the asphalt. "We should've brought some bread for them."

Steve folded then unfolded his length to get out of the car.

"I'll feed those damned birds when they learn some manners. Last time I offered a bunch of them a free meal, I didn't like what I got in return."

Conan smiled at that. "You have to stand to windward." He started across the ragged lawn toward the bare rocks at the point, and Steve fell into step with him.

"Conan, what are you looking for? You know something about Beryl Randall I should?"

"No, and I'm not assuming she's responsible for the fact that her car was found here the morning after the murder. I'm not even assuming that it had anything to do with the murder. I'm just—"

"—curious. Okay. Well, it's as good a place as any to be curious. Damn—look at that wave!"

A breaker hit the rocks at the point with a resounding thump and threw up a wall of white that disintegrated into a splatter of rain blackening the basalt. The wind carried a fine spray, and Conan smiled as he felt its chill against his cheeks.

The sea liked to remind its audience that its reach exceeded their grasp of its power.

This rock-buttressed point of land lunged out past the breakers to engage its adversary where the heavy swells began to feel the drag of the sloping shelf fifty feet beneath the surface, and the encounters of sea and rock were almost always spectacular. At the forefront of the rock bastion, the patient, ravening water had cut a transverse channel, and the meeting of wave and counterwave within the confines of that chasm was terrifyingly beautiful.

Yet Conan stopped before he drew close enough to see the channel. He stopped because a chain link fence barred his way, and this was why he seldom came to Shag Point any more.

A few years ago, before the fence, two people had been swept to their deaths in the chasm, imparting the harsh lesson of the terror in the beauty. The state in response to the terror put up the fence, enclosing the seaward periphery of the park, putting the terror out of reach, but with it the beauty.

Conan could, and had, climbed over the fence in defiance of it, but its very existence rankled him. He didn't object to being protected from dangers which could not be anticipated and the risks assessed before they were encountered, but that wasn't the case here, and he considered this fence as unreasonable as a barricade closing off an interstate highway. People died on highways, too.

He turned north as the ocean exploded a new wall of white into ephemeral existence. Steve walked beside him silently, while Conan studied the occasional scraps of litter caught at the bottom of the fence. He followed it for a while, then left it and crossed a short distance to another chain link fence, but this one he didn't take exception to, and it had been here for twenty years.

It enclosed a square ten feet on a side, and he didn't object to it because it offered protection from a danger which could not be anticipated. The rock was rough and irregular, like a field of huge, fused boulders, and within this enclosure, the fissures served to camouflage a gaping hole. It wasn't bottomless; somewhere within the black fastness of rock below, it found an outlet to the sea.

Conan leaned against the railing, listening to the faint thumpings and gurglings from its depths, and finally the juxtaposition of wave and current came right and from the hole spewed a geyser of sea water broken in its forced passage through the rock into a cold steam of spray.

Steve shouted and backed away, like Conan, unexpectedly drenched. These pseudo geysers were called spouting horns, and there were hundreds along the coast, but this was one of the largest. Conan took out a handkerchief to wipe his face and sunglasses, laughing with Steve in startled exuberance more than amusement as they started back toward the car.

"You know, I've been here maybe ten times," Steve said, "and stood over that thing with Jamie waiting for something to happen, and this is the first time it ever did."

"Next time bring Jamie during the winter at high tide."

"I'll call ahead for a schedule."

When they reached the car, Conan ignored it and walked on across the drive toward the picnic area.

Steve asked hopelessly, "Where are you going *now*?"

"Oh, I just want to poke around a little."

He poked around in every garbage can in the park, finding most of them empty; the park had few visitors this time of year. He also poked into the trash containers in the restrooms, both of them, then went to the stone-walled picnic shelter, looked in the four garbage cans there and into the cooking fireplaces at each end. The first hadn't had a fire in it since it was last cleaned, but the second was a different story. He turned back the grate, then picked up a charred stick that someone else had used to stir a fire.

The ashes were piled a foot deep in gossamer leaves.

"Steve, look at this. Paper."

He was looking and agreed with that determination, but still asked dubiously, "So?"

Conan prodded cautiously, but was rewarded with nothing but flurries of ash snow.

"So someone burned a lot of paper in here, and it wasn't very long ago or this would be a sodden mulch."

"Papers. You're thinking of the Surf House records?"

"Well, yes. I guess so."

"Don't give me that I *guess*. Okay, you've got a pile of paper ashes, but bookkeeping records aren't kept in loose bunches; they're kept in ledger books, things with hardboard covers and metal binders and rings. Things that won't burn."

Conan nodded, probing still deeper.

"I know, and there's nothing of that description here."

"And in any of the trash cans you've been poking in?"

He sent up a choking cloud of ashes with a final sweeping probe, then rose and wiped his hands with his handkerchief.

"No, Steve, nothing here nor in the trash cans, but I can't poke around in the most obvious disposal receptacle."

"What's that?"

"The spouting horn."

"Yes, I guess you do have a problem there." He frowned out at the receptacle in question, and it obligingly spouted. "Conan, what makes you think these ashes came from burning the records? I mean, how often do the park service people clean these places in the winter? Once a week?"

"More like once a month, probably. Come on, it's nearly three. I have to get back to the station."

"*You* have to—" He spluttered a moment, then caught up with him. "Don't tell me *you're* getting lonesome for Earl."

"No. For Marc Fitch. Look, I know those ashes don't mean a damn thing. Maybe some hitchhiker was just getting out of the rain and warming up with a newspaper. I guess I just don't like the coincidence of Beryl's car ending up here, but I'm well aware that coincidences do occur." He took his keys from his pants pocket. "Here—you drive."

"Sure. Who says cops are never around when you need them? We even play chauffeur for absent-minded—"

"This just may be your last chance to drive a twelve-thousand-dollar car, friend, so shut up and enjoy it."

He laughed and started the motor with a gratuitous roar, but by the time he turned onto the highway, he was frowning.

"Okay, Conan, so how do *you* explain Beryl's car ending up at Shag Point?"

"I don't. Maybe it *was* stolen; some kids out for a little good, clean fun."

"Then the car conked out on them, so they pushed it off the highway into the park where it probably wouldn't be found before they got home?"

"No, it didn't conk out on them. I talked to Rafe Driskoll—he's the mechanic who worked on the car—and he said it ran beautifully *once it started*. It just didn't always choose to start. But if it started for the thief or thieves—and obviously it did—then it was stopped at the wayside purposely. It stayed here because it didn't choose to restart. Of course, there are reasons for car thieves to stop there. It's a local lovers' lane, for one thing, and off the highway, which makes it attractive to someone trying to avoid the highway patrol, and it has nice clean restrooms sheltered from the wind and rain."

Steve was approaching the Holliday Bay bridge, but he didn't seem to notice the speed limit signs. "Okay, but if that car wasn't just stolen by some fun-loving kids, you think it was used to transport pilfered goods? Like the Surf House records?"

Conan shrugged unhappily. "Maybe."

"Sure. Maybe. And if those pilfered goods were disposed of at the wayside, the pilferer had a problem afterward; the car wouldn't start. So, what'd he do? Walk home?"

"Why not?—if the pilferer lives in Holliday Beach. Once he got past the bridge, he could stick to back streets to avoid being seen, or even the beach, depending on the time. It was a rough sea, but low tide was about one-thirty that night. It'd be a wet, miserable walk, but not at all impossible."

"It was Beryl's car, so here's the jackpot question: Does that mean she's the pilferer—and the killer?"

"A car's driver isn't always synonymous with its owner, and I still can't connect Beryl with a motive against Brian. Or against Nye, for that matter, unless her books didn't balance as well as she says they did, and Nye found the imbalance. But even then, I can't believe she'd set Brian up as a scapegoat. The records were disposed of, but not the body. That should have been her—or any murderer's—*first* concern, unless leaving it where it was served a purpose. Anyway, that long walk probably would be impossible for her, along with dragging an inert man into the freezer, plus the general excitement that goes along with murdering someone. Remember, she has a heart condition."

Steve slipped under the town's traffic light on yellow, breezily barreling along at fifty in a thirty-mile zone.

"You figure somebody else used her car for disposal purposes? Why? All your suspects have cars of their own."

"That's one I can't answer or even hypothesize about."

"Damn, you mean I caught you with your hypotheses down?"

Conan managed a laugh, but for the rest of the ride sat in sober silence trying to remedy his embarrassment. He didn't succeed.

Marcus Fitch's silver Continental was slumming among the city employees' cars at one side of the police station, and when Conan and Steve went in, Marc was at the front desk signing in to see his client.

"Conan, you're supposed to walk in with the real killer under cuff and key. Is this all you could come up with?"

Steve snorted. "You got it backward. He's all *I* could come up with. How are you, Marc?"

"Beautiful, of course. Should I ask about you?"

"Probably not." He frowned toward the glass-paneled door of Kleber's office; the chief was on the phone, but waving for Steve to come in. "I'll see what he's got on Hancock."

Marc raised an arched brow. "Hancock? Isn't he—"

"The night man," Conan replied absently; he was listening for what Kleber said when Steve opened the door.

"Hold on a second, Dave." That was into the phone, then to Steve, "We got a line on Hancock. Found his car."

Conan started for the door, staving off Marc's questions with a vague, "I'll talk to you later."

Steve had left the door open, a purposeful oversight Conan appreciated. Kleber was still on the phone, and by the time he concluded his call, Conan was on his window bleacher seat, and Kleber was too smugly preoccupied to object.

"That was Sheriff Dave Gould up in Tillamook." Then as if Steve was a visitor from Florida, "It's fifty miles north up the coast. One of Dave's men found Hancock's van."

Steve sat down while he lit a cigarette, his eyes reduced to slits in a bed of crow's feet.

"Where?"

"In the parking lot at the bus depot in Tillamook. Well, naturally, Dave asked around in the depot, and somebody checked a suitcase in the name of J. Hancock for Portland at about a quarter to twelve; the Portland bus leaves at twelve-ten. The baggage man remembered the suitcase—it was so beat up, he was afraid it'd fall apart before it got to Portland—and he remembered who checked it, but it *wasn't* Hancock."

Steve frowned at having to ask. "Who was it?"

"Well, nobody could give Dave a name, but it was an old lady; white hair, medium height, a little on the heavy side. *And* the guy at the ticket window remembers an old lady, same description, buying two one-way tickets to two different places, and one of them was to Portland."

"What about the other one?"

"He couldn't remember. Maybe Astoria, but maybe Westport. Anyway, I figure Hancock conned the old lady into buying his ticket and checking his suitcase for him so he wouldn't have to show his face. Probably just picked some woman who happened to be sitting in the depot.''

Conan observed mildly, ''Odd that he'd be so careful about showing his face when he checked the suitcase in his own name and left his car in the parking lot.''

Kleber shot him a cold look, then shrugged.

''Listen, when you've seen as many dopeheads as I have, you don't call anything they do odd. Right, Mr. Travers?''

''Mm? Uh—yes. Right. When is the twelve-ten due in Portland?''

''Three-fifteen.'' He looked at his watch. ''About ten minutes ago. Dave called Captain Sade at the state Narcotics Bureau, and he sent a couple of men to meet the bus. Even if Hancock doesn't show up on this bus, he's got to pick up his suitcase sooner or later, and somebody'll be waiting.''

''Well, next time you talk to Sheriff Gould, tell him thanks for me. He's fast on the uptake.''

If Conan detected a strained note in that, Kleber was oblivious to it.

''Dave's been sheriff in Tillamook for over twenty years. You learn a thing or two after that long.''

Steve nodded unenthusiastically, then, ''Where are you going?'' That was to Conan, who had left his windowsill and crossed to the door.

''To jail,'' he replied, ''to confer with my client and associate.''

Steve didn't respond to that, but in the brief meeting of their eyes was a silent understanding. The motions must be gone through, but neither of them shared Kleber's confidence that Hancock would ever pick up his suitcase in Portland.

CHAPTER 19

Marcus Fitch lounged elegantly at one end of the bunk, taking electronic notes with the cassette recorder held in one diamonded hand, while Conan occupied the wooden stool and Brian paced his cage, settling occasionally on the other end of the bunk only to rise again within seconds.

Conan did most of the talking, bringing them up to date on developments and adding his speculations. Fitch was intrigued with Van Roon and questioned Conan closely, but he was only grasping at the straw of an alternative that might cast reasonable doubt. Brian didn't seem capable of recognizing a straw when it was presented to him; he was more abstracted than before, constantly asking to have things repeated, but still losing track of the conversation.

At length, a little hesitantly, Conan broached the subject of Tilda. He addressed his question to Marc.

"Can you get enough leverage on Kleber to make him loosen up on visitors for Brian? Tilda's been asking—"

"*No.*" Brian turned from the window, his face at first

ashen, then mottled with a sick flush. "I—I don't want to see her."

Conan shrugged acceptance, and Brian's flush deepened. He looked down at his hands, then sought something to do with them, and finally put them away in his pockets.

"I guess what I really mean is . . . I don't want her to . . . to see *me*. Not here."

Conan considered that an error, but he didn't argue it. To do so would be both unfeeling and futile.

"I'll tell her Kleber is holding the line on visitors."

Brian said through an oppressive sigh, "Thanks."

After Marc and Conan were released from Brian's cell and the ward door closed behind them, Marc shook his head.

"Conan, your boy is hanging on by his fingernails."

"I know. Where are you staying, Marc?"

"I'm not. I'm a commuter. But I'll be happy to tarry long enough for dinner at the Surf House—you're laying out for it, of course—and you can give me a tour of the scene of the crime."

Conan sent him a slanted smile.

"Whatever's fair. The bar is the logical place to start the tour. I'll meet you there in"—he checked his watch—"in an hour."

"Bring the chief." He cocked a thumb toward Kleber's office, but he was referring to Steve Travers, not Kleber. "Unless he doesn't want to be seen with the opposition."

Conan waved him on. "Steve's not that choosy about his company. He's occupying *my* guest room."

Conan went into the office without knocking; Kleber was absent, and Steve had taken over his chair and phone. A little unavoidable eavesdropping revealed that he was again unraveling knots in the Salem office. There was a second phone on the desk. Conan helped himself to it.

Claude Jastrow's home number yielded a negative result, so he tried Van Roon's office. Also negative. At Van Roon's home, he got an answer, but it wasn't Conny. Mavis Van

Roon volunteered that her husband was in Portland on business and offered to take a message.

Conan identified himself and declined to leave a message, but asked, "When did he leave, Mrs. Van Roon? I had an appointment with him this morning."

"You did?" She sighed. "Guess Conny forgot. I mean, this trip came up so suddenly, you know."

He didn't know, but he hoped to find out.

"Well, it was the trip I wanted to talk to him about. He told you about the, uh, Portland property, didn't he?"

"Portland? I didn't know he had any listings . . . Well, no, he doesn't usually tell me about his business deals. Was that you who called him last night?"

Jackpot. It came so easily, he wasn't quite ready for it.

"Oh . . . you mean about nine?"

"I thought it was later; maybe ten. Probably didn't look at the clock right. Was something . . . wrong, Mr. Flagg? Conny seemed so—well, sort of upset."

He said lightly, "I'm sure it's nothing for you to worry about, Mrs. Van Roon. When did he leave this morning?"

"About eight o'clock. You want me to have him call you when he gets home tonight?"

"No, I'll talk to him tomorrow. Thanks."

He hung up and offered Steve, who was still engaged with his lieutenant, a noncommittal smile in response to his questioning frown, then punched another number.

Beryl Randall answered after only two rings.

"Oh, Mr. Flagg, I'm so glad you called. Mr. Barnstad told me you came by today, and I *did* want to thank you. It was so thoughtful of you."

"Well, I just wondered—"

"There was really no cause for concern, but the last few days *have* been rather trying, and when one has harbored a heart condition for any length of time, one learns that the subtle first symptoms *can't* be ignored."

"Yes, I'm sure one does."

"Usually a day or two of rest will avert any serious problems; that's why I decided to take the day off today. What time did you come by? Mr. Barnstad said about one.''

"I think it was about—''

"Well, I was sound asleep then. In fact, I spent most of the day sleeping, and I *do* feel so much better. Actually, I'm rather a light sleeper, so I always use earplugs when I nap. Sometimes I even have to use them at night. I do so love the sound of the rain and the surf, but there *are* times when they're just too much. Have you seen Brian today?''

Conan was caught with his attention wandering.

"What? Oh, yes. I just left him.''

"Well, I hope you told him that everything is under control at the restaurant.''

"He isn't worried about that, Mrs. Randall.'' That was the least of his worries. Then he added as if it had almost slipped his mind, "By the way, Johnny Hancock was bailed out this morning and immediately departed for parts unknown, and Kleber is out for blood. Especially for the blood of the person who put up his bail.''

The only hint of hesitation was the time necessary for a ladylike snort of disgust.

"Well, I hope Chief Kleber doesn't think anyone at the restaurant would be that foolish. Of course, Brian *has* put up bail for various employees in the past, but only for minor offenses like drunkenness. Never for anything as serious as drug possession. And in his absence that decision would be left to me, and I've *never* considered it an employer's responsibility to put up good money to get employees out of trouble of their *own* making. You just tell the chief that. Or *I'll* be happy to tell him. If he thinks—''

"I'll tell him, Mrs. Randall, and I'm glad to hear you're feeling better.''

"Oh, it was nothing serious, you know, but one must—''

"I'm relieved to hear that. Good-bye.'' He hung up before she got a fresh start and leaned back for a respite and a cigarette.

"What are you so relieved about?" Steve asked as he hung up his phone.

"Beryl didn't have a heart attack. Anything from Portland?"

"Hancock's suitcase is still at the bus depot. Damn, I wish we could get a line on that old lady."

"Too bad they don't get names for bus tickets like they do for plane tickets, but I'll make you a side bet: it wasn't Hancock who conned her into buying the ticket and checking the suitcase. Someone else was shy about showing his face."

"No bets. Who're you calling now? Kleber doesn't consider that a public phone, you know."

"My taxes help pay his phone bill." He punched the number, then took a quick puff on his cigarette; that's all he had time for.

"Tally's Surf House Restaurant, may I help you?"

"Tilda, this is Conan." Then to forestall any questions about Brian or visiting privileges, he went on quickly, "I only have a few minutes now, but I'm coming down to the restaurant later. I wondered if Claude is there."

"Yes, he's here *now*," she replied irritably, "but he only arrived a few minutes ago—an hour and a half late."

"Did he say why he was so late?"

"No, he's in one of his moods. All I got was Shakespeare."

"I hope it was appropriate. Did you get a chance to ask around about any phone calls he had last night?"

"Oh, yes, I did." She paused uncertainly. "Conan, can you tell me why that's so important?"

"Loose ends, Tilda; I'm just trying to tie up a few."

"Oh. Well, one of the waitresses said there *was* a call for Claude, but she didn't remember what time it was, except that it was after eight."

"All right, Tilda, thanks. I'll see you later."

"Wait! Conan, just one question."

He braced himself. "Sure. What is it?"

"Did you ask Mr. Fitch if he could do anything so I can see Brian?"

"Uh . . . yes, I talked to Marc. I'm sorry, but there's just no way to force Kleber to loosen up on that."

He thought he managed that fairly well. She seemed to consider it for a while, then said flatly, "Brian doesn't want to see me."

And what could he do with that? Conan frowned and decided not much.

"It's just that . . . well, he doesn't want you to see him in . . . I don't know."

"I do, Conan." Her voice was a bleak weight in his ear. "I understand. Just tell him . . . I'll be waiting for him."

"All right, Tilda."

He hung up and took a long drag on his cigarette, vaguely annoyed at finding himself an intermediary between lovers, especially when one had become such a strangely reluctant lover.

Steve asked, "Well, what've you got?"

"A problem for Dear Abby, and a couple of unexplained phone calls and unexplained absences." And a witness vanished, courting death in a feckless pursuit of greed.

CHAPTER 20

On the morning of Friday the thirteenth, Conan was awake early enough to have breakfast with Steve. At least, to sit at the same table with him while he downed three eggs and a dozen slices of bacon. Conan concentrated a great deal on the view, a flat, grayed vista with no sunshine to bring to life the jade lights under the breakers. Still, he found it preferable to lacerated eggs drenched in catsup.

Steve politely suggested that there was nothing Conan could do at the police station; perhaps he'd like to catch up on things at the bookshop this morning.

Conan informed him that there was never anything to catch up on there that Miss Dobie couldn't take care of. She was entirely self-sufficient and only supported his delusion of authority out of courtesy, or even fondness, and perhaps a pragmatic recognition of the fact that he provided a certain amount of color, as well as the capital to see the business through the long winters.

Steve didn't argue that pessimistic assessment, but neither did he show any enthusiasm for Conan's company, and at the station it soon became apparent that he was right: there was nothing for Conan to do.

But he refused to concede that.

At least he could see his client.

That occupied half an hour even if it produced no fresh insights and seemed to have no discernible positive effect on Brian's state of mind—he was still in emotional shock—nor on Conan's.

Well, then, he could go over the file on the case, the progress reports, lab findings, statements, photographs. The file was fairly thick by now and occupied nearly an hour.

But Steve *did* have something to do here, only part of it concerned with the Nye case; he also had three other homicide investigations to supervise by remote telephonic control. And Earl Kleber had an investigation into the fatal shooting of the town's traffic light last night, probably perpetrated by a gang of juveniles whose predilection for midnight drag-racing on the back streets of Holliday Beach had earlier this morning brought forth an angry assemblage of local citizens to protest the situation to Kleber personally.

As a result, the chief's face became increasingly red as the morning progressed, and his tolerance for Conan's civilian meddling in police business diminished accordingly.

Even Steve's tolerance was wearing at the edges.

Finally, he suggested, "Conan, get out of here."

Conan got out, satisfying himself with Steve's promise that he would call if anything broke.

He went to the bookshop where within an hour he succeeded in putting Meg into an offended pout, filing a stack of rental returns on the wrong shelves, losing forever two unpaid invoices, alienating a book salesman and three old customers, and reducing Miss Dobie to long, disconsolate sighs.

Finally, she suggested, "Why don't you take a walk? On the beach, maybe."

"Because there are no phones on the beach."

At noon she suggested, "Go get some lunch. It'll help."

He couldn't fathom what it would help and he wasn't hungry, but if she wanted to go next door to the Chowder House, he'd be happy to tend the cash register for her.

She stared at him, contemplating the potential damage to orderly business procedure and customer relations, then sighed, again, threw up her hands, and walked out.

The phone rang while Mrs. Hollis was concluding a purchase, examining the bill she took from her purse carefully before offering it in a fragile, age-freckled hand. Conan juggled her change and the receiver, cursing the cast under his breath.

"Steve?"

"Holy mud, Conan, have you been sitting on that phone all this time?"

"Mr. Flagg . . ."

He looked at Mrs. Hollis, who was frowning over her change, but a look was all she got from him.

"What's happened, Steve?"

"Something broke. We just got the word from Sheriff Gould up in Tillamook County. The state patrol has a body."

"Mr. Flagg, you gave me too much—"

"A body? Hancock?"

"Probably. Description fits, anyway. It was dumped in the ocean twenty miles south of Tillamook on 101. Gould has divers there, but the body's at the bottom of a two-hundred-foot cliff. They haven't got it up yet. I'm driving up with Earl to have a look. But, Conan, if you—"

He didn't wait for the cautionary admonition that doubtless followed, but hung up with a short, "Thanks, Steve."

Nor did he wait to see why Mrs. Hollis was thumping her cane so impatiently.

"Mr. Flagg, you gave me too much *change*. Mr. Flagg? Oh, for pity's sake!"

He was gone, leaving the door—and the cash register—wide open.

Half an hour later he was urging the XK-E around a curve at something more than a safe speed. He was on the inside of the curve with a bank of basalt on his right, a spare lane of highway and a stone balustrade on his left. Beyond that was a brooding expanse of sky. He could see the horizon of sea, but the surf was two hundred feet below the road.

At the next curve a patrolman held up a sign ordering him to slow down. He did, but when he rounded the curve, ignored the next patrolman's waving command to drive on.

The stone barrier bulged seaward to accommodate a graveled area where cars could pull off the narrow, harrowing road. The space was crowded with an ambulance, a winch truck, two state patrol cars, a car from the Tillamook County sheriff's office, and another from the Holliday Beach police department, but there was enough room left for the Jaguar.

Conan strode to the back of the ambulance. The winch truck and the men in wet suits had finished their work; a stretcher heavy with a blanketed burden was being loaded into it.

"Wait! Let me see him." He reached for the blanket, and the two deputies carrrying the stretcher, perhaps intimidated by his tone, paused.

He turned the blanket back from the face.

The straggling hair, dark because it was wet, made hideous streaks across it like blood. Yet there was no actual blood. The sea had washed the skin clean, given it the pebbled, purpled aspect of some invertebrate creature of its own, given the unblinking eyes the nacre of shattered shells. An alien zoomorph, this visage; it seemed to have three eyes.

"What the hell do you think you're doing, Flagg?"

Kleber. Conan covered the face, flushed in death, and looked around into Kleber's face, flushed in anger.

He didn't give Conan a chance to answer his question.

"I put up with you nosing around in the Nye case, but I'll be damned if I can see what right you got in *this* one!"

"This is still the Nye case," he said curtly, noting that Steve was occupied with the only civilian present, a middle-aged man who seemed to have mixed feelings about the whole affair.

"What do you mean, the *Nye* case?" Kleber demanded. "Some dopehead gets himself dumped in the ocean, and you figure that's got something to do with—"

"Yes!" Conan flared. "Johnny Hancock may have been a dopehead, but don't tell me it's just coincidence that he happened to be in the kitchen at the Surf House when Nye was murdered, and now he just happens to be *dead*!"

Kleber spat out, "So, you figure Johnny witnessed that murder? Trouble with that, Flagg, is the only person who'd have any reason to shut him up is already behind bars. The man *Nye* pointed the finger at himself!"

The initials. Those damned incomprehensible letters.

"If you'll just for once look at the *other* evidence—"

"All right, you two, just cool down." Steve had ambled up beside them. "You can fight this out later—in private."

Kleber mumbled something about Sheriff Gould and stalked away, while Conan went to the stone balustrade and let the chill wind beat against his face. At the foot of the cliff, the surf simmered around the rocks in patterns of white on azure green as exquisite as a flower jasper.

Steve joined him in contemplation of the view and said, as if he were answering a question, "He was found on a fluke. Ben Selzer—he lives in Cloverdale—" He glanced over his shoulder at the one civilian, who was answering questions for Gould and Kleber. "He had a flat tire and managed to limp in here where he could get off the highway. Then he thought he heard some sea lions barking and looked over the edge here. Hancock's body was caught down there in the rocks."

Conan nodded and looked around the graveled area.

"No hope for tire tracks, I suppose."

"Not now, anyway. Gould thought he had a simple case of drowning till his divers got down to the body. I called Dan Reuben to do an autopsy, but the cause of death is clear enough: a bullet between the eyes. Small caliber, probably, and close range; looked like tattooing around the wound. But there was no exit wound.''

Conan's eyes narrowed. ''Well, that's a piece of luck. Reuben can recover the bullet.''

''Sure. Then all we have to do is find the Saturday night special it came from. Can't be more than a thousand of them in Taft County alone.''

''Well, you might start with the one Conny Van Roon keeps in his desk.''

''We'll check it as soon as Dan gets the bullet out. Does anybody else on your list own a small-caliber gun?''

''I don't know. I'll try to find out.''

''I'll check gun registrations—for what that's worth. Any suggestions about who I should check, other than Van Roon?''

Conan felt Steve's intensely inquiring gaze, but didn't try to meet it.

''Claude Jastrow and Beryl Randall.''

''She's still on your list?''

''Yes, I guess so. I still can't tie her in with a motive against Brian.''

Steve snorted. ''But she collects Victoriana.''

''*Good* Victoriana, but apparently that runs in the family. Steve, she was in a crucial position at a crucial time Monday night. She's the last person who admits seeing Nye alive, and there's a period of at least ten minutes unaccounted for when she was supposedly in the ladies' room.''

''But she was seen leaving the ladies' room, and Van Roon was in a crucial place at a crucial time, too. And what about Jastrow? Nobody's sure exactly when he left the bar, and he was in the kitchen to chew Hancock out about those scuff marks just minutes after they were made—according to your theory.''

''And that chewing out may have been simply an audacious smoke screen?'' He frowned, then answered his own question. ''Well, it has Claude's style about it.''

''Mm. Well, I'll leave the style to you. My money's still

on Van Roon.'' He gave Conan a tight smile. ''Earl got a call from the FBI about him today.''

Conan shifted his field of focus abruptly from the surf to Steve's face.

''Why was the FBI asking about Conny?''

''Well, they're running a routine surveillance on some guys who happen to be visiting in Portland—from Las Vegas. Two of them are just hired on for their muscle content: Sonny Fisk and Otto Curtin. The big boy is Lucien Gysing. They call him Lucy, he's such a sweetheart. The FBI says he's with the syndicate collection division.''

Conan smiled grimly. ''So, that's where Conny comes in.''

''Probably. Anyway, Lucy and friends had a late lunch with Conny at the Fernwood Inn just outside Portland yesterday about three o'clock. The FBI got Conny's name from his car license. The conference lasted an hour, and he came out of it alive.''

''Three o'clock.'' Conan considered that, then nodded. ''He left home at eight in the morning, so he had plenty of time to make a detour to Tillamook and reach Portland for the meeting. He could've met Hancock in Tillamook and shot him in his own car. Maybe he parked his car in an alley where it wouldn't be noticed, and a small-caliber gun doesn't make much noise. Then he hid the body on the floor of the car, drove Hancock's van to the bus depot, found the little old lady patsy, walked back to his car, drove south until he came to a good dumping spot—like this—then went his merry way.''

''To Portland to report everything under control. He might not even tell Lucy and friends about Hancock. After all, he took care of that little problem. What's the matter? You don't like that theory?''

Conan frowned, watching an approaching squall drag its gray veils over the sea.

''It fits the facts, Steve, but Jastrow could've played the same scene, deleting the trip to Portland and the three evil

crones from Nevada, of course. What I don't like about the
theory is the risk involved for the killer in staging the murder
in Tillamook.''

"But he had to get Hancock's van and suitcase to the depot. If he didn't stage the murder close by, what did he do
for transportation after he left the van there?''

"Well, here's another scenario for you: maybe the killer
met Johnny somewhere else—for instance, in Holliday
Beach—then rode *with* him in his van this far, probably keeping him at gunpoint, killed him here and pushed the body
over the cliff, then drove the van on to Tillamook.''

"And walked home again?''

"No. Took a bus.''

That called up a sigh of resignation.

"Well, I guess I'll go on up to Tillamook and see if I can
pry out anything more at the bus depot.'' He grimaced testily
at the sky; the wind was tossing raindrops at them. "One
thing I found out already: between noon and five yesterday,
eight scheduled buses went out of that depot headed every
direction but west. You want to come with me?''

"No, I'll leave the prying to you.'' He noted, but didn't
feel it necessary to comment on the fact that Steve hadn't
mentioned the one piece of evidence that seemed to negate
all their prying, the piece of evidence Kleber never let him
forget. The initials.

That omission, Conan knew, wasn't simply an act of
friendly consideration; Steve just didn't like to close any
doors until he was sure what was behind them.

A minor traffic jam was taking shape as the official cars
moved out. Conan waited until the scream of sirens faded as
the ambulance departed—and that was gratuitous; there was
no hurry getting that victim to town—then started for his own
car.

"I'm going back to Holliday Beach, Steve.''

"What for?''

"Well, I live there, for one thing.''

"Sure. Well, good luck.''

"At what? Living?"

"At whatever you've got in mind."

Conan took a last look back at the stone wall.

"I wish I *had* something in mind."

CHAPTER 21

Because it was at the north end of town and he passed within two blocks of it on his way, Conan stopped first at the police station. When he told Brian about Hancock's death, the news seemed to have as much personal impact as an earthquake in the Arctic Ocean, but that wasn't callousness; it simply didn't register. Vestiges of the stoic front were still evident, but badly eroded. Conan didn't stay long. Brian didn't need company; he couldn't cope with it.

Because it was only a few blocks farther south, Conan's next stop was F. Conrad Van Roon's office. The sign on the door proclaimed it open for business, but no lights were on, and the sign was probably only an oversight. Van Roon was present, but not necessarily accounted for.

He slumped with his elbows on his desk, past putting his bottle away, and it was almost past offering him solace; there was only a scant inch of whiskey in it. Conan walked over to the desk, wondering why alcoholics so often bought their ruin in pint bottles; fifths would at least be more economical.

"Hello, Conny."

197

Van Roon looked up, mouth sagging, one eyelid drooping lower than the other. The gun lay on a yellowing pile of paper near his right hand.

"Who . . . who're you?" Then he blinked laboriously. "Oh. Wha'd'you want?"

Conan found a pencil, hooked it through the trigger guard, and picked up the gun. A Bauer .25-caliber automatic. It looked like a toy, but there was ominous potential in the weight of it. He sniffed at the barrel.

"Been doing a little target practice, Conny?"

Van Roon pushed himself upright. "Gimme that! It's *mine*!"

"Yes, I know." He sat down on the corner of the desk and put the gun down beside him, out of Van Roon's reach. "They found Johnny Hancock's body."

At first, Van Roon only stared at him, the color draining unevenly from his slack features.

"Now, waita minute—jus' waita minute. . . ." He was sobering up rapidly, the rabbit eyes coming into desperate focus. "Wha's it to *me* if they found . . . found his body?"

"You don't seem surprised that he's dead."

"Well . . . well, *sure* I'm s'prised." But he didn't yet have his eyes under control; they wandered to the gun.

Conan asked lightly, "Are you celebrating?"

"What d'you mean?"

"Celebrating the successful conclusion of your meeting with Lucy Gysing and friends."

At that, he had to seek the remainder of the solace in the bottle. His frail body shuddered with it.

"I don' know what you're talkin' about."

Conan spelled it out for him. "You met with Lucy and his amiable sidekicks to tell him that the Surf House deal is still on. Brian is conveniently out of the way, and that little unforeseen problem—the witness to Nye's murder—well, you took care of that. Or did you even tell Lucy about it? Probably not. Why worry him with details?"

Van Roon's gelatinous face quivered.

"Get out! Damn you—I tol' you once! Get *out*!" He made an abortive lunge toward the gun, but stopped short when Conan let his hand hover over it.

"Tell me about your trip to Portland, Conny."

"It's none of your business!"

"It's Brian's business, and that makes it mine. You had a phone call Wednesday night from Johnny, didn't you?"

"From who? Johnny Hancock? No. He never—"

"I *know* you had a call."

"Mavis," he pronounced with indignant disgust. "But it wazh—wasn't Johnny Hancock! I swear it wasn't! It was—it was Gysing!"

"He called you at your home? That seems a little careless. All right, so you left Thursday morning at eight."

"Right! Left at eight and went straight to Portland. That's what the call was about. He told me where I was sh—s'posed to meet him."

"And when? What time was your appointment?"

"It—it was . . . ten. No. Maybe . . . eleven."

"No, Conny, that was when you met Johnny, not Gysing."

"Johnny?"

"Remember—Johnny Hancock?"

"Now, wait. . . . No, I didn't—I never saw . . ."

"It's a two-hour drive to Portland, but you didn't meet Gysing until three o'clock. That means you have five hours to account for."

"*No*. The meet was at eleven! I swear—"

"Should I believe you or the FBI? They're interested in people like Gysing when they wander out of Nevada."

"The . . . FBI?" He fumbled for the bottle, and it seemed to come as a profound shock when he found it empty.

"Yes. The FBI. So, tell me about that five hours."

"I . . . I left early. Couldn't take Mavis bitching about . . . And—and anyway, I had things to do in town." He drew himself up piously. "Business to take care of."

"Of course. Potential clients, other real estate dealers to see—that sort of thing?"

He nodded eagerly. "Yeah. That's it. Business."

"Who did you see? Give me one name, Conny."

He floundered with that, staring reproachfully at his empty bottle, then looked up and found Conan.

"Who I saw's none of your business!"

Conan laughed. "Because there *wasn't* any business, not with anyone in Portland except Lucy Gysing. Damn, Conny, if you told me you spent the day in a bar working up your nerve to face Gysing, I might believe you."

Van Roon went livid. "You got no right to say that! I had *business* to take care of!"

Conan rose, shrugging indifferently.

"By the way, I can testify to the caliber of this gun and to the fact that it was in your possession at this time, and that it's been fired recently. If it should suddenly disappear, you might as well sign a confession."

Van Roon's mouth moved aimlessly before he could get out any coherent sounds.

"Wait a . . . listen, what're you—you can't . . . but I didn't *do* anything! That gun—I just use it to . . ." His frenzied gaze jerked erratically around the office. "The rats! I just use it to kill *rats*!"

Conan stared at him, pity vying with disgust to choke off anything he might have said. Then he turned abruptly and went to the door.

His next stop in geographical sequence might have been the bookshop, but Conan drove past it without even the usual proprietary survey, winging like a homing pigeon to the Surf House Restaurant, where he found Tilda presiding over only a few occupied tables.

"How is Brian?" she asked, and Conan saw the same numb detachment in her eyes as he'd seen in Brian's.

"I don't know, Tilda. Not good, but maybe better than he should be. Is Claude here?"

"Yes, he's in the kitchen."

"What about Beryl?"

"She's here, too; downstairs in her office."

"Then she recovered from the subtle first symptoms."

Tilda gave a mirthless laugh. "Oh, yes. The Widow Bea always recovers. But that was catty. I'm sorry."

"Was it? Is she prone to hypochondria?"

"Well, yes, but it was catty because she never lets it interfere with her work. Oh—excuse me, I have a customer."

He nodded. "And I have Claude."

He found Jastrow in the cooking area. Five plates, empty except for a garnish of romaine and spiced apple, were lined on the counter under the pass-through, but the chef had his back to them, presiding like a white-uniformed Vulcan over the array of grills, ovens, and broilers, which poured out waves of heat even the exhaust fans couldn't contain. The backup cook, a harried young man with a sweating and corrugated brow, hovered about like a surgical nurse to provide tools and ingredients at Jastrow's command.

"Sliced!" Jastrow snapped as he flung a handful of mushrooms into the garbage can. "For Stroganoff, the *sliced* mushrooms, Benjy." He pushed a skillet of tenderloin strips to the back of the stove grill and uncovered a huge stockpot, squinting into the fountain of steam it belched out.

Conan was standing by the refrigerator at the end of the narrow space, and when Benjy lunged for it to remedy his error with the mushrooms, Conan had to move fast to avoid a literal encounter with a swinging door.

"Benjy, I have another order of steamer clams coming up," Jastrow informed him as he accepted the bowl he proffered, "and a brochette. And Benjy—sherry! There's not half an ounce in this bottle." He said that as if it were Benjy's fault, but he was out of range, whisking past Conan as if he didn't exist.

Jastrow recognized his existence with a dubious glance as he shifted to the main grill.

"Hamburgers!" he said contemptuously, shouting against

the roar of the fans. "The All-American gastronomical abomination! Are you here to study culinary art, Mr. Flagg?"

"No. To ask some questions."

He frowned, but it seemed to be at the waitress at the pass-through who shouted, "Razors, D-3!" Without taking his eyes from the grill, he reached behind him for a garnished plate, scooped two grilled clams onto it, then a few steps to the right to the microwave oven where he procured a baked potato, and by this time Benjy was back, a neat exchange of plate and wine bottle was made, and Benjy cut and plumped out the potato, then sailed the plate up to the dish-up counter where the waitress fielded it.

"I'm busy, Mr. Flagg," Jastrow said, as if he were explaining something to a three-year-old.

"So am I," Conan replied and waited stolidly while the hamburgers, Stroganoff, and steamer clams went out through the pass-through.

Meanwhile, another colander of clams went into the stock-pot, and Jastrow couldn't resist leering at Conan through the steam and pronouncing, *"Double, double toil and trouble . . ."* Then catching the spirit of the role, he took the plate of tenderloin chunks Benjy provided and with a haggish cackle, tossed them into a skillet.

" 'Eye of newt, and toe of frog . . .' " And with a handful of chopped onions, *" 'Wool of bat, and tongue of dog. Finger of birth-strangled babe . . .' "* That as he poured in the last of the old bottle of sherry. *". . . Ditch delivery by a drab!' "*

When he climaxed the performance with a suitably fiendish laugh and aimed the empty bottle at the garbage can, Conan said, "They found Johnny Hancock's body, Claude."

For the span of a heartbeat, he seemed paralyzed, then he turned with a quick shrug and began impaling hunks of meat, green pepper, onion, and whole mushrooms on a skewer.

"They found his body? That, I assume, means he's dead."

"Yes. Shot between the eyes."

Jastrow consigned the brochette to the broiler and checked the order wheel; two new slips were up.

"Benjy, a T-bone. From the cooler." He opened the refrigerator—but Conan, anticipating him, was out of the way—took out four hamburger patties and flung them on the grill. "If you expect to see me prostrate with grief, Mr. Flagg, I'm afraid I'll have to disappoint you. I can only say, as the Bard did so aptly, *'Nothing in his life Became him like the leaving it.'* On the broiler, Benjy. Mark it well done, heaven help it."

Conan countered, "The Bard also said, *'Foul deeds will rise, Though all the earth o'erwhelm them, to men's eyes.'* "

"Ah, very good, but do you call Johnny's murder a foul deed? Of course, you didn't know him."

"I call murder most foul whoever the victim. You had a phone call Wednesday evening. Who was it from, Claude?"

He stiffened, then busied himself painting liquid pseudo-butter on hamburger buns.

"And what gives you the right to question the identity of the people who choose to call me?"

"Johnny Hancock's becoming death. And Eliot Nye's."

Jastrow dropped half a bun into the oil, swore in terms the Bard would have understood, threw both halves at the garbage can, then glared at Benjy.

"Go . . . check the salad. The soup stock. Something!" Then when Benjy prudently retreated, "Mr. Flagg, if I'm under suspicion of a crime, it's my right to be so informed."

"I'm not a policeman, but can you give me one good reason why I shouldn't tell Steve Travers that you received a call the same evening Johnny phoned an unidentified benefactor to blackmail him into putting up his bail, or that you weren't home yesterday from ten in the morning until four-thirty, when you arrived an hour and a half late for your shift?"

That morning hour was a shot in the dark, but Jastrow didn't argue it. His lip curled in lofty indignation.

"What I did with my time yesterday is no concern of yours or the police!"

"Isn't it? You own a small-caliber gun, don't you?"

Another shot in the dark, and apparently it hit home.

"Who *doesn't* own a gun in these out-of-joint times? But if you're saying—oh, *damn*!" The odor of charred meat reached him; he leaped to the grill and flipped the hamburger patties to the back, then jerked the broiler door open, pulled the T-bone and brochette out from under the flames, left them smoking, and rescued the tenderloin in the skillet, all the while emitting an amazing stream of foul malediction.

A waitress appeared at the pass-through and shouted, "Steamers, A-2!"

Jastrow's face went slack.

"Oh, my God, the *steamers*!" He lunged for the stockpot, grimacing as the steam erupted. "Ruined! *Ruined!*"

The lid clattered into a corner where he flung it.

"You! Damn you!"

Conan ducked behind the refrigerator as the colander and two dozen steamer clams rocketed toward him, the former crashing into a shelf and triggering an avalanche of jars and condiments, the latter raining on tables, the floor, and a passing busboy like a fall of shrapnel.

Benjy came out of the cooler, eyes going round.

"Holy Moses, what *happened*?"

Conan didn't stay to explain.

CHAPTER 22

Conan retreated into the silent depths of the banquet rooms. The west wall on this level was also made up of windows; another squall was mustering to the southwest, the sea was pale against lowering clouds, and on the horizon a line of orange-pink glowed.

The office was tucked in behind the staircase, and Beryl Randall was tucked in behind her desk and a barricade of ledgers. Her jeweled glasses flashed in the light of the desk lamp as she looked up at him.

"Oh, Mr. Flagg, I'm so *glad* you came. I've been *so* worried about Brian, and I was just thinking about calling you." She moved a stack of guest checks from the chair by the desk. "Here—do sit down, and forgive the disorder. It only takes one day away to get behind here, and the dairy and produce deliveries come on Fridays, plus the liquor order for the weekend. I suppose he's terribly discouraged."

Conan sat down in the chair she had prepared for him.

"Brian? Well, he hasn't much to be encouraged about." She shuffled the guest checks absently.

"Oh, it just seems . . . I mean, Brian, of *all* people. Mr. Flagg, you don't think it will ever *really* come to—to a trial, do you?"

"I hope not."

"But surely you don't think . . . I mean, you *know* he's innocent."

Conan bit back an annoyed rejoinder at that blithe *non sequitur*, but his tone was still sharper than he intended.

"Yes, *I* know he's innocent."

"Then how . . . well, I guess I'll never really understand how *anyone* could think him guilty."

"The initials, Mrs. Randall. Nothing short of a confession from the killer will negate the evidential weight of those initials."

"The initials?" she asked dazedly.

"The initials Nye left in the freezer written in his own blood. I told you about them."

"Oh." She looked down at the guest checks in her hand. "Yes, of course. Oh, I really *don't* understand that. It's so . . . mysterious. The writing on the wall. Like—like a divine judgment."

He stared at her, wavering between instant rage and laughter. In the end, he only said, "I'd call it a *mis*judgment, and something other than divine."

"Yes, well, that was only a figure of speech, of course. At any rate, I'm *sure* something will come up—*you'll* find something to clear him. Oh, I've already been through these." She stacked the guest checks and threw them into a wastebasket.

Conan frowned, and more to change the subject than out of real interest, asked, "Don't you keep those for your records?"

"Oh, no. We'd soon run out of storage space. Actually, the real records are on these cash-register tapes." She produced an example, rolled and rubber-banded. "We run two tapes; one on the register in the dining room and one on the kitchen register. All orders are rung up on the latter, you see, so we can check it against the one in the dining room where the cash comes in. That way if a waitress decides to pocket the ticket *and* the customer's cash, the discrepancy will show up when I cross-check the two tapes."

"Couldn't a waitress just neglect to ring up the order on the kitchen register?"

"Not if the order is to be filled. Only a properly rung ticket will be accepted, unless the *cook* is in on the fraud, too, but Brian watches—at least, he always . . . well, there isn't much chance of that occurring."

"But if someone could get at both registers and run new tapes that would match, then destroy the old ones, the discrepancies wouldn't show up."

She said coolly, "No one has access to the register tapes but Brian and me. I assure you, that *isn't* possible." She opened a drawer to put the tape away; a drawer stacked with bundled bills.

He lifted an eyebrow. "Do you usually keep that much cash on hand?"

"No, and this is more than usual since I missed a day, but a great deal of cash *does* go through here every day. There was nearly ten thousand dollars this morning." She took a cloth bank bag from another drawer and began counting the bundles into it. "I hope you noted that I said the money passes *through*. I don't think Mr. Nye ever really understood that. Tomorrow, for instance, is payday, and all this will be reduced to pennies, literally."

"It's still a large temptation. Do you keep a gun here?"

She stopped and stared at him.

"A *gun!* Heavens, no. I wouldn't have one around, and thank goodness, Brian feels the same way about them. Don't worry, Mr. Flagg, this is going to the bank right now." She checked her watch and frowned. "Oh, dear, I didn't realize it was so late. Well, I can always put it in the night depository."

Conan waited while she filled out a deposit slip, then brought out his stock opening gambit.

"Mrs. Randall, they found Johnny Hancock's body to-day."

The lines around her mouth deepened, but she didn't look up until she put the deposit slip in the bag and jerked the drawstrings tight.

"Well. And I've already written his paycheck. Now I'll have to adjust the balance. How did he die?"

Conan rose and went to the door, not sure he could trust himself to answer that civilly.

"Of a bullet between the eyes."

"A . . . bullet . . ." Her chin came up. "Is *that* why you asked me about a—a *gun*?"

"Yes."

"Well, I *don't* know why you'd—" She stopped, and her indignation ebbed. "Oh. I suppose if we *did* keep a gun here, any number of people might have access to it."

"That occurred to me."

She smiled tolerantly. "As I said, we *don't* keep a gun and never have."

"Do *you* own a gun, Mrs. Randall?" He put that in not because he expected a meaningful answer, but simply out of pique; to remind her that she was not above suspicion. Her face reddened satisfactorily.

"Of *course* not, Mr. Flagg! I told you, I don't *like* guns, and I *won't* have one around."

He looked at his watch. "If you leave in the next few minutes you'll have time to make the bank before it closes."

"Oh." She scrambled for the deposit bag. "Yes, I'll just make it. I *know* those night depositories are perfectly safe, but I always feel better if . . ."

He didn't hear the rest; he was already halfway up the stairs.

If Conan expected to find a haven in the bookshop, he was doomed to disappointment. At the door he met Jasper Hanks, who related in clinical detail his recent gall bladder surgery, and inside the shop, the Morrises related in equally clinical detail their recent tour of Europe. They didn't like it. Next year they were going to the Far East. Conan refrained from suggesting another destination while he escaped into his office and closed the door. He left a small opening to let Miss Dobie know she wasn't excluded.

It was nearly closing time. He poured the last cup of coffee from the pot and sat down behind his desk while Meg gave him the Treatment, which was usually reserved for him on his return from a long absence. It consisted of pointedly ignoring him, but always from a distance of about five feet so he couldn't ignore her.

Her choice today was a corner of his desk where she curled herself as if for a nap, putting her back to him. But it didn't work; he was too preoccupied to realize he was being ignored. At length, she capitulated and presented herself in his lap so he could make his peace without stretching. He responded with a laugh and offered the expected petting, while she offered a murmuring purr.

Finally, Miss Dobie came in, offering a languishing sigh.

"Those Morrises! They don't like it *here*, either; too much rain. I suggested Southern California." She hefted the coffee pot, then pulled the plug. "How goes the case?"

He said curtly, "My client is still in jail."

She sank into a chair and intoned, "'. . . 'the law's delay, *The insolence of office and the spurns That patient merit—*' "

"Miss Dobie, please—I've already had enough Shakespeare thrown at me today, along with an order of steamer clams hot off the stove."

Her eyes widened. "Oh, dear. That must've come from Claude Jastrow."

"It did."

"I guess he has quite a temper."

"Yes."

"Was it his temper that did in that Hancock person?"

Conan choked on his coffee, and when he recovered asked irritably, "Is that hot off the grapevine—about Hancock?"

"Well . . . in a way. The news about Hancock's body

being found was on the radio this afternoon. Mrs. Rickey told me about it. They said he worked at the Surf House Restaurant. *Was* it Chef Claude's temper?''

"Maybe."

Her auburn curls seemed to come to attention.

"Does Hancock's murder have anything to do with Eliot Nye's?''

"*I* think so, but Kleber doesn't.''

"Oh, what does *he* know? Did Jastrow kill Nye, too?''

"I don't know that he killed anyone. He isn't the only suspect on my list.''

She might have simply asked who was on his list, and he might have told her, but Miss Dobie always preferred the oblique approach.

"What about Howie Bliss? I never did trust that man since he rented that first edition Stewart Holbrook and never brought it back. I should've known better; he doesn't read that sort of thing. Probably sold it somewhere.''

"Possibly."

"Or Tilda Capek." Then she frowned. "No. Women like that always use poison, don't they?''

Conan couldn't restrain a laugh. "Women like what?''

"Oh . . . beautiful and exotically foreign, I guess.''

"She grew up in Chicago. But according to Steve Travers, Nye's *wife* would use poison.'' He rubbed Meg under her chin, watching her tilt her head blissfully.

"Nye's wife? I didn't know he had a wife. Well. Now, *that* offers possibilities. I'll bet she has a lover.''

"Yes. A sporty type who looks like Lorenzo de Medici and drives a Ferrari.''

"Ah! Well, Lorenzo wouldn't limit himself to poison.''

"No, but unfortunately both wife and Lorenzo have been eliminated for reasons beyond my control.''

"Oh. Too bad. Well, that leaves . . .'' Her eyes narrowed on a speculative glint. "Beryl Randall.''

"What makes you think she should be on my list?''

"Well . . . it's just that I never trust anyone who works so hard at seeming to be more than she is."

The game was getting interesting; Conan willingly played to that lead.

"What do you mean, more than she is? Is she so little?"

"I mean that to-the-manor-born air she puts on. The only people she'll deign to associate with around here is the local chapter of the DAR, and how she got into that I'll never know. Probably a forged family tree." She frowned thoughtfully, then shrugged. "Maybe not. Some of those founding fathers did a lot of fathering. But if any of her ancestors were born to any manors, it was quite a few generations back."

She had Conan's full attention now. He was remembering Beryl in her miniature mansion pouring coffee from a silver pot and sighing over "her only heritage from a more gracious time. . . ."

"How do you know she wasn't to the manor born?"

"*Well* . . . I have a second cousin—actually, a cousin by marriage—or maybe she's a third cousin. Her husband was my mother's brother's nephew, or something. Winifred Toller. Well, you met her once—remember? Anyway, Winnie was born and lived all her life in Sweet Home."

Conan was already thoroughly confused, but he let Miss Dobie run her course, confident that all would be made clear eventually, and part of it was with her next words.

"Beryl comes from Sweet Home, too, you know. Anyway, Winnie runs a secondhand bookstore, and we get together now and then to see if we can fill out each other's wanted lists. The last time she was here . . . let's see, that was in April. Or maybe it was May. No, it was April. You were gone. That was the time you took that trip to London and ended up in Bangkok. Well, Winnie came over for the day, and we had lunch at the Surf House, and while we were there, Beryl came into the dining room. She didn't seem to want to recognize Winnie, but—well, she's hard to snub. Anyway, afterward, Winnie had quite a lot to say about Mrs. Randall."

She stopped to take out a cigarette, and Conan obliged her by lighting it and asking, "What did she have to say?" He lit a cigarette for himself while Miss Dobie elucidated.

"Well, Winnie remembered Beryl Randall when she was still Beryl *Henty*. It seems her father—oh, what was his name? Jake. That was it. He was a logger when he was sober, which I guess wasn't too often. The Henty family was—well, if you'll pardon the expression, the poor white trash of Sweet Home, and Beryl was the oldest of seven children. When the seventh was born, it was too much for Jake; he vanished without a trace, leaving Mrs. Henty to raise the brood, and that wasn't easy, since she only had a sixth-grade education. She managed by taking in laundry and doing housecleaning, and of course the children had to help, and that included Beryl." Miss Dobie paused to catch her breath and deliver a weighty sigh. "I'd really admire Beryl, you know, if she wasn't such an unmitigated snob. I mean, when someone pulls themselves up by their bootstraps—and an advantageous marriage in this case—you have to admire that. But I really *can't* admire pretension. Not at all."

Conan took a long drag on his cigarette, then when Meg stirred restlessly, resumed her massage. He didn't admire pretension, either, but he was more concerned with a pragmatic consideration: Beryl's heritage, that incredible collection of museum quality bric-a-brac, wasn't a heritage at all if Winnie Toller's story was true, and he had no reason to doubt it. The pretension Miss Dobie found so objectionable in itself inclined him to accept Winnie's veracity. But that collection—however dubious he was about Victoriana, the collection was one of impressive monetary value, and no matter how frugally Beryl lived otherwise, her bookkeeper's salary wouldn't stretch far enough to buy that heritage.

"Miss Dobie, what did Winnie tell you about this advantageous marriage of Beryl's?"

"Well, when Beryl was still a teen-ager helping feed Jake Henty's deserted brood, she worked as a housekeeper for the Randalls. Now, they're the upper crust of Sweet Home; they own about two thousand acres of prime farmland and filbert orchards and live in a beautiful old mansion on top of a hill. Well, Winnie said Vanessa Randall—she's Theo's sister, and he's the one Beryl finally married—took Beryl under her wing and helped her finish high school and go on to business school. Let's see, Theo's first wife must've died before Beryl started working at the Randall house. He had two children, a boy and a girl. They were only a few years younger than Beryl. Anyway, she went to business school and worked in Portland for a while as a secretary and bookkeeper, then eventually met Theo again. He hired her as his private secretary and about a year later married her.''

"A modern Cinderella," Conan observed. "So, she became mistress of the manor then.''

"With a vengeance.'' Miss Dobie's eyebrows flicked up meaningfully. "From what Winnie said, she didn't make herself popular with Theo's children, or his sister, or the people of Sweet Home, and I guess she spent money like she was trying to go through the whole Randall fortune single-handedly, but luckily there was a lot of fortune. Winnie said somewhere around five million.''

Conan's eyebrows flicked up at that. "How much of it went to his widow?''

"Winnie didn't know. He willed most of it to his kids, but she was sure Beryl got her share—one way or another.''

And that would account for a very valuable heritage.

"I wonder why she didn't stay in Sweet Home as mistress of the manor.''

"Because with Theo gone, the children and Vanessa didn't hesitate to let her know they didn't *want* her. I guess there was quite a family row. That's when Beryl moved down here.''

"I suppose she chose to work as a bookkeeper simply out of boredom.''

"Yes. I suppose so.'' Then the avid glint rekindled in her eyes. "*Is* Beryl one of your suspects?''

He laughed. "She'd be more of a suspect if you hadn't

provided her a visible means of support other than her salary as a bookkeeper.''

"Oh." Miss Dobie seemed both perplexed and disappointed. "I'm sorry about that."

"Does pretension rankle with you that much?"

Her face turned pink. "That's not what I meant. I wasn't sorry for her sake—I mean, I *was* sorry for your—oh, never mind. Who else is on your list?"

She'd worked around to the direct question, Conan noted, and he gave her a direct answer.

"Conny Van Roon." Then while she puzzled over that, he asked, "What does the grapevine have to offer on him lately?"

"Well, let's see, there *was* something. . . . Oh, yes—Mrs. Higgins was in today looking for that new Victoria Holt. For heaven's sake, the advance copies have just gone out to the reviewers; I don't know how she expects us to have it already. Anyway, she lives next door to the Van Roons, and she said they're moving. Sold their house, and this morning Mavis was packing the china."

Conan's eyes went to black ellipses. "Moving?"

"Yes. Mrs. Higgins was just dumbfounded, it was so sudden. Of course, it's no secret that Conny's business has been going downhill for years, but—well, where would he get the money for a fresh start? The sale of the house, maybe, if the buyer paid cash, but that doesn't happen very often."

"Did Mrs. Higgins know where they're going?"

"Well . . . she was a little vague. Something about south and the desert and some big housing development. Maybe Conny got a job as a salesman."

South and the desert. Nevada. And perhaps Conny did get a job; a reward for another job well done, or so close to done, his benefactors were acting on the assumption of its completion.

Conan gently shifted Meg to the desk and rose.

"Well, maybe the desert will be good for Conny."

"Dry him out, you mean?" Miss Dobie asked archly.
He couldn't bring himself to laugh at that.
"One way or another, I suppose."

CHAPTER 23

As Conan drove to the police station, the pallid dusk faded prematurely with the gusting onset of a violent squall that seemed to drive the villagers into hiding; the rain-veiled streetlights shone on highway and sidewalks as lonely as midnight.

When he reached the station, he found Kleber in conference behind his closed door with Steve. He interrupted them only long enough to learn that Steve's inquiries at the Tillamook bus depot had garnered nothing but a description of the woman who had checked Hancock's suitcase that would fit half the female Caucasians over sixty-five in the country.

He limited his questions to that, reading the clear warning in the set of Kleber's jaw, closed the door quietly, and went directly to jail.

The guard saved himself a trip when he took Conan to Brian's cell by carrying the prisoner's supper with him. It made for slack security—both his hands were occupied with the tray when he entered the cell—but the risk of this prisoner attempting an escape was something less than minimal.

Brian lay on the bunk, his face to the wall; he didn't stir when the guard announced the arrival of supper and a visitor. Perhaps he'd been playing solitaire earlier; cards were scattered negligently around the bunk with some magazines and newspapers. The guard left the tray on the floor and locked the door as he departed.

"Brian?"

He wasn't asleep. Still, Conan had to repeat his name before he finally moved. He turned over as if it were an exhausting effort and lay staring at him, then at length made a further effort and sat up on the side of the bunk.

"Conan. I didn't know it was you." And perhaps didn't care. There was nothing personal in that; he seemed past caring about anything. The blue of his lifeless eyes had faded to lusterless gray, and his face had already assumed the pallor of long confinement.

"Your dinner is served," Conan said lightly. "Potato château, beets julienne à l'Anglaise, coq au vin . . ."

Brian focused on the tray and tried to smile, then fumbled a package of cigarettes out of his shirt pocket. It was empty. Conan offered one of his, lit it, then sat down on the wooden stool near the bunk to light his own. Percy Dent was back in his accustomed cell rendering "You Made Me What I Am Today" in a frail, faded tenor.

"Well, live entertainment with dinner," Conan quipped.

Brian successfully presented a smile, even if it was short-lived.

"And with lunch and breakfast. That's his favorite song. That's his *only* song."

For a while they both listened to Percy's song, neither moving except for occasional puffs at their cigarettes, but even when the song lapsed into soft snores melding with the rush of rain on the window, Brian maintained his listening pose, and Conan maintained his silence, watching him, wondering where he wandered in his thoughts—to the past or to the future.

Finally, Brian looked at his watch and frowned.

"What time is it? I guess I forgot to wind my watch."

Conan checked his. "Five-forty."

"No, I didn't forget. Just seems . . . later. Damn, I hate winter. All my life I've lived where winter only gives you half a day and leaves you a night and a half."

"Where did you live before Oregon?" It struck him as strange, sad somehow, that he didn't already know that.

"Oh, California for a while. I did part of my Army hitch at Fort Ord and just never got around to going back east again. But I grew up in Minnesota." His eyes clouded with memory, an equivocal mix of regret and pleasure. "My dad ran a dairy farm. I mean a *real* dairy farm. Made the ones up in Tillamook County look like 4-H projects."

Conan hesitated before asking, "Is your father retired?" He was afraid he might be dead.

"Yes. Sold the farm and he and Mom moved into one of those retirement complexes near Rochester." He leaned back against the wall with a sigh that seemed forced out of him by the very weight of the atmosphere. "I was thinking about Dad today, and I wanted so damn much to talk to him."

"That could probably be arranged."

"No, I—well, not yet. I don't want him to know I'm . . . here. Or Mom. They'll have to know sooner or later, but it won't hurt if it's later. Anyway . . ." He shrugged listlessly. "Well, I don't really know what I'd say to him."

Conan didn't know what to say to that, but Brian didn't seem to notice his silence, nor its length. The rain was coming harder, drowning Percy's soft snores.

At length, Brian leaned forward to grind out his cigarette in the plastic ashtray among the debris on the floor, then propped his elbows on his knees; it seemed too much of an effort to reach the support of the wall.

He asked, "How . . . how's Tilda?"

It was the first time since his incarceration that he'd asked about her, yet there was no hope in it; none of the special kind of hope that lives in love even when it dies in everything else.

Conan called up a smile with his reply.

"The show goes on, and Tilda's a good trouper. She's confused and frightened for you, but she's keeping her chin up and her upper lip stiff."

Brian assayed a short laugh. "That's too pretty an upper lip to keep stiff." The laugh slipped away from him, and he frowned as if he'd forgotten something he meant to say. Then he dismissed it with another listless shrug and asked, "Have you been down to the restaurant lately?"

"Lately? Well, yes. I've become sort of a fixture there. My last visit was this afternoon. Business wasn't booming today, but then it's February."

He nodded, his rueful smile a little steadier.

"Tell me about February. I opened that place in February, and for a solid month the cook and I sat around playing poker till . . ." Again, he seemed to lose track of what he was saying, but after a moment apparently recalled the general subject. "How's Bea taking everything?"

Conan shrugged. "Another good trouper; business and balances as usual. At least, she's back at her post today. I was beginning to wonder yesterday."

"Yesterday? What happened?"

"She called in sick, and since she has a heart condition, I thought I should worry a little, but I guess it was just preventive recuperation."

Brian gave an odd, knowing laugh that surprised Conan; it was so uncharacteristically cynical.

"Poor Bea," he said, shaking his head. "The old heart condition. She could just ask for a day off now and then; she works so much overtime, she deserves it. But every time she wants an extra day off, I get that heart business."

Conan stared at him, feeling a chill sensation at the back of his neck.

"What do you mean—that heart business?" His tone must have been sharper than he realized; it erased the smile from Brian's face.

"Well, I just mean you don't need to take her heart condition seriously. But I shouldn't laugh about it because she does take it seriously.''

"You mean she *doesn't* have a heart condition?"

"No. I guess her blood pressure's a little high, but it's not bad, and there's nothing else wrong with her."

"Are you sure? How do you know?"

Brian hesitated, a little intimidated by his insistence.

"Look, what difference does it make? So she needs an excuse to coddle herself once in a while. So what?"

Conan pulled in a deep breath and got his impatience under control.

"So . . . well, it could make a big difference. I just need to know if you're sure about the state of her heart."

Brian was still frowning, as if he felt himself somehow out of his depth and wasn't sure how he got there.

"Bea doctors with Nicky Heideger, and so do I. A couple of years ago I asked Nicky about Bea. It wasn't really any of my business, except I was wondering what the hell I should do for her if she keeled over with a heart attack at the restaurant. Well, Nicky and I trust each other, and she knew I'd keep it to myself, and I have till now. She said Bea's heart is as good as mine, but she likes, or needs, to think she's got a problem. It's psychosomatic. But like Nicky said, it's not hurting her; she's not making an invalid of herself, and it's not hurting anybody else. So, if an old lady wants to baby herself once in a while, what difference does it make?"

Answers to that question were clamoring in cacophonous confusion in Conan's mind, tension as constricting as fear clamped on his throat, and he had to make two tries to get a word out.

"What . . . you called her an old lady. How old is she?"

Brian seemed to absorb his taut doubt, but in him it translated into apprehensive bewilderment.

"Well, I . . . I'm not really sure, but I know she could be collecting Social Security if she wasn't working."

That meant she was over sixty-two.

Yet she claimed—and looked, if one didn't look too closely—forty-eight.

Old lady.

The words reverberated in his consciousness.

"Brian, doesn't she have another source of income that would put her over the Social Security minimum?"

"What do you mean?"

"Her husband was a very wealthy man. Doesn't she have any income from her inheritance?"

Brian shook his head. "No. He was wealthy, all right, but he didn't leave much of his wealth to Bea. She told me about it one night when she had a few martinis too many. I guess the thrill went out of their marriage a long time before Theo died. She says his sister and kids poisoned him against her. I don't know. Anyway, all he left her was the house she's living in and ten thousand dollars; enough to get her moved with a little cushion for her to live on till she found herself a job."

The confusion of answers was beginning to take coherent shape. Conan neither moved nor spoke, and the only thing in his surroundings he was aware of was the rain against the barred window.

Finally, Brian pleaded, "Conan, for God's sake, what's all this about Bea?"

Bea. It sounded exactly like the letter B.

"Have you ever been in her house, Brian?"

"What? Yes. Not very often, but I've been in it."

"She has a collection of antiques in that little bungalow worth—god only knows how much. Tens of thousands of dollars."

"Sure, she does. All that came from her family. I mean, it was hers before she got married."

Conan finally brought his eyes into focus on Brian's face, and perhaps it was only his own fearful surmise he saw reflected there.

"No. Beryl Henty's family had a hard time feeding itself.

There was no gracious heritage for Beryl, no heritage at all except avaricious shame."

Brian seemed to recoil, his pallid features cast with gray.

"But that . . . that's impossible! I mean, if she—Where . . . where did all that stuff come from?"

Conan almost replied, *from out of your pocket*.

And yet she loved him.

In her own way. In her own autistic way, and to the degree she found it expedient, or was capable of loving any human being.

Bea. B. Bea. B. Bea. B. . . .

Conan came to his feet and stared distractedly around the cell; the bars seemed to have moved in closer. Then he snatched one of the magazines from the floor, stood a moment longer, still searching, then went to the tray in which Brian's supper cooled into inedibility.

Brian protested, "Damn it, Conan, what are you—"

But Conan shook his head to quiet him and knelt beside the tray. The beets lapsed in a separate dish in a pool of margarine-filmed juice. The wrong color of red. Not that it mattered.

He turned the magazine to a page that was nearly all print, folded it back on itself, then held it in front of him in his left hand. It was awkward with the cast, but he needed his right hand free. He dipped his index finger into the crimson liquid, then made a vertical line on the page.

Brian was kneeling beside him, silenced in baffled attentiveness; the rain smashed against the dark window.

Conan dipped his finger again and began at the top of the vertical with a horizontal line, moving to the right, then looping back to the vertical, then out and back in a second loop. The letter B stood luridly on the page.

He dipped into the dish again and made a second vertical, then began another horizontal at the top and a little to the left of it, eyes half closed, focused as much on the remembered original as on this facsimile made with a facsimile of blood. He pulled the horizontal line across, then let his finger drag, the line end in a curving smear.

B. T. The initials seemed a palpable weight on the page.

He said, "Eliot Nye stopped here because he either lost consciousness or died at that moment. But he didn't finish his message, Brian. He didn't *finish* it."

Brian's face was only inches from his, his breath coming in quick, shallow whispers.

"He didn't . . . finish it?"

Conan dipped his finger again, and beginning where he left off, continued the downward curve only hinted at until it met the vertical in a loop, then drew a straight line down and away from the vertical at a 45-degree angle.

The initials still weighted the page, red on white, B. R..

Brian spoke; the sound was a choked moan.

"Beryl Randall."

Conan nodded. "Yes. Bea."

CHAPTER 24

Brian crouched, staring at the initials, his eyes reflecting light like glazed porcelain, his face devoid of expression, drained of life. He might have been a wax figure except for the faint, uncontrollable tremor in the fine muscles under his skin.

"Bea . . . oh, damn, she . . . *she* killed that poor son of a . . . but why? In the name of God—*why*?"

Conan dropped the magazine and took a hard grip on both his arms.

"Brian, the important thing is that this is the answer. This is your *freedom*."

But Brian neither heard the words nor felt the pressure of his hands.

"She's been ripping me off, hasn't she? All these years, she's been . . . and that's why we weren't showing enough profit to please the IRS . . . and Nye—he found out, didn't he? He found *out*! And that's why—*Ahhuh!*"

He surged to his feet, sending Conan sprawling, kicking the tray aside in an eruption of food and rattling plastic. His

224

fists closed on the barred door, wrenching at it as if he meant to break the lock and wrest the door from its steel hinges with his bare hands. The clatter echoed against the cement walls and wakened Percy Dent to a wail of alarm.

"She put me in here! She did this to me! She—"

Conan knocked one hand away from the bars, flinching at an unexpected stab of pain—he'd used his left hand for the chop—then spun him around and pinned him against the bars.

"Brian, listen to me! You've got to hold on just a little longer. Don't you understand? I've got the truth now. *That's* the key to this door!"

As if that were a cue, the rattle of a key sounded in the ward door. Brian sagged, eyes closing, then opening to come into lucid focus on Conan's face.

"Sure. I'm all right now. I'm . . . all right."

Conan released him and stepped back to give them both a little breathing room.

"Just give me a chance, Brian. Please. Let me talk to Steve before you do anything or—"

"Damn it, what's going *on* back here?"

The guard stalked into the ward, slamming the door behind him, and with remarkable poise, Brian gave him an ingenuous grin and a shrug.

"Nothing, Charlie. I just tripped over that damn stool and fell into my supper. Busted my shin good." Then raising his voice, "Hey, Perce, everything's okay. Go on back to sleep."

Conan watched that performance with narrowed eyes, but it was effective; Charlie relaxed into annoyance, and Percy stopped his anxious wailing and began cursing the disturbance to his sleep in a droning monotone.

The magazine with its carmine letters lay face up on the littered floor. Conan hurriedly picked it up and went to the door.

"Let me out of here, Charlie. I've got to talk to Steve Travers. Is he still in Kleber's office?"

Charlie sorted through his keys, brow furrowed.

"I don't keep track of who's in and out up in front. You'll have to see for yourself."

Conan waited impatiently while Charlie mumbled and fumbled at the lock. Brian was listlessly surveying the scattered ruins of his supper.

When the lock finally clicked, Charlie said irritably, "Okay, Tally, you just stay back—*Hey!*"

Conan was suddenly catapulted forward, flinging the door open as he hit it.

He collided with the guard and fell with him in a flailing pile, Charlie protesting with indignant shouts until his impact with the floor knocked the breath out of him. But before Conan could even get past the fact that he'd been pushed from behind, he was dragged to his feet. He clamped his teeth on an angry cry of pain.

"Damn it, Brian, you'll break my arm!"

His right arm was twisted behind his back, Brian's hand like a vise on his wrist while his left arm was thrust under Conan's left and flexed to immobilize him and bring the barrel of a .38 police special to rest against his head just in front of his ear.

Brian eased the strain on his arm with a considerate "Sorry." Then, "Charlie, don't try anything!"

Charlie was crouched, blank-eyed and openmouthed, slapping futilely at his empty holster. The ward door crashed open and two officers rushed in only to stumble to an abrupt halt when Brian snapped, "Hold it right there! Get your hands up!"

Conan sighed. He sounded like a TV crime drama script.

"Brian, if this isn't the stupidest—"

"Be quiet, Conan. You can't talk me out of it. You guys—" This to the gaping policemen at the door. "Start backing out. You, too, Charlie. Keep your hands up where I can see them."

The quivering tension in Brian's muscles transmitted itself to Conan's body. He didn't argue further, nor object to being made a flesh-and-blood shield. If Brian had made up his mind to escape—and obviously he had—Conan knew he was his only hope of getting out of this building alive. He felt no fear for the gun at his head; Brian would die before he pulled that trigger. The fear was for Kleber and his men. For their guns.

Charlie and the two officers backed cautiously into the hall while Brian and Conan followed in a grim lock step. In the distance, the radio emitted spurts of voices and static.

Conan counted steps, concentrating like a dancer on Brian's movements, anticipating and co-ordinating his own with them. Perhaps there *was* something to fear in the gun at his head: if Brian tripped, it might accidentally go off.

Eighteen steps to the end of the hall, and Brian's breathing quickened. The radio muttered and stuttered, but the dispatcher was no longer attending it. He was staring dazedly at the strange procession emerging from the hall. So was Earl Kleber and two more of Holliday Beach's finest, as well as Steve Travers.

Brian faced them with his heart pounding; Conan could feel it. His voice was husky and nearly unrecognizable.

"I'm walking out of here, and don't try to stop me. I don't want to hurt anybody."

Kleber was standing near the front door, shoulders hunched, right hand hovering over his holster.

"Tally, you goddamned fool—"

"Get away from that door, Chief!"

Conan caught Steve's eye, but there was no way to let him know that he considered himself in no real danger; the danger was to Brian. And it was impossible to determine how worried Steve actually was; his face always tended to go tautly blank under stress.

He said quietly, "Okay, Tally, you're calling the shots," and began moving back toward the wall, motioning the others to follow suit. "Give him a clear path, boys. Earl, you better open that door."

He did, then backed away from it, his eyes angrily slitted, never leaving Brian's face.

Conan braced himself to resume the grotesque, lock-step dance, looking out beyond the door where the light caught on whirling motes of rain against blackness that seemed to have no finite dimensions.

Ten steps. The rain reached them in an astringent spray at the door. And in all that time—and it seemed intolerably long—no one moved, and there was no sound except the remote and unheeded voices from the radio.

Beyond the door, the rain slashed at their faces.

"Where's your car, Conan?"

"To the left on this side of the street."

Brian turned, and his next words were directed back into the station.

"Everybody stay right where you are. I've still got this gun at his head."

Everybody stayed, at least as long as Conan had them in view, which was only a few seconds. Brian began the lock step again out into the rain and across the gravel that made for treacherous footing. A tree under the streetlight cast reeling shadows as it whipped in the wind.

Brian released his right arm. "Give me your car keys."

"Let me go with you, Brian."

"No way!"

They were only a few steps from the car; the driver's side was toward them. Conan knew he could probably free himself now, but he didn't try. When they reached the car, Brian turned with him toward the station, and Conan saw Kleber and his men at the door; saw the flash of light on their guns. Brian still needed his human shield.

"The *key*," Brian insisted, shaking him as he might a recalcitrant child.

Conan pulled his key ring out of his pocket and it was immediately plucked from his hand.

"Brian, for God's sake, take me with you!"

"No. I—I have to . . . oh, damn, Conan, I'm sorry!"

Sorry for what, Conan wondered, but when the back of his head imploded with pain, he understood.

His knees buckled and he sprawled in the gravel, the roar of the Jaguar's motor searing white-hot in his head.

But Brian hadn't hit him hard enough.

Strange lights darted behind his eyes as he scrambled to his feet and staggered against the car, his right hand locking on the door handle.

Brian shouted, "Get away, Conan!"

The car reeled forward, wheels spinning mud. From the station, Kleber's apoplectic bellow echoed Brian's order.

"Flagg! Damn you, get away from that car!" Then when a shot sounded, "Hold your fire! *Flagg!*"

The XK-E swerved, gears snarling as Brian reached out the window and tried to push him away, but he refused to surrender his hold, even when the car lurched into the street and began to pick up speed.

Kleber yelled in a frenzy, *"Flagg! Get out of the way!"*

But Conan stumbled along with the car, clinging stubbornly to the door handle, despite Brian's frantic pummeling, despite the car's acceleration.

He held on and kept pace with it, his head pulsing and rattling with the erratic chain-saw spew of the motor, Kleber's receding shouts, Brian's curses that sounded almost like sobs. He held on and kept pace until the car was half a block into the murky dark before he lost his grip and the rain-slick metal jerked out of his hand. He ran a few more steps, fighting for balance, and pitched headlong into a muddy pool lined with bruising shards of asphalt, while the XK-E, with a triumphant roar, leaped into the darkness and out of range of the fusillade of shots that exploded from the station.

Conan remained prone in his makeshift foxhole, praying for deliverance from ricochets, until Kleber's shouted orders ended the volley, then he began pulling himself up out of the mire, spitting out a mouthful of water that tasted foully of exhaust fumes. The rain offered a sluicing shower, but its primary effect was to chill him thoroughly rather than wash away the coating of stinking mud he had acquired.

"Conan? Where are you? Conan!"

Steve was slogging toward him, looking like an animated scarecrow with his suit jacket pulled up over his head against the rain.

"Here, Steve!"

He was on his feet when Steve reached him. Kleber was only a few paces behind, but his anger preceded him.

"Damn it, Flagg, didn't you *hear* me? If you'd just got the hell out of the way, we'd've *had* him!"

Steve asked, "Conan, are you all right?"

He was in the process of trying to ascertain that; his eyes didn't seem to be focusing too well.

"Yes, I think so. No new breaks, anyway, unless he broke my skull." That and an old break were making themselves known; his left hand ached to the elbow. He turned and started for the station, but Kleber blocked his way.

"Flagg, if I ever find out you and Tally *planned* this, by God, I—I'll—" He lapsed into stuttering rage, then got his tongue, if not his temper, under control enough to demand, "Where's Tally going?"

Conan pushed past him. "How the hell should I know?"

Kleber apparently didn't have an answer to that. After two gasping snorts, he headed for the station, too, overtaking and passing them in a few strides.

Conan was hardly aware of him.

"Steve, I need your car."

"You know where Tally's headed?"

"Maybe." He balked at lying outright to Steve, but there wasn't time for explanations. "Will you let me have your car, or do I have to hotwire a police car?"

They had reached the parking area in front of the station, and Steve paused to search his pockets for his keys.

"You're in enough trouble as it is. Here—the car's at the side of the building. Hold it!" He grabbed Conan's arm before he could run out in the path of a police car launching itself toward the street, lights flashing, siren screaming. A second car hurtled after it, then Conan slipped away from him and started across the gravel at a lope.

Steve shouted, "Wait! Where are you going?"

Conan, back over his shoulder said, "Stay here at the station, Steve. I may need to get hold of you fast."

"Damn it, Conan, where are . . ." His shoulders slumped, he stood disconsolately, blinking into the rain, and watched yet another car leave the parking lot—his own.

Conan drove the Ford as if it were his Jaguar, covering the two blocks to the highway in seconds, making a careening turn, and rocketing southward out of sight.

Steve pronounced fervently, "Hell," then turned toward the station. But something in the gravel near the street caught the light and his eye. He detoured to investigate and found a .38 police special.

He said even more fervently, "Damn it to hell," and ran for the station.

Kleber was standing over the dispatcher giving orders into the mike. Steve heard the red-flag formula, ". . . armed and dangerous."

"Earl!" He leaned over the counter with the gun. "Hold the armed and dangerous. Here's Charlie's gun. Tally dropped it outside."

Kleber stared at the gun blankly. "Are you sure?"

"How many police specials do you usually have lying around in the parking lot? He's *not* armed, and you'd damn well better get that through to your men!"

"What about Flagg's car? He's licensed to carry a gun."

"He doesn't usually carry his gun in his car."

"Doesn't *usually*? You think that's going to make some cop's widow feel any better?" But he did make a concession of sorts when he said into the mike, "Tally *may* be armed. Repeat. *May* be armed."

Steve turned his back and sagged against the counter, scowling at the pool of water accumulating on the floor as the rain drained from his clothes. A minute later Kleber breezed by on his way to the door.

"State patrol's setting up roadblocks north and south of town," he said in passing, but at the door he stopped, perhaps realizing he had more to say than distance to say it in. "Me and my men are covering the restaurant, Tally's apartment, and his girl friend's apartment. You want to come with me?"

"No. I'm staying here."

"Suit yourself. Where's Flagg?"

"He's gone to look for Tally."

"Where?"

Steve sighed. "Damn it, would I be standing around here if I knew?"

CHAPTER 25

The Ford's speedometer hit sixty when Conan passed the bookshop, and he heard the wail of a siren behind him with a sinking chill. He didn't have time for a speeding ticket.

But he dutifully slowed and pulled over to the shoulder, sagging with relief when the police car screamed past without pause, every light flashing disaster.

Then he spun out onto the highway, reaching again for a mile a minute, passing Laurel Road with only a glance, although it was the most direct route to his objective. But with the rain it would be a morass of mud, and he had no more time for digging out of a mudhole than for a ticket. He could only hope Brian had made the error of taking the direct route and might even now be extricating the Jaguar from muddy bondage on Laurel Road.

But that hope was too faint to lighten his foot on the accelerator.

The triangular yellow warning of an approaching curve he ignored, leaning close to the windshield, straining to see through the torrents arrowing out of the darkness to smash into the glass between the frantic sweeps of the wipers. He was looking for a certain cross street, one that was paved and would take him without risk of getting mired in mud to Front Street, which was also paved.

A street sign swam into the headlights. He braked too hard and skewed into a flamboyant skid, his breath stopping until he had the car under control and reeled into a right turn. The pounding of his heart set his head aching in blinding pulsations. He floor-boarded the accelerator as if he could leave the pain behind, hurtling past houses with their windows full of warm yellow light like a howling apparition from a nether world. Only three blocks. The sign announcing Front Street sprang into the lights.

He slowed, but not enough, and this turn produced a skid almost as hair-raising as the last. He came out of it muttering an expression of gratitude that was probably a prayer and careened north into the stilettos of rain. When the headlights flashed on curved, metallic surfaces, he surrendered the hope that Brian had been waylaid by mud.

The XK-E was parked in front of Beryl Randall's out-wardly and deceptively humble home.

He slid to a stop fifty yards short of the house. The alarm whined to remind him he'd left the keys in the ignition, but he only slammed the door to silence it and struck out for the house, as much blinded by rain as darkness. The front door was open, and he didn't stop to wonder if that was a stroke of luck or simply an almost inevitable oversight in the confusion of Brian's unexpected arrival.

He approached the door from the right, and when he reached it paused, listening, before he leaned far enough past the jamb to look down the shadowy tunnel of the hall. There were voices; no, only one voice now, unintelligible against the wind and rain.

Brian was in profile to him, standing with his back to the fireplace, intent on something—rather, it would be some-one—across the room from him. His chin was thrust for-ward, his hands open at his sides as if he were ready to attack, but the incredulous chagrin drawing his features tight made it evident that his stance was defensive.

He was facing a gun. And more: an incredible truth.

Conan slipped into the hall, pressing close to the right-hand wall, and moved like a shadow in the shadows toward the light, toward Brian, toward that voice. He recognized it, and now could understand the words.

". . . what could I *do*, Brian? Theo left me penniless. And I never took enough to really hurt you. You didn't even *miss* it. No one did until the IRS came in, until that Nye person started poking around. It was *all* his fault."

Conan was watching Brian; he didn't want to attract his attention. Not yet. But there seemed to be no danger of that. Brian was too morbidly fascinated, like a doomed animal hypnotized by a predator.

He asked huskily, "But . . . why—why did you *kill* him?"

"Oh, but I *didn't*," the voice responded with earnest candor. "It was an accident. You see, I *had* to talk to him after what he said to you in the bar, and when he told me he *knew*—I mean, he'd figured it out from the records—and I couldn't just . . . well, we went to the kitchen. We could talk in private there. And he . . . he slipped and hit his head on the cutting table. Oh, it made a *terrible* sound. I thought he was dead. Really, I did, Brian. . . ."

Conan came to the end of the wall and reached the metal screen that served as a room divider. There he stopped and looked through the pattern of gold-colored arabesques.

An old woman was standing in the middle of the room.

An old woman caught in the shimmering light of a chandelier that flashed on glittering gilt, on blood-red ruby glass, on cleaved crystal planes, on simpering miniature goddesses and prudish nymphs, on ebony animal appendages clawing crystal spheres, on quivering fringes and tangled laces, on china writhing with bloated flowers; knickknacks; bric-a-brac; a grotesque assemblage of inanimate *things* that seemed to smirk and giggle among themselves.

An old woman who was considered only an innocent dupe

at the Tillamook bus depot; an old woman with a thin, sad
crown of white hair, her face ungraced with cosmetics to give
warmth to the tired skin, her creased mouth sunken in the
absence of false teeth, her naked, browless eyes vague and
unfocused without the glasses. She wore a full-length bathrobe now, a bulky, quilted garment designed to ward off the
chills to which old joints are so sensitive, but no doubt in
Tillamook she had worn a heavy coat to add apparent weight,
and then, as now, there would have been no elastic under-
garments to restrain the lax sag of aging flesh.

But there was one thing about this old woman that wouldn't
have been exposed in Tillamook.

The small automatic in her hand.

Conan found an ambiguous irony in that gun. She'd been
so meticulous about leaving no incriminating evidence, yet
she hadn't disposed of the weapon with which she shot
Johnny Hancock.

Perhaps she still considered herself above suspicion.

". . . never, *never* intended for you to be blamed, Brian.
If you'd *only* gone home when you should have, everything
would've been fine. I waited in my car for you to leave. I
waited and waited, but you *would* choose that night to get so
drunk you passed out on the bar."

Brian shook his head at that tone of annoyed rebuke and
whispered, "Oh, God . . . oh, God help me. . . ."

"Well, what could I *do*? Finally, I decided I'd better get
rid of the records. Nye found out about—well, about my little
fudging from them. I was going to come back to take care
of . . . of him. I thought surely you'd be gone by then. But—
oh, that *car*! It wouldn't *start* again. I had to *walk* all the way
home, and without a car, I couldn't very well do anything
about Nye. I mean, it would be difficult enough to get him
from the freezer to my car, but to dispose of his—of him
without a car—"

"Bea, you . . . you just walked home and went to bed
after leaving a man in—leaving him to *freeze* to death?"

"I *told* you, I thought he was dead when—"

"Oh, I can't *believe* this!"

His hands knotted into fists, he took an unsteady step toward her, and the gun came up, her eyes lost their ingenuous vagueness, turning cold and obdurate.

"Brian, you mustn't let your temper get out of hand."

"My *temper*?" He stared at her hopelessly. "You—oh, God, you're *crazy*! What're you going to do now? Kill *me*, too?"

She prefaced her answer with a long, plaintive sigh.

"Well, I suppose I'll have to. Oh, Brian, really, you give me no *choice*. Don't you see that?"

His face was contorted not with anger, but with an inner torment that could find no verbal expression. She raised the gun, sighting on his heart, but he only stared at her. Perhaps he still didn't believe he was face to face with his own death. Or perhaps he was too deep in shock to care.

Conan moved along the screen; the gun wavered, then abruptly swung around toward him.

"Who's there? Who's *there*?"

He dropped into a crouch. The gun cracked, the bullet ringing when it hit the screen.

"Who's there?"

Another brittle crack, a screech of alarm. Conan was past the screen, springing to the attack, but Brian was ahead of him, his strangled cry raw with unleashed rage. Then both alarm and rage were stifled in grunts of impact. The gun cracked again, the sound muffled in a tangle of bodies as they hit the floor and tumbled against the far wall.

Beryl came up shrieking—short, gasping screams that didn't stop even when Conan scrambled for her, rolled with her, straining for the gun, while she kicked, bit, and clawed with feline viciousness. The gun went off twice more, but he had her arm; the bullets smashed harmlessly into the wall. He banged her hand against the floor unmercifully while her shrieks turned to howls of pain, and finally the gun went skating under a chair.

He dived for it; the chair crashed over, knocking a painting off the wall, and as soon as the gun was in his hand, he twisted around to face her.

But she didn't launch a new attack.

She was incapable of that, lying hunched on her elbows, her strength spent, toothless mouth sagging open, every panting breath rasping in her throat.

Conan thrust the gun in his pocket, watching her numbly as she began crawling, crawling toward Brian.

He lay on his side, knees drawn up, both hands pressed to his chest to contain the red flow that welled between his fingers and spread across his shirt. A dark stain was forming on the rug beneath him.

"Oh, Brian . . ."

She stretched out a shaking hand to him, and his lips pulled back from his teeth, loathing vying with pain to make every word a wrenching effort.

"Get—get *away* from me, you dotty old bitch! *Get away from me!*"

She recoiled as if she'd been struck.

"Brian, how can you *say*—"

Conan cut off the incredible question as he dragged her to her feet and pushed her down onto a plush settee, stomach rebelling at her look of pained insult. He turned away, stumbling against a side table; it toppled, its burden of bric-a-brac cascading to the parquet floor. Beryl shrieked in dismay and sank to her knees among the shattered ruins.

He left her to the debris and knelt beside Brian, his fingers seeking the pulse in his throat. He was still conscious, but too bound in pain to speak, his pulse faint and erratic, his breathing almost undetectable. His forehead was wet with perspiration, his cheeks wet with something else; with tears. That was for another kind of pain.

Conan rose and found a telephone—a brass-and-porcelain monstrosity—and dialed the police station. Steve Travers was on the line in a matter of seconds.

"Conan! Is that—Where *are* you?"

He felt the weight of the gun in his pocket as he watched

Beryl gathering the pieces of a cobalt vase into a little pile. She'd cut her hand, but didn't seem to notice the bloody prints it made on the floor.

"I'm at Beryl Randall's house, Steve. I have a killer and a murder weapon for you. And another victim. Get an ambulance here fast."

Beryl droned monotonously, "Oh, look what you've done. . . . Look what you've *done*. . . ."

CHAPTER 26

The jangle of the phone jarred Conan from a deep sleep plagued with amorphous dreams, but he let it ring twice more before he made a move toward it in order to orient himself and be sure this was in fact his own bed, that it actually was the morning sun flashing on the breakers outside.

The fourth ring sounded while he propped himself on one elbow and fumbled for the phone; the fifth ring was cut off when he finally lifted the receiver.

"Hello."

"It's Steve, Conan. How're you feeling?"

That, he decided, was something better left undiscussed on this aching morning after.

"I'm all right, Steve. Where are you?"

"The police station. Where else? Look, I think you better get down here. Luther Dix arrived a few minutes ago."

"Damn. What does he want?"

"It'll be easier to explain if you'll just come on down to the station."

After a moment, he agreed reluctantly. "All right. Give me fifteen minutes." Then as he began levering himself out of bed, "No, make that twenty."

It was actually twenty-five. He kept lapsing into musings that made slow work of the automatic processes of showering, shaving, and dressing. The odors of hospital and jail melded in memory, calling up vagrant fragmentary images.

Brian at the hospital. Conan had called Nicky Heideger; he couldn't remember when, but she was there, and it took her an hour in surgery to excise the bullet in Brian's lung and repair the damage it had done. When she emerged from the operating room, her succinct assessment was that he had the constitution of an ox; otherwise, he probably wouldn't be alive.

Conan, she credited with the pigheadedness of a mule. That was while she repaired the damage he had sustained, including putting a new cast on his hand.

And Beryl Randall at the police station. Beryl in hastily donned street clothes and wig, protesting through every stage of her incarceration the inconsiderateness of it. "But you can't expect *me* to stay in one of those filthy jail cells. . . ."

The cells weren't filthy, whatever else they were, and by now she would have been transferred to the county courthouse, which had segregated facilities for women prisoners. No doubt she would find them equally offensive.

She admitted nothing. She refused to answer a single question and considered the booking officer's inquiry about her age particularly impertinent. But Steve had her gun for ballistics comparison with the bullet recovered from Johnny Hancock's body, and he had Conan's detailed statement recounting the confession he overheard while Beryl made her ritualistic rationalizations to Brian.

And Kleber had an explanation for the initials in the freezer. He accepted it with laudable grace.

Conan was still so preoccupied when he drove to the police station, he nearly forgot why he was going there, but two blocks before he reached it, as if that was the range of some unknown frequency that Luther Dix broadcast, Conan remembered, and by the time he arrived at the station, the muscles of his jaws were pulsing with tension.

Dix was in Kleber's office with the chief and Steve. Conan didn't pause to knock, and would have dispensed with amenities altogether if Kleber hadn't offered such a warmly courteous, "Good morning, Mr. Flagg."

Mister Flagg. It was remarkable.

"Good morning, Chief." Then with a glance at Steve, who was standing at one side of the desk, "Hello, Steve," then finally to Luther Dix, who sat sternly upright in one of the chairs in front of the desk, "Mr. Dix."

"Mr. Flagg." He seemed surprised to see him and not too happy about it.

Steve took an envelope from Kleber's desk and handed it to Conan.

"Mr. Dix brought this. It was written by Eliot Nye last Monday, probably less than twelve hours before he died."

Conan took the letter, but before he could even assimilate its existence, Dix protested, "Mr. Travers! That letter is IRS business—or perhaps police business at this point—and I certainly don't think—"

Kleber said, "Well, now, I figure Mr. Flagg's got a right to know about it. He's been in on this thing from the beginning, and he was the one who broke the case."

That was more than remarkable; it was astounding.

Conan murmured gratefully, "Thank you, Chief."

Dix was equally astounded, especially when he saw that Steve was in agreement with Kleber. He sagged back into his chair in blinking silence while Conan unfolded the letter.

It had a fastidiously formal look about it, typed with no errors on heavy bond under the IRS letterhead. Conan scanned it hurriedly first, then gave it a second, closer reading.

Holliday Beach
February 9

Re: Brian Tally audit (Social Security
Number 475-32-5087, Document Locator
Number 83434-115-50733-7.)

Dear Mr. Dix:

I will discuss this matter with you later today by telephone, but I feel it imperative that I offer my recommendation in writing as quickly as possible so that it may be
acted upon promptly.

On the basis of the second audit and my investigation
of accounting and inventory procedures at the Surf House
Restaurant, I am convinced that the deficiency in reported
profits which I noted in my previous audit was not due to
purposeful misrepresentation on Mr. Tally's part, but to
fraud of which he was himself the unknowing victim.

I shall present the evidence upon which this assumption
is based in detail in a future report, but I am convinced at
this time that Mr. Tally is—and has been for several years—
the victim of embezzlement, and the money thus stolen
from him accounts for the low profit ratio which led me
to recommend levying a tax deficiency against him. I am
also convinced that only one person could possibly be
responsible for this embezzlement scheme, and that is his
bookkeeper, Mrs. Beryl Randall.

In view of this development, I am recommending that the
tax deficiency claim against Mr. Tally be dropped, and that
the seizure order due to be executed next Friday be re-
scinded, or at least deferred pending further investigation.

Sincerely,

Eliot Nye

Conan studied the tidy signature and wondered what there
was about the letter that awakened grief he'd never felt for

the man who had written it. Finally, he put it back in its envelope and looked at the postmark.

"Mr. Dix, this was mailed last Monday. When did you receive it?"

"It arrived in the afternoon mail on Wednesday."

Conan felt the anger congesting his throat like something alien his body was trying to expel.

"Wednesday? And you didn't bother to tell Steve or Chief Kleber about it until today?"

Dix said stiffly, "It was necessary to consult our legal department before I could take any action on it. That, of course, took some time; they're understaffed and always very busy."

"Busy! While your legal department was so damn *busy*, a man was murdered! A human life, Mr. Dix, lost while you went through channels, and maybe Johnny Hancock's wasn't much of a life, but it was *his*, and he wouldn't have lost it if you'd called Steve as soon as you received this letter. Nor would Brian Tally be lying in a hospital recovering from a bullet wound that nearly killed him; nearly made him a *second* victim of your official caution."

Dix turned lividly pink under that attack.

"Mr. Flagg, I object to your taking that tone with me! I had no way of seeing into the future, and you have no way of proving that my retaining that letter for a few days had any effect whatsoever on the subsequent course of events."

Conan didn't argue that. All at once it seemed darkly, futilely humorous. But he couldn't laugh at it.

"What about the IRS claim against Brian?"

Dix took a deep breath, his mouth pursed.

"In light of Eliot's recommendation and the fact that the pertinent records have been lost—*if* it can be shown that Tally had nothing to do with their loss—the case will be dropped." Then he added piously, "You'll note that the seizure order was *not* carried out yesterday. I put an indefinite hold on it when I received Eliot's letter."

Like a gift from heaven. Brian's bitter words. Conan thrust the letter into his jacket pocket and strode to the door.

"Steve, I'm going to the hospital. I'll return this."

Neither Steve nor Kleber offered any objections, but Dix popped out of his chair.

"Wait a minute! You can't take that letter!"

Conan turned on him. "I *will* take it. It was written in Eliot Nye's blood as much as the dying testament he left— *tried* to leave—in his death chamber. The letter was addressed to you, but the message is addressed by circumstance to Brian Tally."

With that, he stalked away. The glass in the door rattled as he slammed it.

He slammed the front door of the station, too, and he was thinking bitterly that undoubtedly the Bard had said something appropriate to this occasion.

All that came to mind was:

> *The evil that men do lives after them;*
> *The good is oft interred with their bones;*
> *So let it be with Caesar.*

And should Eliot Nye fare better than Caesar?
Yes.

ABOUT THE AUTHOR

M. K. WREN, a widely acclaimed writer and painter, was born in Texas, the daughter of a geologist and a special education teacher. Twenty-five years ago, she found her soul home in the Pacific Northwest, where she wrote CURIOSITY DIDN'T KILL THE CAT; A MULTITUDE OF SINS; OH, BURY ME NOT; NOTHING'S CERTAIN BUT DEATH; SEASONS OF DEATH; WAKE UP, DARLIN' COREY; and the science-fiction trilogy, THE PHOENIX LEGACY. As an artist, Ms. Wren has worked primarily in oils and transparent watercolors and has exhibited in numerous galleries and juried shows in Texas, Oklahoma, and the Northwest.

GENE THOMPSON

"A FINE, LITERATE WHODUNIT IN THE CLASSIC VEIN...

Publishers Weekly

Available at your bookstore or use this coupon.

___ **A CUP OF DEATH**   35881 $3.50
The sixty-year-old San Francisco lawyer Dade Cooley and his wife Ellen try to solve
the murder of Dade's old friend Paul Van Damm. He was killed by an intruder who had
stolen what appeared to be a piece of worthless costume jewelry.

___ **MURDER MYSTERY**   29892 $3.50
Wealthy Miriam Welles is crushed to death in her garage by her Rolls Royce. When
Dade Cooley, her lawyer arrives in town for the funeral, he quickly sees that things
aren't quite what they seem.

___ **NOBODY CARED FOR KATE**   31198 $3.50
Kate was an eccentric, unpleasant lady . . . but why was she killed? and by whom?
An official inquiry is to be held and the family is joined by Dade Cooley and his wife
who had been mysteriously summoned by Kate prior to her death.

 BALLANTINE MAIL SALES
Dept. TA, 201 E. 50th St., New York, N.Y. 10022

Please send me the BALLANTINE BOOKS I have checked above. I am
enclosing $.............. (add 50¢ per copy to cover postage and handling).
Send check or money order — no cash or C.O.D.'s please. Prices and
numbers are subject to change without notice. Valid in U.S. only. All orders
are subject to availability of books.

Name _____

Address _____

City _____ State _____ Zip Code _____

12   Allow at least 4 weeks for delivery   TA-230